AT WHAT COST

AT WHAT COST

A Detective Penley Mystery

James L'Etoile

CROOKED
LANE

NEW YORK

Copyright © 2016 by James L'Etoile.

Published in the United States by Crooked Lane Books,
an imprint of The Quick Brown Fox & Company LLC.

Crooked Lane Books and its logo are trademarks of
The Quick Brown Fox & Company LLC.

Library of Congress Catalog-in-Publication data available upon request.

ISBN (hardcover): 978-1-62953-995-9
ISBN (paperback): 978-1-62953-996-6
ISBN (ePUB): 978-1-62953-997-3
ISBN (Kindle): 978-1-62953-998-0
ISBN (ePDF): 978-1-62953-999-7

Cover design by Denis Kohler.
Book design by Jennifer Canzone.

Printed in the United States.

www.crookedlanebooks.com

Crooked Lane Books
34 West 27th St., 10th Floor
New York, NY 10001

First Edition: December 2016

10 9 8 7 6 5 4 3 2 1

The borders which divide Life from Death are at best shadowy and vague.
Who shall say where the one ends, and where the other begins?

Edgar Allan Poe, "Premature Burial," 1844

ONE

Raindrops played off a drumhead of blue-tinged flesh at John Penley's feet. It was human, but it wasn't a body. Ragged lacerations exposed thick strands of muscle and crushed sections of pale-white bone. Remnants of a headless, limbless shell of a male torso rested at the river's edge. An open chest wound became a flesh-lined catch basin for the pelting rain. Each drop sounded with a deep plunk and swirled up a pink froth from within.

Portable halogen lights, erected on the levee road, bathed the muddy bank in a harsh glare. Red plastic flags atop thin metal rods sprouted up from the mud, marking the area around the torso. The little flags whipped and rattled in the wind that ran up the levee bank. Penley pulled up the collar of his raincoat against the driving rain, but the chill he felt didn't come from the elements.

The malformed tattoo of an Aztec warrior on the victim's chest was familiar to Detective John Penley. The unique prison tattoo identified the partial corpse as Daniel Cardozo, a high-ranking gangbanger.

Everything that made Cardozo human—and there were those who debated whether the violent drug addict was part of the species—was missing. The man's chest held only a shallow pool of bloody rainwater. The remains were little more than a husk of a man.

A sucking sound in the mud behind Penley pulled his focus away from the broken gang member. David Potter, a crime-scene technician, struggled for footing in the thick ooze. Penley shielded his eyes from the lights as Potter made his way down the bank, mud leeching to the ankles of the technician's rubber boots with every step. The burden of bulky equipment and heavy nylon satchels threatened to topple the one-hundred-thirty-pound man.

"Where do you want me to start, Detective?" Potter asked.

"Let's get some photos of the riverbank, below the body, before the rain washes everything away." Penley pointed to a section of slick mud indentations that ran from the water's edge to the torn human remains.

Potter placed the equipment cases down on a small patch of bent grass, avoiding the viscous mud closer to the riverbank. He unpacked a thick-framed digital camera and pulled a stack of numbered yellow signs from one of the nylon satchels. Potter took a wide approach to the riverbank, well away from anything in the area he was going to photograph. A yellow marker with the number one went into the ooze at the spot where the water met the slope of the levee. The mud held an impression, a deep, V-shaped indentation in the bank. The flash from Potter's camera bathed the spot in artificial daylight for a moment and revealed several deep footprints.

"Detective, someone hopped out of a boat into the mud and sank at least calf-deep. The bow left a nice indentation."

"What kind of boat?" Penley asked.

"It wasn't one of those flat-bottomed jobs or a big fiberglass deep-hull boat either. It's too sloppy to get an impression, but I'd be willing to bet it was a lightweight aluminum fishing boat—maybe ten to twelve feet."

"Why go through all the trouble of dumping a body up on the bank? Had to know we'd find it," Penley said.

"Maybe they wanted you to," Potter said in between camera flashes.

The sound of car doors echoed down the bank from the levee road. Penley shielded his eyes against the halogen spotlights once more and saw the outline of Elizabeth White, deputy medical examiner, on the levee road. The detective pointed in the direction of the flags marking the trail to the body.

"Should we set up a tarp over the body?" she asked as she approached.

"Your call," Penley said. "But he didn't leave us anything. He was careful. He's always careful. This is the third dump in the last six weeks, and we haven't pulled so much as a carpet fiber from the bodies."

Penley gestured to the remains. "Meet Daniel Cardozo. Gang member, drug dealer, and pimp."

Elizabeth knelt next to the open torso and pulled up on a flap of rib cage with her latex-gloved hand. Severed arteries, torn diaphragm muscle, and an esophagus draped against the spine. "Have you located the rest of him? A limb? Anything?"

"Nothing, and we won't. Just like the other two victims," Penley said.

She traced the lines of the tattoo on the victim's chest with her finger. "This is different. The others had no physical markers, no characteristics to identify them. Why did he leave this?"

"Might be the only thing Cardozo did that was worth a damn."

"What?"

"Getting inked. That tattoo—it gives us a place to start. We don't have to work through missing persons reports and hope for a DNA hit in the system. We know who the victim is this time."

"You're that certain?"

"When I was on the gang task force, we tracked Cardozo and the other West Block Norteños gang members. I never had enough to nail Cardozo, but he always ran on the fringes, you know? If drugs were moving across the river, he had a hand in it. Weapons? Same deal. So I've seen that tattoo more than a few times."

Penley followed the trail of plastic flags back up to the road, leaving Elizabeth and two of her assistants to document the remains and pack what was left of the gangbanger in an opaque plastic sheet.

The killer did society a favor when he got rid of Cardozo, Penley figured. But the hairs on the back of the detective's neck prickled looking at the lump of flesh wrapped like a birthday present. The feeling wasn't from the savage brutality of the attack but rather from an unanswered question.

Why did the killer dismember Cardozo and the victims before him?

TWO

John spent the rest of the morning mulling over the Cardozo killing. Flashbacks to the ripped and dismembered body distracted the detective to the point where conversation with his wife was forced at the breakfast table. Melissa could have told him she was pregnant again, and it wouldn't have registered. He grabbed his pager, clipped it to his belt, gave Melissa a practiced kiss on the cheek, and said a mumbled "Love you," then he was out the door.

Police activity evaporated with the first light, and the only indication that a life had ended along the remote levee road was a torn length of yellow crime-scene tape on a rusty metal guardrail.

John pulled the car off the narrow levee road into a sparse, brown, grassy patch a few yards upriver from where Daniel Cardozo's remains had soiled the muddy bank a couple of hours ago. He got out, leaned on the fender, and out of habit, patted his jacket pocket for his cigarettes. The rattle of nicotine gum when he expected to find the cigarette pack darkened his mood. He tossed back one of the chalky gum pieces and worked it with his jaw while he looked for anything out of place along the water's edge. Crime scenes always looked different in the daylight.

The sunshine revealed scores of muddy footprints that traced from the asphalt down to the water's edge where Cardozo had turned up. Thick, dried chunks of mud clumped on the road's surface, evidence of the foot traffic from everyone who had worked the scene. If he hadn't known better, John thought the site looked like an amphibious landing zone. It wasn't so much the mud or mud-print patterns John had come for—it was the river.

The killer selected this open spot on the riverbank, where heavy brush, less than twenty yards in either direction, provided more seclusion for his body dump. He hadn't bothered to hide Cardozo's body under the water's surface, and it hadn't accidentally washed up on shore. Leaving the gang member's remains out in the open, in plain view, was deliberate by design.

John stood at the edge of the road, kicked a small chunk of crumbling asphalt down the embankment, and watched it tumble down the levee. The black hunk of tar and rock made it halfway to the waterline before it lost momentum and toppled over on its side. It sat alone in the trampled mud, where it stood out on display among the clumps of clay and native grasses. It was an insignificant piece of asphalt on exhibit in the open space, unlike the fleshy billboard display of the killer's latest handiwork.

Across the river, five ducks formed a quick-moving, V-shaped flock, searching for a place to land in the marshy rice fields. The wind carried the deep, muffled report of two shotgun blasts from the far side of the river. One bird tumbled down, followed by another splashing in the rice field. Another dead creature along the waterway.

John's cell phone buzzed. "Penley here," he responded.

"John, it's Tim," the caller said.

"What's up, Lieutenant?" Tim Barnes was the ranking supervisor in the detective bureau and one of the few John trusted to have his back when it mattered.

"We've got one of Cardozo's next of kin in one of the interview rooms. You heading in, or do you want Paula to run with it when she gets here?"

John watched the river current push through without an echo of last night's activity. Life goes on—for some. "I'll take the interview.

I dropped by the crime scene again but should be back in the office in about twenty. By next of kin, you mean . . ."

"One of his West Block Norteños gang brothers we rounded up. We're trying to run down his wife."

"Who filed the missing person's report on Cardozo?"

"The wife reported his disappearance. So did Manuel Contreras. We have Contreras on ice in the interview room," Barnes said.

"Anyone make contact with the wife?"

"Gang unit. They couldn't wait to go make that notification."

"No love lost between the gang unit and the Norteños," John said.

He hung up and headed back to his sedan, convinced the body dump was an obscure message from the killer. A warning to other gangbangers, or the act was a personal vendetta against Cardozo. Either way, he wanted attention.

THREE

Manuel Contreras posed in the spartan interview room, chest puffed up and his thick arms crossed in defiance. Gang tattoos laced up his neck from under his black shirt and painted a toxic camouflage that proudly displayed the gang member's hatred. That hate was presently focused on the uniformed officer who stood at the door.

Penley opened the door and tossed a notepad on the table.

"Mr. Contreras, I see you're wearing black. You in mourning for Daniel Cardozo?" John asked.

"What the fuck you talking about?"

"Cardozo was killed this morning," John said.

"So I hear."

"Who'd want to punch his ticket?"

Contreras shrugged and said, "Could be a long list. Danny pissed off a lotta people over the years."

"You on that list?"

"Nah. Since the dude got out of the pen last year, he ain't been into nothing but his wife and daughter. Damn shame. His little girl got real sick. Some kind of cancer, they say."

"So you and the other Norteños picked up his slack?"

The gangbanger shook his head. "All I'm sayin' is that his head wasn't in the game no more. He was still one of us. He did his part over the years. Nobody affiliated with the West Block Norteños had nothin' to do with his death."

"Who'd stand to gain by his death?"

"Like I said, he ain't been in the game. He went back to prison for a bullshit weapons beef, and while he was behind walls, his little girl got bad. Nothing he could do but watch her get worse from the prison visiting room. I'm sayin' when the dude hit the streets, all he did was take the kid to doctors' appointments and shit."

"Anyone think Cardozo wasn't pulling his weight?" Penley asked.

"Nah, it wasn't like that. Danny was a hardcore dude from way back. Nobody—and I mean nobody—questions that." Contreras leaned back in the chair, his thick arms tensed.

Penley changed course. "You mentioned his daughter. Cancer treatment's not cheap."

"You talk about gangs—damn doctors are a gang, extorting people for money they don't have. They promise one more treatment or some new surgery—if you can pay for it. How is that right? A dude like Danny, he got no insurance, and it's like no pay, no play."

"How did he pay the medical bills?"

"We take care of our own. We took up collections, held fund-raisers in town, that kind of shit."

"By fundraisers, you don't mean taking down a liquor store?" Penley asked.

"No, man. Danny got respect from everyone, and people willingly gave for his kid's cancer treatment. We collected twenty-two thousand for the girl. No one complained. Danny even did some jobs on the side to pay his kid's bills."

"What kind of jobs?" Penley asked.

Contreras shrugged. "I dunno, that's just what I heard."

"What about people he came up against before he went to prison?" Penley questioned.

Contreras thought for a moment. "There may have been a couple who didn't like what Danny had to say."

"Got any names for me?"

"Nah, ain't my style. But I can tell you who had it out for Danny—the city attorney and the West Sacramento chief of police. They made up all kinds of shit to scare people into getting that gang injunction passed. Anyone who got beat down, they said it was us; anyone who got robbed, they blamed us; and anyone who got themselves killed, we got the heat. We'd have to be a thousand deep to pull off all the shit they tried to lay on us."

"With Danny out of the picture, you have complete control now, right?" John asked.

"You sound like one of them organized crime cops from the feds. If there was anything to control, Danny wasn't at the wheel no more. It ain't up to me who fills his shoes."

"Who would want him dead?"

Contreras locked eyes with Penley. "I honestly don't know. You'd better find out before I do."

"Where were you between midnight and six this morning?"

"Don't try and lay this one on me."

"Answer the question."

"Man, from ten o'clock last night until you guys dragged me out of bed this morning, I was home. You know the gang injunction curfew says I can't be in no public place after ten."

"Where was Cardozo?"

"How should I know?"

"When did you see him last?"

Contreras shifted in his seat. "Danny left my place about eight last night."

"What did you guys talk about? Did he say where he was going after he left your place?"

"Mostly, we talked about his kid. It was ripping him up. She wasn't getting no better, and the doctor bills kept coming. Dude said he might have a way to take care of her and had a big score lined up. He was on his way to the job when he left my place. I guess his little girl ain't gonna get no help now."

"You don't have any idea what kind of job he was talking about?" Penley pressed.

"Nah. He was quiet about that kind of stuff. He didn't tell me nothin' about what he was doing, but I got the feeling that he was on to something—something big, you know. It was like he found gold."

A sharp rap on the door announced the arrival of Joseph Morrison, the on-call attorney representing the West Block Norteños when their various criminal endeavors fell apart. Morrison's gray-flecked beard reminded Penley of a barnyard goat, especially when the lawyer chomped away on a wad of gum as he did now.

John patted his phantom cigarette pack and felt the letdown of the nicotine gum container. Not that he could sneak a smoke in a public building; the cigarette pack was a touchstone, a security blanket.

"Mr. Contreras has nothing to say to you, Detective." The attorney put his pricey briefcase on the table between Penley and his client, a leather-bound barrier of legal protection.

"We were having a friendly discussion about the life and times of Daniel Cardozo," Penley responded.

"And dude was just getting to the part where Danny was up to no good," Contreras said to his attorney.

"That's enough, Manuel," Morrison said to his client. He turned to Penley. "What are you charging him with? I'll remind you that the terms of the gang injunction apply in Yolo County, not over on this side of the river."

"We found the body of one of your clients on the Sacramento side."

"Mr. Contreras has no knowledge of that."

"We were about to find out," Penley said.

"Are you charging him with murder? With anything?"

"No." Penley shook his head.

"Then we're done here. Mr. Contreras, let's go."

The gang member stood and started out the door behind his attorney. He paused and said, "You'd better find him. Danny was a respected man. This could get out of hand if you don't get whoever done this."

Morrison turned and grabbed his client by the sleeve. "That's it. Don't say another word until we get in the car."

"Dude deserved better than this. It ain't right what they did to him," Contreras complained as he pulled away from his lawyer's grip.

"I can't help him unless you tell me who 'they' are," Penley said.

"I dunno who, but Danny was one tough dude who could handle himself. It had to be a setup, a trap."

"That, or someone he thought he could trust," Penley added.

"It better not be that, or someone else will be floating in the river," Contreras said.

The attorney jerked on his client's arm once more and pulled him from the room. Morrison's face flushed with anger. "Give him a reason to lock you up, why don't you?"

Contreras pulled free from Morrison and walked ahead. Morrison turned toward Penley and said, "Leave my client alone. You have anything further, you come to me, understood?"

"What do you know about Cardozo's murder?" Penley asked the attorney.

The rate of gum chomping increased, and Morrison said, "If I knew anything, attorney-client privilege would bar me from telling you. In this instance, I assure you that Daniel Cardozo's death was not gang related. If someone inside the family did this, it would be tantamount to suicide. Even their wives and children would be green-lighted for retaliation."

"Nice family."

"It is what it is, Detective. You need to find another angle, is what I'm saying."

Penley watched the attorney catch up with his client down the hall, and the duo disappeared around a corner.

Penley found a dead end as far as the street gang connection was concerned. He had to admit the desecration of Cardozo's body didn't carry the usual hit-and-run characteristics of a gang kill-ing. The body dump was calculated and purposeful. Disposing of a well-known gangbanger out in the open was bold. The killer could take anyone anywhere and wasn't concerned about the police. He wasn't going to stop.

FOUR

John Penley's work area consisted of two battered metal desks pushed together so that he faced his new partner, Detective Paula Newberry. The two desks were a study of contrasts in organization and individual styles. They reflected the personalities of their respective occupants. Penley's well-ordered desktop had files stacked neatly in one corner with his computer angled precisely on the opposite corner. The blotter in the center held a single binder and a notepad. Paula's desk looked like a photo from a FEMA disaster area. Crime-scene photos, computer printouts, reports, and files littered the surface. Her computer keyboard balanced precariously atop an overfilled in-box, and four paper coffee cups incubated a filmy layer over coagulated coffee remnants.

John and Paula were partners of last resort. She came from internal affairs after a short but rocky assignment investigating other officers, and most detectives welcomed her like a communicable disease. Paula was an outsider in a world that valued having your partner's back above all else. The lieutenant paired them up, and his only direction to Paula was to "leave the IA baggage behind."

Paula perched in an old desk chair she rescued from a thrift store. The chair lifted her five-three frame so that she could work at her desk without feeling like she was at the kids' table at Thanksgiving. Most of her personal belongings rested in a box under her desk, uncertain if, or when, they would find a permanent place to rest. She examined a series of photos of the Cardozo crime scene she had placed on a whiteboard on the wall behind her desk. Paula didn't look away from the graphic images of the mutilated torso when John Penley entered.

"Let me guess—Manny Contreras says he didn't do it," Paula said.

"That's right. I'm thinking he might be playing it straight on this one. When did you get back home?"

"It was a five-hour drive to San Luis Obispo. You know they call that prison the 'men's colony'? Sounds nice, huh? Anyway, five hours down, ten minutes of testimony at a lifer hearing, then turn around and drive five more hours. I haven't been home yet."

"Is this the guy who killed his neighbor over an argument about their backyard fence? Is the Board of Parole Hearings gonna release him?"

Paula shrugged. "Don't know. He's old and sick, so they might give him a date. But anyway, about Contreras, he always has some angle going. What makes you believe him now?"

"If our victim was laying down on the gang business—and we'd have to get the Yolo County sheriff and West Sac. PD to confirm that—then I don't see any benefit to a hit on Cardozo."

"Why would Cardozo end up this way"—she gestured to the photos—"if it wasn't about him?"

John lowered himself into the chair behind his desk and made sure that the notepad and files remained in place on the desktop. "Manny thought that Cardozo was onto a big score or something,"

"Like what?"

"He claimed he didn't know. Some kind of job," John said.

"Our other victims, Johnson and Mercer, didn't have any score going on—anything we know about anyway. They were gang members, like Cardozo. All three ran with different gangs but had the same lifestyle."

"Hustling, moving a little meth, some protection racket action. All the usual stuff." John pointed at the photos from the Cardozo crime scene. "That is not your typical gang killing."

"I don't need the medical examiner's official report to tell me Cardozo, Johnson, and Mercer were all killed by the same guy. We haven't leaked the details of the murders, but this," she said, pointing to a photo of the open carcass, "is our guy's signature."

"Question is, what's our guy do with the parts he doesn't leave behind?" John asked.

Paula swiveled in her chair. "Other than sending a message to gangbangers?"

"What? You think our killer is cleaning up the city? I mean, sure these victims had gang ties, but why them? They weren't the worst of the worst."

"Maybe he's a vigilante, making a statement about gangs. Cardozo ran with the West Block Norteños, Mercer was a Crip, and Johnson was a Skinhead. I'd say it was a little equal opportunity roadside cleanup, except for the way they were mutilated," she said.

"If this was gang on gang, we'd have heard about it. If this is some kind of gang move, what does it mean when the killer leaves you behind without your arms, legs, and gooey bits? Did the profile the lieutenant got from the FBI mention anything?"

Paula pulled a thick file folder from one of the piles on her desk, which caused a mini-paper avalanche. She ignored the disarray, thumbed open the file, and glanced at the contents. "The usual psychobabble about a loner with narcissistic tendencies. Here we go—the profiler said the mutilation could be symbolic of a 'psychic injury' experienced by the subject, or displaced rage. Killers who display their victims in this manner often experience abandonment by parental figures."

"Doesn't tell us much we didn't know."

"Other than he may have 'mommy issues.'"

"The lieutenant told them about the gang connection on the first two victims, right?" John said.

She flipped a page, ran a finger down the print. "Yeah, the profiler said further field intelligence from the gang unit is needed to rule out racially motivated gang activity. Get this: 'Considering the symbolic nature of the mutilation, investigators should consider the victims were chosen specifically. The killer literally spilled their guts, indicating they may have been seen as informants.'"

"Cardozo takes the racial angle off the table. Black, white, and now Hispanic victims. From my dealings with Cardozo, I didn't take him for a snitch. Contreras seemed to back that up."

"Would Contreras tell you if dearly departed Daniel Cardozo was an informant? If he wasn't, then we have a killer taking out gang members at random. How do you warn anyone when you don't know what the killer wants? I'm not ready to admit this guy is a Zodiac or Son of Sam targeting gangsters at random."

"How can you work like that?" John said, indicating her desk.

"What are you, my mother? I have a system that works for me—that's what matters."

"Your desk looks like an episode of *Hoarders*. It—"

"Rubs your OCD the wrong way? Get over it." She flicked her hand dismissively.

"I'd hate to see your house. I hope you have GPS on your cell phone so the rescue crews can find you when you get lost in your living room."

"Are you done?"

"For now."

Paula glanced back at the file in her hand. "We interviewed the Johnson and Mercer next of kin for any connection to one another. I seriously doubt they ran in the Yolo County gang circles with Cardozo. Maybe Cardozo's wife can tell us something about Daniel's decision to turn his back on the homeboys. That had to have pissed off someone."

"Maybe," John said. "Manny Contreras thought it had nothing to do with the West Block Norteños."

"What else is he gonna say?" Paula swung her hands open wide to emphasize her point, knocked her computer keyboard off its perch, and sent it clattering to the floor.

"Would you at least get rid of those coffee cups before they spill all over the files?"

Paula retrieved the keyboard and tossed it on the desktop, where it toppled over one of the paper cups. The thick, dark-brown sludge remained solidly adhered to the bottom reaches of the container. She grabbed it along with the others that littered her work area and disposed of them in her trash can. Paula held the can up. "Happy now?"

"A little."

"As I was saying, Contreras and all his gang buddies will say nothing to implicate Daniel Cardozo in their business. The Yolo County DA would swarm all over them for any violations of the injunction."

"Were you able to locate who reported finding the body?"

"An anonymous caller. Didn't call nine-one-one but called in on a direct line to the watch commander."

"So no recording?"

"And no trace on the number. The caller said where to find the body, and the first black-and-white found Contreras. No one else was there," Paula said.

"What time was the call?"

"Four fifteen in the morning."

John's desk phone rang, and he picked it up. "Penley."

He listened to the caller and shifted his eyes to Paula. "Where can we meet?" Another pause, then he said, "How about thirty minutes? Fine—see you then."

"That was Cardozo's wife. Manny Contreras told her that she should call us and talk."

"You mean he told her what to say. We should pull Contreras back in for obstruction. He's tainted our investigation talking to the next of kin," Paula said.

"Why don't we hear what she has to say before you go all medieval on his ass? She sounded like she wanted to talk—"

"Oh, she will. Whatever Manny told her to say."

"I'm interested in what she knows about Mercer and Johnson. If she can lead us to a connection there, I don't care what Contreras told her."

"Where we meeting her?" Paula stood and grabbed her jacket from a pile of shoes and sweats on the floor behind her desk.

John opened a desk drawer and removed a fresh notebook, tucking it in his jacket pocket. "She's staying with her mom, here in Sacramento. The projects off Broadway."

Paula shrugged into her jacket. "Neutral territory, at least."

FIVE

The brick-and-mortar public housing projects were anything but neutral territory, as far as a half dozen street gangs were concerned. Drug deals took place on the sidewalks in plain view, watched over by sweat shirt–hooded sentries posted on the ends of Kit Carson Street. Before Penley piloted the unmarked police sedan onto the street, the signals went out by cell phone from the watchers, warning the dealers and their runners of the approach.

The thugs' body language was easy to read. Penley saw hands in pockets, undoubtedly clutching various weapons. The dealers planned to protect their turf from all rivals, other gangs, or narcotics officers. Tense and ready to run and gun.

Penley slowed the car and pulled to the curb. "Roll your window down," he said to Paula.

"Is that George Watts?" she asked.

"Yeah. When did he get out of prison?"

"I dunno. He probably got kicked because of overcrowding," Paula said.

"We should say welcome home."

Penley leaned over toward Paula's open window and yelled at a knot of men. "Hey, George! Got a second?"

One man, slightly older than the twenty-year-olds with him, squinted, and recognition spread across his face. He spoke in hushed tones to the men around him, and the group relaxed slightly. A few hands came out of pockets, but most important, the hands held no semiautomatic weapons. The older man separated himself from the group and walked toward the unmarked car.

"Detective Penley, what brings you 'round here? You get busted back to narcotics?" George chided. He held a gold-framed smile provided by an elaborate grill of gold and diamonds in the shape of a marijuana leaf over his front teeth.

"We're here about a murder," John said.

"Ain't been nobody killed here in more than a week."

"You hear about Daniel Cardozo?"

George nodded and said, "Yeah, damn shame too, if you ask me. He seemed to be getting his life together since he got out of prison."

"Did you see him around here recently?" Paula asked.

"I ain't talking to you, Newberry. You're the reason I gotta wear this." George put his foot on the passenger-side window frame and pulled up his pant leg to reveal a GPS ankle monitor. "Cause of you, I got no privacy and can't go more than a quarter mile from here."

"I didn't make you sell pot over at Kennedy High," Paula said.

"I wasn't selling nothing."

"Only because you got busted before you had a chance. That's why you got twenty-four months instead of sixty," Paula countered.

"Man, you had them take away my medical marijuana card. That ain't right. I got a right to smoke to help my condition."

"George, you had three pounds of weed, and there's nothing wrong with you that jail time can't cure," Paula said.

"That's harsh, Newberry," George complained.

"Now about Cardozo—you seen him?" she pressed.

"Last couple of weeks, he was here a lot. His wife moved in with her mom, Theresa, and they took care of the kid—I think the girl is sick or something. Cardozo was straight up about layin' down on the West Block Norteños and convinced the South Side Pirus that he weren't gonna cause no drama."

"How'd he convince them he was done with the gang?" John asked.

"Paid 'em."

"How much?" John demanded.

George shrugged. "Don't know, but I figure it had to be a bundle since the Piru shot-caller lifted a 'hit-on-sight' order on the dude."

"Why did Cardozo have a hit on him?" John asked.

"From what I hear, it went back years to when Cardozo was a heavy with the boys. A drug rip-off. He took down a Piru runner and left with the product."

"Is Rotten Ricky still the Piru shot-caller?" John questioned.

"Yep, dude takes a cut of all the action out here in exchange for protection and so forth."

"Including yours?" Paula asked.

"Man, why you always gotta be like that? If I was into anything, then yeah, Rotten Ricky would get his."

John pointed to a first-floor unit with a long, wide sidewalk in the center of the housing complex across the street. "Seven-twelve. That's where Cardozo's wife is staying, right?"

George nodded.

"Thanks. If I park my car here, am I gonna have all my tires and rims when I get back? You being an entrepreneur and all?" John said.

George smiled. "Depends on how long you're gone. I'm doin' my own number, so alls I can say is that I won't bother your broke-ass ride."

John took the keys from the ignition and opened his door. "Good enough for me."

George strolled back to his posse of young thugs, all of whom eyed the two cops with unveiled contempt. The group listened as George spoke and gestured toward John and Paula. From the street, the conversation was unheard, but the message was clear: George ordered the men to stand down and leave the two cops alone.

Paula joined her partner on the street, and the pair walked across the neglected asphalt to the sidewalk. "What did he mean by 'doing his own number'?" Paula asked.

"When you're in prison, no one else is gonna do your time. You have to do your own—your own number. It also means you aren't taking on anyone else's time by taking a beef for someone."

"You think he meant it—that he isn't involved in anything else around here?"

"By the reaction he got from his protégés over there, I'd say George has his hand in every ounce sold in the projects," John said.

A wide cement path provided access to four units in the complex. The sparse crabgrass lawn ensured that anyone who approached the place was visible. A curtain pulled back in an upper window. There was no sneaking up on the residents in this neighborhood.

Painted numbers marked the unit on the left as 712. Penley rapped his knuckles on the door and took a step back from the threshold. A slight shadow crossed the peephole, a dead bolt scraped open, and the door pulled inward a few inches. Deep-set, red-rimmed eyes peered around the opening and greeted the detectives.

"Mrs. Cardozo?" John inquired.

"You're the detective I spoke with? It's true then? Daniel was . . . butchered?"

"I'm Detective Penley, this is Detective Newberry. May we come inside and speak with you?"

The woman pulled the door open, turned away from the door, and retreated inside the residence. John took the open door as an invitation and followed Mrs. Cardozo.

The newly widowed Mrs. Cardozo was in her early thirties, John guessed. Thinly built and wrapped in an oversized sweat shirt, she perched on the edge of a sofa. She turned her tear-filled eyes away from John. "Manny told me that Daniel was murdered. I always knew that could happen when he ran with the West Block boys, but not now."

"I'm sorry, Mrs. Cardozo," John said.

"Please, call me Maria."

"Do you have anyone here to help you? You need me to call someone?"

"My mother is in the bedroom with Cielo, my daughter."

"Can you tell me what Daniel was up to over the last few weeks?" John asked.

"He wasn't doing anything illegal, if that's what you mean," Maria said.

"No, that's not what I mean. Manny Contreras made it sound like Daniel found some work. Do you know what that was?"

She shook her head. "No, he didn't tell me what it was, and that worried me some. He said I needed to trust him. Danny worked at the Port of Sacramento unloading cargo ships and even got in with the union. He worked after hours to make extra money so we could pay for Cielo's doctors."

"Manny told me about Cielo—her being sick." The words about a sick child felt thick on his tongue.

Maria nodded, and a new trail of tears started down her cheek. "Danny was doing everything he could to pay all the medical bills, and that's why I was so surprised that he quit the job at the docks."

"When did he quit?"

From the back room, an ancient voice called out, "Maria, time for Cici's medication."

"Sí, Mama." Maria stood, picked up a plastic tub that held a dozen prescription bottles, and turned to the hallway.

Paula stood. "I can take that to your mother. Please, sit."

Maria handed the tub to Paula and sat, clearly exhausted and emotionally spent. She wiped her eyes with her sweat shirt sleeve.

Paula retreated down the hall with the tub of prescriptions. Maria kept an eye on her until she disappeared into the bedroom.

John nudged her attention back when he repeated, "When did your husband quit the job?"

"About two months ago."

"Did he say why?"

"He wouldn't tell me. We had a big fight about it. I hope it didn't have nothing to do with his brother Puppet. All he said was that I needed to trust him and that he would be able to take care of us again."

"You have no idea what he did?"

"No. I asked him, and he got all quiet and uptight. That's how I could tell he was into something that he shouldn't be, you know? He promised me, after he got out the last time, that he would stay out of trouble and take care of us. I guess he lied—again."

"Manny claims that Daniel wasn't into anything with the Norte-ños. Moving you here across the river seems to back that up," John said.

"I know what Manny said. But it doesn't add up. My Danny cuts ties with the boys, he starts this new job and shows me a huge wad of cash for a couple days' work. That kind of money—money like that wasn't from a straight job. Danny swore to me that he wasn't doing anything illegal. I told him it wouldn't do our daughter any good if he went back to prison like his brother. He said there was nothing to worry about."

"Did he tell you who he worked for?" John questioned.

Maria shook her head and looked out the window at George and his thugs as they sold a small package wrapped in tinfoil to a young man on a ten-speed bicycle. "I hope Cielo is able to grow up and live in a better place. I worry about what is ahead for her. The treatments and the medications she has to take. Then, if she's lucky, she has to survive out there. It's not fair."

A pang of familiar parental fear iced across John's shoulders. "I'm sorry, Mrs. Cardozo. Can you tell me what Cielo's going through?"

"Hell, that's what she's going through." Her tone was sharp. Maria collected herself, and the exhaustion seeped through her once more. "The doctors have a fancy name for it, but Cielo has cancer. She isn't old enough to understand what could happen. It tears me up inside when I see her at the clinic, hooked up to those machines—she's so little."

A telephone rang out somewhere deeper in the small apartment. Its harsh chime echoed off the walls in high-pitched tones, so loud and sudden that Maria jumped.

"I'm sorry, my mother is hearing impaired, and she has one of those special phones. I hate that thing. I'd better go check on her," she said as she left the couch.

Paula returned from the rear of the apartment and leaned in toward John. "Get anything from her on what our victim was into?"

"Not much." John stood and rolled his stiffened neck, tightened by the pain he felt in Maria's voice when she talked about her daughter's failing health. "Cardozo quit a good job at the port and started some new gig. He brought home some cash—more than Maria thought he should have from a legit job."

From the rear of the residence, Maria's voice grew frantic. "Mama—Mama, we have to go now! Get Cielo up! We have to take her to the hospital! It's time!"

"What's wrong?" Paula asked.

Tears fell from Maria's cheeks. "We have to get Cielo to the hospital. It's finally time for her surgery. Mama! Ay Dios mío, she can't hear me. Mama!" She ran to the rear of the apartment.

"Surgery?" John's chest tightened with the thought of a child on an operating table.

"Man, I thought the little girl looked bad, but wow," Paula said.

"Cancer. Nothing like a being a parent with a sick kid. All your emotions are balanced on a razor's edge. That is one helpless feeling, believe me," John added.

Maria burst from the back of the apartment and stuffed medication bottles and a few clothing items into a plastic grocery bag. She ran to the kitchen and picked up the phone. She entered the number for a taxi service taped to the wall above the phone.

"Hello, I have an emergency. Please send a taxi to—" Maria said, trembling.

John placed his finger on the receiver and disconnected the call. "Which hospital?"

Confusion settled on Maria's face. "Central Valley Hospital. I can't pay for an ambulance, if that's what you're thinking." She started punching in the taxi company's phone number once more.

"We'll drive you," John offered.

"You will?" Maria said.

"Get your daughter and let's go. Central Valley isn't that far."

Maria regarded the cop with a narrowed eye. She retreated to the rear of the apartment.

"What are you doing? It's against policy to transport medical cases," Paula said.

"It shouldn't be. You know that whole 'protect and serve' thing? This is the serve part. You've seen what she's up against—no money, no husband, and a sick kid. She needs our help."

"Yeah, yeah, I get it," Paula said.

Maria told her mother to call the rest of the family while she carried Cielo and struggled to pick up the bag of clothes and medication. John pushed forward and took the sickly girl in his arms. She was limp and rail thin. Her small face was puffy, but her features were delicate and frail. The girl looked up at the stranger who held her with an expression of mild interest. At this point in her treatment, the child had experienced dozens of nurses, doctors, and technicians touching and moving her, so one more unfamiliar face didn't concern her.

John knew that listless gaze, and it tore at his chest. The pain of a helpless, fragile, and vulnerable child was soul crushing. He broke off eye contact, not for the child's benefit, but for his own.

John carried the child to their car while George and his thugs watched. Maria dropped the bag of medications and clothing in the back seat, spilling a half dozen prescription bottles with familiar-looking labels bearing long drug names that seemed like pharmaceutical alphabet soup. John scooped them up and tossed them into the bag.

As they drove away, he couldn't help but think that was a lot of medication for one little girl.

SIX

A stack of pink message slips waited for John when he and Paula returned to their desks. No one bothered to leave messages on Paula's desperate landscape of a work surface, so anything that needed to get under her nose went on John's desk. He took the messages from his blotter and shuffled through them. Two from a local television news reporter went into the trash. The remaining messages included one from the police officers' credit union, a message from Jimmy Franck—a longtime CI, a confidential informant who traded information when he needed a get-out-of-jail-free card—a message for Paula from her mom, and one from someone named Mario Guzman.

"That little girl, dealing with all that medical shit—that's sad," Paula said.

John shifted in his chair at the mention of the Cardozo girl's condition and forced his focus on the message slips.

"Call your mom," he said, passing the pink slip to Paula.

"Oh God, I forgot." She tugged on the ends of her shoulder-length hair.

"Birthday?"

"Worse," Paula said. "She's got it in her head that she has to play matchmaker. She keeps arranging for me to meet guys from her church group. I totally spaced on dinner at her place last night."

"Ouch. I didn't know you were that desperate."

"She sets up these little dinner parties, and her church friends happen to show up trailing their unmarried sons. You can imagine the caliber of that stagnant dating pool; a bunch of mouth-breathing momma's boys."

"Come on, give her a break. She's trying to help. It can't be that bad," John said.

Paula leaned over her desk, lowered her voice so the other detectives couldn't overhear, and said, "Really? You think it can't be that bad? Last month, she pulled off one of these meet and greets, and the guy was a 290 registrant. A frickin' child molester we locked up a couple years back. He nearly shit himself when he saw me, so I knew his mommy didn't know what his deal was. So yeah, it is that bad."

"At least you know he's not gonna cheat on you with another woman," John joked.

Paula threw a pencil at him. "Shut up."

"Well at least you're not trolling the web on one of those Internet dating sites."

Paula didn't respond.

"No, tell me you're not," John pressed.

"You're such an ass." Paula flipped him off, swiveled her chair so that her back was to him, and after dialing her phone, said, "Hi, Mom. Yeah, I know, I'm sorry," into the receiver.

John reshuffled the pink message slips in his hand and spotted one from Jimmy Franck. Jimmy ran in the fringes of the methamphetamine trade in the Central Valley and tipped John to three lab operations last year. John suspected the labs belonged to Jimmy's rivals or to someone who demanded that Jimmy make good on his drug debt. John wasn't in the mood to deal with the methhead's hustle.

John picked up the message from the police credit union and dialed the number.

"This is Janet," she said.

"Janet, John Penley returning your call."

"Thanks for calling back, Mr. Penley."

"No problem. You have some good news for me?"

"I'm afraid not, Mr. Penley. We cannot refinance your home at this time."

"Why not? The interest rates you are handing out on new mortgages are a good three points lower than what we're paying now. We haven't missed a single payment."

"I know, Mr. Penley. The market is still very much upside down, and the appraisal on your property came back too low to support a refinance at this time. When the market values go back up, I'm sure we can do something then. Right now you owe more than the property is worth, and we cannot loan against equity that doesn't exist."

"What about the bailouts I keep hearing about? Don't we get some credit for paying on time?" John asked.

"I'm very sorry, Mr. Penley. If you consider a short sale, perhaps we can help you get something out of the property."

"I don't want to sell. We can't do anything on a refinance? A smaller amount? How about another appraisal?"

"No, Mr. Penley. We have no options at the moment. I'm sorry."

John hung up and sank into his chair. He closed his eyes and rubbed the pain that sprouted beneath his temples. It felt like a vise clamped down on his head. Stress and nicotine withdrawal competed for his attention.

Paula hung her head, doing more listening than talking on the phone with her mother.

John peered across the desks and low-slung partitions that made up the warren that housed the detective bureau. Lieutenant Barnes stood by his office door and motioned for John. He pushed back from his desk and cut across the space. "Lieutenant?"

"Look at these misfits, Penley. Half of them walk around in eight-hundred-dollar suits and spend all day posing in the men's room mirror taking selfies. Then I got a bunch who look like hoodlums, and when they go canvass a crime scene door-to-door, we get nine-one-one calls for attempted home invasions."

"The times are a-changin', Lieutenant," John said.

"Listen, I need to talk to you about your case. The A chief hit me up this morning and used the S-word."

"The assistant chief? Serial killer?" John said.

"Yeah, and when that happens, everything changes. The city council will pressure the chief for a quick close, and calls for the feds to take over will start. The politics behind all this will get really messy. If this killer ends up being called the Sacramento Slasher or something, the politicians will line up at the chief's door, and it won't look good for the city."

"I get it. I never liked serial-killer labels based on location, like The I-5 Killer, Hillside Strangler, Green River Killer, and East Side Rapist. That kind of thinking limits the scope of the investigation. If you're focused on a specific area, you're gonna miss what's happening somewhere else. So no River City Stalker," John said.

"Give it some thought. The brass and the media-relations folks are gonna have to call him something. Better it come from the detective than the politicians," Lieutenant Barnes added.

"I contacted the FBI Violent Criminal Apprehension Program and spoke with the contact you gave me, Mike Thompson," John said. "They had nothing in their files that matched our guy, but he was able to get us a preliminary profile on our killer. Lucky us— this guy is new and unique. The feds can't offer anything we don't already have."

"I'll brief the A chief and try to buy us some time. Let me know when you have anything new that I can feed to the brass."

"Will do," John said.

After a pause, Lieutenant Barnes asked, "How's your son?"

"He handles all the doctors and drugs like a champ. I wish I was as strong."

"How's Melissa holding up?"

"She's amazing. We take turns propping each other up."

Lieutenant Barnes nodded and said, "If you need some time off with your family . . ."

"We have a serial killer to deal with."

"I have closed a few cases myself, you know," Barnes said.

"Tim, I appreciate the offer, but it's better if I keep busy here. If I sit around and dwell on everything, I'll go crazy and be useless to Melissa and the kids."

"I get it," Barnes said. "If and when you need some time—let me know."

From across the office, Paula called out, "Penley, the ME wants to start the post on Cardozo down at the morgue. We gotta go."

"New partner working out?" Barnes said.

"She needs to put in some clean time to show everyone what she's about."

"Newberry took a lot of heat after the Carson investigation."

"I didn't know she was on that case. Paul Carson was an asshole. A twenty-year cop selling dope out of the evidence room deserves to go down."

"Yeah, but Carson was a popular guy, and your new partner set up surveillance on the buy. Some say she set him up."

"You color outside the lines and you run that risk," John said.

"The brass said she didn't exactly fit the mold in IA."

"That's not necessarily a bad thing." John glanced at his coffee mug and tossed the thick, burnt coffee in the sink. "I better get going before Paula throws a stapler to get my attention."

"She couldn't find one on that disaster of a desk. Do something about that, would you? You're the senior detective."

John strode back to his desk and stashed his coffee mug in the bottom drawer. He grabbed his jacket and met Paula, who waited at the door to the detective bureau.

"I'm surprised that the ME is doing a post so soon. It's been less than twenty-four hours. Things must be slow in the body shop," John said.

"Dr. Kelly said this one won't take long because there's not much left to examine," Paula reported.

"Then why the rush?"

"She said something was different with Cardozo."

"What's that?" John asked.

"Cardozo was alive when he was gutted."

SEVEN

Plain walls, tall columns, and expansive windows belied the gruesome tasks carried out within the building on the corner of Forty-Ninth and Broadway. It seemed more suited to scruffy-bearded software designers until the plain-lettered sign came into view—Sacramento County Coroner. John pulled into the parking lot at the rear morgue entrance. He avoided the front public lobby where families waited to claim the remains of their loved ones. Good news never came to those who gathered there, and John felt the lobby held a suffocating cloud of misery from years of accumulated sorrow.

Dual glass doors parted for the detectives as they walked in from the covered bay, past the coroner's white nondescript minivans, used to harvest the dead for examination. A pair of attendants rolled a white-sheeted gurney from an industrial scale toward a wall-mounted X-ray machine. Movement and control of the remains that passed through this building required the skill of an air traffic controller. Dr. Sandra Kelly was equal to the task. During her tenure as coroner, budget cuts hit the operation along with the loss of half of the forensic pathologist positions and the elimination of the chief forensic pathologist. Only two forensic pathologists remained, and they were on call twenty-four-seven to handle the load. Each performed more than six hundred autopsies a year, more than twice the national average. Criminal defense lawyers pounced on the slightest hint of a miscalculation or procedural error due to the workload. So far, Dr. Kelly aptly doused the embers of doubt when called as an expert witness. The look on her face changed when she noticed John and Paula cut through the six open bays of the autopsy suite. These three recent murders tested the coroner's office resources and her own reputation. This was personal.

Dr. Kelly grabbed a file as the two detectives entered.

"Come with me," Dr. Kelly said. No polite conversation, no banter. The doctor led them to the homicide suite, one of two enclosed autopsy spaces.

A sheet draped a lump in the center of the stainless-steel table. Too small for a corpse; the remnants of Cardozo's body hid under the cover. The size of the bundle betrayed the violence inflicted on the former gangbanger.

One wall in the suite displayed a dozen photos of the Mercer and Johnson autopsies. The wounds were identical, grisly bookends of one another. A single, long gash ran from victims' throats down the length of their torsos.

"Let's start here," Dr. Kelly said. "Mercer and Johnson exhibited a common single wound track running from the sternoclavicular joint, where the collarbone and sternum connect down to the pubic arch. Deep, straight, and precise."

Dr. Kelly pulled back the sheeting and exposed Cardozo's carcass. "You see anything different here than what we found with Mercer and Johnson?"

John stepped forward to the steel table where the torso sat like an empty shell, void of its life-sustaining contents. The lump of flesh and bone was sickly white under the autopsy room lighting, more grotesque than it had been in the moonlight. The chest cavity had sunk in on itself because the ribs no longer connected to the sternum. Each rib bore evidence of a sharp cut severing the rib cage from the breastbone. The victim's skin was drawn and puckered like the leather of an old baseball glove. This, too, was evident in the prior two victims.

"Looks the same to me," John said.

"And you call yourself a detective," Dr. Kelly said behind a smirk.

The coroner pressed her gloved hand down on the incision, at the point where the incision began. The severed rib, cartilage, and muscle tissue, while cleanly cut, bore reddish, mottled stains. "Along with the histamine levels in the tissue, this indicates that the incision was perimortem."

"This is how you knew he was alive when the killer went to work on him?" Paula said.

"Exactly. Help me turn him," the doctor directed.

John took a purple latex-free glove from a box on the counter and pulled it over his right hand. Along with Dr. Kelly, he turned the torso onto its side.

John saw the bruise before Dr. Kelly pointed it out. "That looks like a ligature mark. I couldn't see that through the mud last night," he said.

"The bruises tell us this victim was restrained before death. There is a narrow gouge in the skin from whatever was used to bind him. I've swabbed it for trace, but I'm not hopeful it will reveal anything."

"Narrow, like rope or a length of wire?" John said.

"I'd be inclined to say wire. It was wrapped tightly around the victim's torso, and it didn't leave any abrasions that I'd expect to see from a rope or drapery cord."

"Mercer and Johnson didn't have any evidence of restraint," Paula said, looking at the crime photos.

"Why did Cardozo need the restraint that the others didn't?" John said.

"The simple answer is he was alive. Couple that with the near lack of lividity, and that means most of the blood was drained before it had the opportunity to pool. See here, there are a few speckles of pooling; not what you would normally expect," Dr. Kelly said as she touched pinpoint purple specks on Cardozo's back.

Together, John and the doctor lowered the torso back down. John snapped his glove off and tossed it into a red biohazard container near the exam table.

He walked to the wall that displayed the Mercer and Johnson autopsy photos. "What are you saying?"

"The evidence points to the fact that they were dead before the incisions occurred," Dr. Kelly said. "This new one was alive. We don't know if Cardozo was conscious or not."

"Sweet Jesus," Paula added. "You mean he may have been awake when this happened to him?"

"It's possible, and the use of the restraint tells me that it was highly probable."

"Cause of death?" John asked.

"I have tissue samples in the lab for a tox screen. He didn't leave us liver tissue, ocular fluid, blood, or brain matter to work with. Just an empty shell. Right now, Cardozo is like Mercer and Johnson—homicide with the exact cause of death undetermined."

"This guy covers his tracks. But the killer had to know that Cardozo's tattoos would give us a quick identification. We needed a DNA hit to identify Mercer and Johnson. Cardozo was different," John said.

"What if the profiler was right about the whole spilling his guts thing, the idea that he was a snitch? Was the killer trying to find out if he was an informant? It might explain why Cardozo was awake when he was gutted," Paula said.

"That's an angle we can explore," John said. "We can go back and check against known informants. Just because the West Block Norteños claim Cardozo wasn't in trouble with the gang doesn't mean they didn't do a little housecleaning."

Dr. Kelly pulled the sheeting back over Cardozo's remains. "Sorry I couldn't be of more help here. There's simply nothing left to autopsy. Everything is gone. It's like it was already done for us."

John turned, took a step toward the door, then stopped and returned to the photo display. His finger traced the incisions on the

Mercer photo and then touched the Johnson photo. He tapped the latter. "What's he doing with the body parts he keeps?"

"I don't know. The precision with which he dissected, removed limbs and all the internal matter is disturbing. This is someone who knows exactly what he wants with the body and goes about it very efficiently."

"Medical training?" John asked.

"You want to look at every doctor, mortician, and veterinarian in the Central Valley?" Paula asked her partner.

"It's a pool to start with," he said.

"It's a frickin' ocean until we know what he's doing with the body parts. There is absolutely no chatter on the street about finding body parts. Is he getting rid of them? He could be making stew like that New York cop for all we know," she countered.

"A disgruntled sous chef, an off-the-rails satanic cult, or a killer getting rid of gang informants, Cardozo is our connection to the 'why.' This killer is skilled and kept his victim alive while he slowly killed him. What did he want from Cardozo?" John said.

"More than his insides?" Paula asked.

"Something made Cardozo special. We find out what that was and we're finally in our killer's head."

EIGHT

On the walk to the car, Paula asked, "You really think the killer has medical training? I don't need another reason to hate going to my gynecologist."

"You heard Dr. Kelly. Every cut was made with exact precision."

"Or lots of practice," she said.

Both detectives got in the car and buckled up. John started the engine and backed from the parking lot. "Remember back in high school biology? Dissecting frogs?"

"Not my favorite day. That smell. Every time I attend an autopsy, that formaldehyde odor reminds me my class was right after lunch. We had pizza that day, and I threw up all over my frog. I was so embarrassed. I never understood why they made us do that nasty stuff."

"That's kinda what I'm getting at, minus the pizza. The killer treats his victims like lab specimens. Every cut is exact, the bodies are opened up—he knows what he wants; he's not bumbling around looking for something, exploring," John said.

"Cold, direct, and all business. We can run a check on doctors who lost their licenses and complaints filed against hospitals or insurance companies," Paula suggested.

"It's a start, and I can't wait for the doctors to start throwing up the 'patient confidentiality' flag as soon as we start digging."

John pulled the unmarked sedan into the police department parking lot and nosed it into an empty slot near the door. Too late in the day for a call to Jimmy Franck, the snitch, as he'd be deep in a dime bag by now. If Jimmy had anything, someone would have called it in. Inside, shift-change briefings started for the evening units before they hit their assigned patrols. John and Paula entered the hallway and passed the briefing room when a graveled voice called out.

"Hey, Penley, you got a minute?"

John backtracked a few steps to the briefing room door and saw Sergeant E. B. Collins leaning on the podium at the front of the briefing room. The thirty-year veteran ran the briefing for the evening shift, where he issued the latest "BOLOs," or be-on-the-lookout notices, officer-safety bulletins, and crime-mapping updates. The latter involved geographic information systems, what Sergeant Collins referred to as "video game voodoo magic." Collins preferred the time-tested approach of word-of-mouth information dissemination.

Seated at a half dozen tables were the patrol partners that made up the evening shift. The group was a mix of younger officers paired with veteran training officers and those who chose the evening shift to steer away from brass-heavy day-shift politics.

John looked over at Paula and said, "I've got this if you want to take a run at getting the medical licensing information on vigilante doctors."

"I'll get it started with the state medical boards," Paula said. She continued down the hall toward the detective bureau offices.

John ducked inside the briefing room. "Sergeant," he said.

"Detective Penley, would you care to give us an update on the body fished out of the river last night?"

Collins retained the same formal approach in public that John experienced when Collins was his training officer years earlier. Although when together in a patrol unit, Collins had softened and even shed a tear when John's daughter, Kari, was born. He said it was allergies.

John approached the front of the room near the podium, and before he started, one of the older officers called out, "Was it that dirtbag, Cardozo?"

"The body was identified as Daniel Cardozo," John confirmed.

"Any relation to Luis 'Puppet' Cardozo?" an officer asked.

"Brother," John said.

The officer high-fived another longtime officer.

"That's enough, Stark," Sergeant Collins chided.

"Cardozo and the West Block Norteños were pains in the ass every time they crossed the river. What's the deal with celebrating there being one less? They breed like cockroaches anyway," Stark said.

"Detective, is it true that Cardozo was dismembered and gutted, like the others?" one of the younger officers asked.

"He was, although we haven't released that publicly," John said.

"The dude had that coming," Stark responded.

John stiffened. "Nobody deserves what happened to Cardozo. The family doesn't even have a complete body to bury. Our killer has taken three victims, and the only connection we have is that they were all associated with street gangs. We don't know why Mercer, Johnson, and Cardozo were chosen. Cardozo's body was not hidden like the prior two; he called us after he dumped the body this time."

"How do you know this ain't the start of a gang war, picking off thugs one at a time?" Stark said.

"We all would have heard something on the street if this was another gang turf problem," John said.

The rookie officer asked, "What does he do with them? I mean the arms, legs, heads—what does he do with them?"

"Who cares. It ain't like Cardozo's gonna need them anymore. Tell you what, Rook, if you pull over a car with a half dozen feet in the trunk, then you know you cracked the case," Stark said to snickers from the group.

"All right, that's enough," Sergeant Collins said, cutting off the response to Stark's comment. "Detective, what do you need us to look for?"

"We feel that Cardozo could be the key. We are holding back the medical examiner's specific findings, but I can tell you the killer treated Cardozo differently from the prior two. Listen to the chatter on the street and see if you can pick up anything that tells us what Cardozo was up to in the last few days. Everything so far supports the claim that he had cut ties with the West Block Norteños, so if you hear anything to the contrary, shoot it to Detective Newberry or me," John said.

"Screw Newberry," an officer in the back called out.

"Somebody better find this guy's footlocker before Stark's foot fetish takes over and he keeps them for himself," an officer commented from the back row.

"That's enough. You heard the detective—you hear anything pertaining to Cardozo or these murders, get back to him. Anything else, Detective?" Sergeant Collins asked, signaling that he needed to get on with his shift briefing.

"That's it. Thanks, Sarge."

John turned and left the room, the rookie officer's question nagging at him. What did the killer do with all the body parts? Nothing had turned up. Not so much as a single arm, leg, or shred of muscle fiber. By the time he arrived at his desk, a concept had crystallized.

He's a collector.

NINE

"What do you mean he's a collector?" Paula said from behind her desk.

"He's deliberate in every aspect of his work. I'd say almost obsessive in his absolute precision, right?" John said. He peeled a square of nicotine gum and tossed it in his mouth.

"Okay, I'm with you so far."

"Everything he does is reasoned and planned."

"There's nothing reasonable about any of this," Paula said, gesturing to the crime-scene photos on the wall behind her desk.

"Arms, legs, and heads removed, and not a one turned up anywhere. What did he do with them?"

"We've said that he dismembered the bodies to stop us from identifying them. Now you think he has a trophy room?" she asked.

"We know the killer dismembered them. What if it had nothing to do with hiding their identity? What if he kept what he wanted? Still with me?"

"Yeah."

"Think about this like any other supply-chain business. He brings in his supplies and needs a place to work. He does something with them, and then what? He'd have to stash his product until he gets rid of it. Think of it like a meth lab—product in and product out."

Paula examined the crime-scene photos again. "That still brings us back to how he selects his victims." She ticked off points on her fingers. "Were all three victims gang informants? If they were, then who stands to benefit with them off the board?"

"The FBI profiler mentioned the symbolic injury the killer is acting out. What is it that Johnson, Mercer, and Cardozo did that put them on the killer's radar?"

"They were all gang members in the lower rungs of society, preying on the vulnerable. If our killer ran in those circles, how is he able to pull this off without having the full weight of the Crips, Skinheads, and West Block Norteños come down on him? We've heard no talk of revenge or retaliation, a very un-gang-like response to losing a member. Now we can add to the list that we don't know where he keeps his body-parts stash."

From behind John and Paula, Lieutenant Barnes chimed in, "That is not very comforting, Detectives. What, exactly, do we know?"

Paula's face reddened. She stood and pointed toward the three photos of the body dump sites. The gruesome similarity of the bodies was unmistakable, each one deprived of limbs, heads, and entrails. "Each of these victims turned up where they would be discovered, sooner or later. Cardozo was dumped on the riverbank, Mercer on the bike trail, and Johnson in Miller Park. All public places and all within the city limits, but none of them lived in the city. Cardozo lived in West Sacramento, Mercer in Rancho Cordova, and Johnson was from Grass Valley." Paula looked at her partner and saw his nod to continue.

She pulled a file from beneath her keyboard and said, "The victims were gang members, but not in the city . . ."

"Something drew them here," Barnes added.

"Or someone," Paula said.

"What's your theory, Detective?" Barnes asked.

She looked surprised that the lieutenant wanted to hear what she had to say. "Um . . . I haven't run this by Detective Penley yet. It's only a theory." She got another nod from Penley. "According to all our interviews with the victims' families, there was no reason for Mercer or Johnson to be in Sacramento. Cardozo moved his wife and kid here but kept his ties across the river. The killer got them all to come to him. What would lure a gang member? Money or power. If our killer got them to meet him with a promise of a payoff or some information they could use to move up the ranks, it means he's not randomly targeting his victims. He knew who he wanted and went after them."

Lieutenant Barnes pinched the bridge of his nose, as if he fought off a headache caused by the puzzle pieces Paula laid out. "He'd have to offer one hell of a payday to convince someone like Cardozo to turn on the West Block Norteños. What is special about this guy that he can be the Gangland Pied Piper and get his victims to come to him?"

"I don't know, but it means he has a way to identify them," she responded.

"Which is . . ." Barnes said.

"I–I don't know yet. He's precise in everything, so why not in his choice of victims?"

"What else?" Barnes asked.

"He has a place where he takes them and kills them. It has to be private and isolated, with access to the river. Cardozo was dumped by boat, the bike trail is next to the levee, and Miller Park is right on the water. Nothing is random about that."

Barnes nodded, then after a pause said, "Find out how he does it, Detective." He began to walk back to his office, stopped, and turned back. "Good work, Newberry." He turned around once more and headed away.

Paula looked back to John, and a pained look grew on her face. "John, look—I'm sorry I said anything. I didn't mean . . ."

"Don't you ever do that again," John said.

"I'm sorry! The lieutenant surprised me, and I blurted it out. I feel so stupid."

"That's not what I mean. Don't ever apologize for doing your job. Not in the past and not now. The lieutenant's right. How long have you been working on the idea that the killer has a place near the river?"

Paula sat behind her disheveled desk and pushed files around like a bad poker dealer until she found the one she wanted. "Yesterday before work, I took a run along the bike trail. I didn't really put it together with Cardozo getting dumped on the riverbank until today. The bike trail is next to the river, and the spot where Mercer was dumped is maybe fifteen feet from the water."

She pulled a city map from the folder and handed it to John. The map had green circles indicating the three body-drop sites.

"If you look at the map, the bike trail curves toward the river in this spot. Ten yards up- or downstream, the bike trail bends away from the water," she said.

John looked at the map, opened a desk drawer, and pulled additional photos from a file. He flipped through them until he found one that showed an angle of the waterline from Mercer's body. "I know we did a grid search of the entire scene, but nothing popped up near the riverbank to indicate the body came in that way."

"Everyone focused on the bike trail and the parking lot a hundred and fifty yards to the west. That seemed like the most logical approach for his body dump." Paula came around to John's desk and tapped the green circle she'd drawn around Miller Park. "The boat ramp at the park is no more than twenty yards from where we found Johnson's body."

"The bodies hadn't been in the water, so we didn't look at the water as part of the MO," John said. He pushed back from the desk, upset he didn't make the connection earlier. "You know what bugs me about this? He's going to a whole lot of extra trouble to make these dumps. Talk about risk versus reward. It would be much easier—and safer—for him if he just dropped the bodies in the river."

"This means that the open display of the victims is as much a part of his work as the body parts he keeps. He isn't dumping them—he's showing us what he can do, like advertising. He wants us to know."

John chewed that last point over in his mind.

"What? You've got the quiet, gloomy thing going," Paula said.

"I'm not gloomy. I'm thinking."

The phone on Paula's desk rang and cut off her response.

John fidgeted with the photos and stacked them neatly. He noticed another pink message slip from a newspaper reporter. It went into his wastebasket. Reporters always wanted the inside scoop from the lead investigator instead of going through the department's public information officer.

Paula scribbled notes as she spoke with her caller, and John picked up the leftover message slip from someone named Mario Guzman. John dialed the number, and someone responded on the first ring. The guy must have been sitting on the phone.

"Mario Guzman?"

"Who's this?"

"John Penley," he responded, purposefully leaving out the "detective" title.

"Hold on a sec." In the background, voices of children faded, followed by the unique sound of a screen door slamming against a doorframe.

"Detective Penley?"

"Yes." Guzman knew who John was.

"Manny Contreras said I should give you a call."

"Let me guess, Manny told you to tell me that the West Block Norteños had nothing to do with Daniel Cardozo's murder. Well, you can tell him that you passed on the message." It was clearly another smoke screen to insulate the gang from murder.

"I don't know if they did or not," Guzman said.

Not the response John expected. "What are you saying?"

"I don't know how the Norteños figure in Danny's death. He's dead because of what he—what we saw."

John's neck tingled. "What did you see?"

There was a pause on Guzman's end of the phone, then, in a raspy whisper, he said, "We saw dead bodies, man."

TEN

John and Paula sat across from Mario Guzman in a booth at a mom-and-pop diner in West Sacramento. The place sat a few blocks south of the interstate, overlooked by truckers, travelers, and tourists. Greasy windows cast a tallow-yellow pallor over the locals perched at the counter. Little more than time was consumed in this place.

"Let me get this straight. Cardozo asked you to help him with a job," John said.

Guzman sat across from the detective and wrapped his hands around a chipped gray coffee mug in front of him. "Yeah. He needed my truck, and I helped him load up."

"When was this?" John asked.

"About two months ago—that's when Danny first asked. He said there was some good money in it for me. So I asked him if this was anything illegal, 'cause I don't want no trouble."

"Sure, Mario, you're a pillar of the community," Paula said.

"A what?"

"Never mind. Tell me about the job," John pressed as he kicked Paula under the table.

"We picked up the containers, loaded 'em in my pickup, and dropped 'em off. That's it. Danny knew when to pick 'em up and where they were supposed to get delivered. I didn't know about any of that. Danny would call me, and I'd have to run right over. He said that was why the money was so good."

"Where did you pick them up?" John said.

"There were four deliveries, all from a big ol' warehouse on Fifteenth."

"The drop-off?" John asked.

"That was always the same too. The airport."

"Get to the part about the bodies," Paula said.

Guzman looked over his shoulder and ensured no one was within earshot. He leaned in and spoke in a hushed tone. "The containers were the same—always. Silver metal boxes with heavy-duty locks on them, you know the kind that bankers use to carry important papers and shit. So I figured that it must be something really valuable that we was lugging around."

"So you snuck a look," John said.

"Danny didn't know what we was hauling. I thought, you know, I could skim off a little of whatever it was and make a quick buck. Danny said the guy we was doing this work for said that he could never, ever open the containers. That told me that we had a big score in the crates. I cut the lock offa one with my bolt-cutters and opened it. I swear I didn't know what we was doing."

"What was in it?"

"A heart. A heart all sealed up in a plastic like a—what do you call it? A trophy."

"You sure about what you saw? A heart?" John asked, trying to hide the anticipation in his voice. He hid his emotions better than his partner, who began to bounce on the seat next to him.

"Yep. It wasn't like one of them beef hearts in the meat counter at the *carnicería*. This one was human. I know it. When I saw the damn thing, I fell on my ass. Danny looked really scared—like he was into somethin' that he got trapped in, you know? I told him to close it up and drop it off like nothing happened." Guzman stopped, looked from John to Paula, and put a hand up like he swore an oath. "I didn't take nothin' and didn't touch nothin' from that box. Neither did Danny. We dropped off the containers at the airfreight terminal like we was supposed to and hightailed it outta there."

"Did you put another lock on the case?" Paula asked.

Guzman's eyes widened. "No. No, I didn't even think about it. We just wanted to get outta there. That's how he knew."

"When was this?" John asked.

"The day before Danny was killed. Now I know it has somethin' to do with what he saw."

"Then why aren't you dead?" Paula asked.

"Because Danny didn't tell the dude I was helping." Guzman sat straight in the booth, and the blood drained from his face. "Wait, you think Danny told? You ain't gonna tell what I saw, are you?"

Paula let him twist for a moment and sipped her coffee. "Does this taste burnt to you?"

"Tastes like it was strained through old gym socks," John said.

Guzman leaned forward again and bumped his coffee mug. He grabbed it before the bitter brew spilled onto the worn Formica surface. "You can't rat me out. That's against the rules."

"Sometimes to get the big fish, you gotta use a little fish for bait, Mario. You"—John tapped on the table—"are the little fish here."

Guzman stood quickly in the booth, and his thighs caught the lip of the table. His coffee mug tumbled off the surface and shattered on the floor. The waitress shuffled over to the booth and dabbed the coffee off the table with a dingy brown towel. She tossed the towel on the floor and used her shoe to mop the spill. Guzman waited for her to leave before he continued. "You can't tell. Look what happened to Danny."

"How did Cardozo contact the guy?" John said.

"I dunno."

"How did you know when to make a pickup?"

"I dunno. That was Danny's deal. I asked him about it, and he told me that the dude always called him. Danny swore he never saw the guy."

"How'd you guys get paid?" John asked.

"When we was done with the delivery, at the airport, Danny picked up an envelope with the cash."

Talking to Guzman was like pulling teeth from a guy with lockjaw. "Mario, put all the shit together in one sentence. Exactly where did you go and who paid you? And don't tell me Danny paid you," John said.

Guzman's brow furrowed, and he bit his lower lip while he contemplated how to respond. Then, like a kid in seventh-grade math class, his eyes brightened when he figured out the answer. "Danny and me drove to the warehouse down on Fifteenth, like I said. Then we loaded the cases, drove them out to the airport freight terminal, and unloaded them. Danny always checked in with a dude that worked for the freight company and got us the money."

When he finished, he looked expectantly from John to Paula for approval.

"You remember the name of the freight company?" John asked.

"The guy wore a dark-blue uniform. I don't remember the name." Guzman glanced at his watch and said, "I did good by you guys, right? You ain't gonna tell that I saw anything, right? I gotta get going to work over at the ball field. I can hook you guys up with some River Cats tickets when they're in town. Sometimes they let me chalk the baselines."

"Yeah, you did fine. Go on, get to work," John said.

Guzman nodded and carefully got up from the table this time. He made for the exit and hit the door in full stride.

"Is this guy for real? He'd have us believe that all he did was loan Cardozo his pickup truck," Paula said. She went for a sip of coffee but thought better of it before the mug was halfway off the table. "You know he held something back. This killer doesn't simply drop off his body parts and call some doofus with a pickup truck."

John shifted in the booth so he faced his partner. "He probably didn't tell us everything. He said they picked up cases of body parts, but he only copped to opening one of them. I bet they looked in more than one crate too. What he did tell us explains why none of the body parts turned up. The killer ships them out. That also means he has someone to help him on the other end of the delivery who picks them up and gets rid of them."

"That's why we haven't heard anything out on the street about body parts in someone's dumpster."

A pair of uniformed Sacramento police officers entered the diner and headed toward the detectives. John recognized Officer Stark from the preshift briefing with a uniform as rumpled and crusty as his demeanor. A younger, thinner, and more presentable officer trailed a few steps in Stark's wake. They sat across from the detectives without asking, and Stark signaled for the waitress.

Stark pulled a small notebook from his breast pocket. "Your CI is a nutjob. Jimmy Franck called nine-one-one, at your behest, and claimed he found a body. We roll on the call to the old ice factory on Fifteenth and meet your CI. You could smell the eight ball on his breath, and he twitched more than an old man with Parkinson's and Tourette's combined. He points out the place, and we go check it out. The lock on the main door is busted. Squatters and homeless got the place all torn up. But in the middle, there's this circle of melted candles, some chalk drawings, and right in the center of it all, there's a body."

"Jimmy found a body?" Paula said. Her eyes popped wide, and she nearly dropped her coffee cup.

"Yep, wings and all," Stark reported.

"Huh—wait, wings?" Paula asked.

"It was a chicken. Your CI called nine-one-one over a dead chicken." Stark forced a laugh that reddened his complexion.

The waitress appeared, put down coffee mugs for the new arrivals, and left the table without much attention. She sensed Stark wasn't a tipper.

The younger officer poured a dollop of creamer in his cup and stirred the light strands of white into the brown sludge. John noted that he was Tucker B., according to his nametag. "Gotta give the little tweaker his due," Tucker said. "It wasn't a chicken, though. It was some kind of hawk. That was a weird sight, what with all the candles and stuff."

"But still—you can't mistake a bird for a human," Stark said.

"You find anything else there?" John asked.

"Nah. We gave the place a once-over. There was nothing else and nobody else in the place. From the flies, I'd say the bird was there for a few days. I didn't call the evidence geeks in for some feathers," Stark said.

"What'd you do with Jimmy?" John asked.

"We ran him over to the Effort for detox," Tucker said.

Tucker looked up from his coffee and caught Paula eyeing him. He smiled and held her gaze until she looked away.

"Tell me about the place," John said.

Stark took a sip from his mug, "Whaddaya mean? It's an empty shell."

"Except for the whole voodoo, dead-bird thing," Tucker added.

"Did you guys give the place a good look?" John asked.

"You trying to tell me how to do my job, Penley?" Stark challenged.

"I'm only asking if you searched the rest of the building."

"I already told you that nobody was in the place."

John pushed back in the booth and clenched the muscles in his jaw. "Do I have to spell it out for you? Did you look for anything in the building, like bloodstains, clothing, or tools that someone might use to cut up and hide a body?"

"Your CI is a flake. I'm telling you for the last time that there wasn't nothing else there—end of story," Stark said. He swung his thick thighs out of the booth and stood. "Let's go, Tucker." The veteran patrol cop didn't bother to wait for his partner and headed toward the exit. Over his shoulder he said, "Thanks for the coffee, Penley. Watch yourself with this one. You wouldn't be the first good cop she brought down."

Paula tensed, and her cheeks flushed an angry hue.

Tucker slid off the worn bench seat and shrugged his shoulders, a gesture that said he was used to Stark's gruff behavior and knew the futility of expecting anything different. "We were in the warehouse for five minutes, tops. Once we found the candles and voodoo stuff, Stark hightailed it outta there. I think it gave him a case of the heebie-jeebies."

"Would it be worth a follow-up search?" Paula asked.

"I dunno. I only cleared the place. Nobody else was there, but there were a couple locked metal doors that I couldn't access. Since they were padlocked from the outside, I figured the owner sealed them so the street people couldn't set up nice little condos."

Tucker pushed a five-dollar bill on the table to cover the coffee that his partner walked out on and headed for the door.

"Sorry about Stark," John said. "He's a special kind of nasty, that one. He went to the academy with Carson."

"I know."

When the officer had departed, John said, "Why would an abandoned ice plant have locked doors?"

"Like Tucker said, someone has to keep the squatters from setting up camp."

"People who lock stuff up have something to hide. If the business went under, then who cares if someone sets up house?"

"You think Jimmy Franck saw something more than a dead bird, don't you?" Paula said.

"I know the guy's a meth-head, but even he wouldn't mistake a bird for a person." John took another sip from his coffee mug. "Jimmy said the warehouse was on Fifteenth. Guzman sat here and told us he and Cardozo picked up the crates at a warehouse on Fifteenth. We gotta go check the place over. Stark screwed up by not conducting a good search when he went in."

"We don't have anything to base a search warrant on. Tucker and Stark went on a dead body call, so they had a reason to enter. They didn't have cause to search the locked rooms. We could find out who owns the property and see if they would give us consent."

John slid out of the booth and dropped another five dollars on the table. "It has to be the same place Guzman was talking about. It might take days to go through all the bureaucratic channels to find out who owns it."

Paula scooted from the booth. "You're not talking about jumping the warrant. There's too much at risk here. If we find anything, any half-awake defense attorney will get the evidence tossed. We have to wait."

"I didn't suggest we peek before the warrant. I don't think we'll need one. We don't need to find the building's owner. We'll get the owner to come to us."

ELEVEN

"This is such bullshit," Paula said.

After a quick stop at the station and a phone call, the detectives parked their unmarked sedan in a potholed asphalt parking strip in front of the vacant ice plant and warehouse on Fifteenth Street. Layers of faded, chipped paint chronicled the delivery of block ice to the city in a time before refrigerators offered the convenience of crushed or cubed ice without leaving home.

"Here he comes now," John said, pointing to a white pickup truck with city plates kicking up a rooster tail of asphalt chunks in its wake. As the truck drew nearer, the code enforcement lettering on the doors came into view.

A stocky man, who John guessed was in his midforties, unfolded from the cab of the small truck. The city worker wore dark cargo pants and a polo shirt with the city emblem on the chest. The code enforcement officer strode toward the detectives and leaned in John's open window.

"You Penley?" he asked.

John nodded and said, "This is Detective Newberry. You call the owner?"

"Yeah. I'm Jackson," the code enforcement officer said, extending his hand. "What's this about?"

"One of our units pulled a dead animal out of this building last night. Homeless probably using the place as a toilet. All kinds of public health violations going on in there," John said.

Jackson sniffed the air. "I don't smell nothing too ripe."

"You're fifty feet away," John added. "Is the building owner coming?"

"Most of the places we roll up on, you can get a whiff a half a block away." Jackson pulled a notebook from his back pocket, thumbed to a page, and said, "The city records show that this building hasn't had a license to operate since 1989, been vacant since. The owner is listed as Margolis Associates. Their property manager is a guy named Brice Winnow. I've worked with him before. Seems to be a stand-up guy."

"Margolis Associates? Any relation to city council member Susan Margolis?" John asked.

"One and the same. It's her company. She bought up a number of old places downtown and in the midtown corridor with big plans for redevelopment and revitalizing the city center. Everything went on hold after she got elected to the city council. She didn't want any conflict-of-interest complaints if she moved forward on any of the properties."

"Jesus, Penley, this is the councilwoman's place. We can't go messing around in there," Paula said.

Jackson jutted his chin toward Paula. "What's her problem?"

"She's a real animal lover, and she's all broken up about the mistreatment of animals in there," John explained.

"Not to mention the political blowback from the councilwoman," Jackson added.

"Not to mention," John said.

A yellow Lotus Elise turned the corner and gingerly made a course around the larger potholes in the parking lot.

"I thought commercial real estate was dead," John commented.

"Apparently not," Paula said.

The flashy yellow sports car pulled up next to the city truck, and the engine purred through twin chrome exhaust pipes. Not an introvert's car of choice; it screamed for attention. The driver's door swung open like a bug's wing, and a pair of high-gloss shoes touched down on the asphalt.

With a politician's glad hand, Brice Winnow greeted the code enforcement officer as if he were a pricey campaign contributor. He sidled up to the police sedan, thrust his soft, moisturized hand to John, and said, "Brice Winnow, representing Susan Margolis."

John knew that statement really meant, "Don't mess with the councilwoman's interests." The detectives got out of the sedan, and John repeated what he'd told the code enforcement supervisor.

"The place is an attractive nuisance. During the last shift, one of our patrol units reported dead animals, human waste, and hazardous debris. Could be a homeless camp or a shooting gallery— whatever, it's unsafe, and we need Mr. Jackson to tag the building," John said.

As Winnow heard the words "attractive nuisance" and "tag the building," he reacted as if slapped. "Hold on now, Officer . . ."

"Detective," Paula countered.

Winnow's eyes narrowed as they shifted and washed over her body. "Detective," he said in a tone that dripped of dismissive indifference. "You have no right to come in here and threaten to tag the councilwoman's property because of the actions of a few street people."

"When it becomes a public nuisance, we do," John said.

"Why haven't I been advised of any problem with the property?" Winnow looked to Jackson, who shrugged his shoulders and walked to his truck.

Winnow pivoted around to face the warehouse and scanned the aged facade. "I don't see any 'public nuisance.' I don't even see any public," he said, gesturing to the empty loading bays, solidly boarded windows, and the absence of so much as a single shopping cart laden with street treasure.

"Can we get on with this? I get off in twenty minutes," Jackson asked as he pulled out a notice for an unsafe building that he retrieved from his truck.

"I demand proof of this alleged nuisance," Winnow said.

"It's your show, Penley," the city worker said.

"Fine, let's head inside," John directed as he and Paula headed for the stairs that flanked the loading bay.

Winnow didn't move; he stood fixed to the asphalt.

"He's not buying it," Paula observed.

"He will," John said as he reached the bottom of the stairs.

Jackson pulled off the adhesive backing on the unsafe-building notice.

From the parking lot, Winnow called out, "Hold on. Let's talk this over. I'm sure there's been some mistake here." He started across the asphalt and scuffed the tip of his shoe on a section of cracked pavement. Winnow climbed the stairs, and his face betrayed the fact that he held Penley responsible for the deep gouge in his shoe. "Show me this great threat to public safety."

"You got a key?" Jackson asked.

"Yes, of course," Winnow said. He thrust a hand into his pants pocket, pulled out a ring with a single silver key, and caressed the metal with a finger. "Here, let's get this over with." He handed the key to Jackson.

"There's your consent to search," John whispered to his partner.

"Keep your key. The lock's busted," Jackson said.

John pushed the door back against rusted hinges, and it opened into a deep black maw beyond the threshold. A stale copper smell wafted from within. "Lights?"

"I had the utilities shut off ages ago," Winnow said.

John fished a hand behind the door and located a gang of switches that once operated the electric roll-up doors and overhead lights. He flicked them up, one at a time. Nothing happened. He reached for the last switch, and a jolt of electricity shot up his arm from a bare copper wire where the switch had once lived. John involuntarily jumped away, banging into the steel door. A white spark sizzled and burned bright spots in John's field of vision.

"You okay?" Paula said.

"Yeah. I guess the power got turned back on." John looked to the code enforcement officer. "Hand me your flashlight, would you?"

John took the thick black flashlight and pointed the beam on the exposed wire. Careful not to repeat his near electrocution, John held the light steady and observed that the switch was missing, replaced with a new strand of heavy yellow Nomex-wrapped power cable. The new strand of cable joined in the switch box in a messy, twisted copper connection.

"You need a better handyman, Mr. Winnow," John said. John ran the light from the box along the path of the new yellow-coated power cable. It ran toward the dark rear of the warehouse and disappeared into a gray metal box mounted above a door.

"Squatters, no doubt," Winnow responded. "Same ones who broke the lock."

"Copper wire and fixtures are stripped from abandoned buildings, not usually added." John took a few steps forward into the warehouse, and a light snapped on from overhead. The light nested above the old industrial fixtures that once illuminated the ice-plant floor. This light was new and included a motion-sensor switch. The beam focused on a particular spot. Illuminated on the floor below was a pentagram, punctuated with melted candles.

"What the hell is that?" Jackson said.

Paula stepped closer and bent on one knee. "This is what Stark and Tucker found. I'll give Jimmy the benefit of a doubt on this one. It is kinda creepy."

"Bird? This is all about a dead bird?" Winnow scoffed.

Jackson gave the pentagram altar a wide birth and made the sign of the cross with a quick motion.

John stood over Paula's shoulder and examined the chalk drawing around the dead hawk. It was unlike any pentagram he'd ever seen, all jagged angles and straight lines emanating out from the hawk's carcass. The design gave off an ancient vibe, almost Native American. That's when it struck him. It wasn't a pentagram; he'd seen this drawing once before. This was a crude replica of the tattoo on Daniel Cardozo's chest.

"There is too much blood under this bird. There had to be another source," Paula said.

"Detective, is this all you came for?" Winnow said.

John ignored Winnow and walked deeper into the building, following the yellow power cable. A faint hum, mechanical and continuous, arose from the darkness. John reached the far wall, where the power cable terminated in an old electrical box mounted above a bank of ancient walk-in freezers. A few freezer spaces no longer had the thick insulated doors, but the one directly under the power box was intact, secured by a shiny new padlock and reinforced steel hinges.

John waited for the others to catch up and then borrowed a set of bolt-cutters from Jackson. After snapping the lock's shank, John drew it back out of the hasp bolted into the insulated door. A tug on the thick handle released the door, and a fine mist of vapor seeped out from the edges.

The humming sound grew louder as the door opened, but the space inside was unlit, filled with a veil of cooled mist that reflected his flashlight beam.

John pulled the door fully back on its hinges, and mist pooled onto the floor around his ankles. The copper scent was sharp. He stepped into the freezer, directed his light on the wall nearest the door latch, and found a switch. Using the end of his flashlight, he forced the switch up, and three banks of fluorescent lights flickered on overhead.

Inside, the freezer was larger than expected. It stretched back thirty feet, with opaque plastic sheeting draped from floor to ceiling. At the rear of the space, a curtain of sheeting separated a section of the freezer. A metallic surface, beyond the plastic barrier, reflected the glare of an overhead light fixture.

The burnished concrete floor told a history of ice blocks being shoved and pushed across the surfaces of the warehouse. Rubber tubing snaked from beneath the plastic curtain and disappeared down an old floor drain in the center of the space. Congealed blood pooled in the drain. The sharp note of bleach in the air failed to cut through the stench wafting from the drain.

As the detectives and Winnow approached the sheeted area, the code enforcement officer stayed near the door and readied to bolt like a sorority girl on a ghost hunt.

John reached the plastic curtain and pushed it aside, revealing a deep-channeled table with high-set sides. John had seen similar pieces, but only at the morgue. The table design served the coroner and morticians well, ensuring human remains, fluids, and detritus remained on the surface and didn't slop onto the floor.

Thankfully, the table was clean, but deep gouges in the stainless-steel surface betrayed heavy use. In the center of the table, a single metal case, slightly larger than a standard briefcase, sat upright.

"What is that?" Winnow said.

"That looks like what Guzman told us he and Daniel Cardozo picked up," John said.

"Guzman and who?"

John placed a hand on the case. "It's vibrating."

Paula moved closer. "There is a tag on the handle." She flipped it over. "It's addressed to you."

Dark, handwritten block letters spelled out *Detective John Penley*. Under the name, the only information consisted of eight letters and numbers, indecipherable gibberish, on the paper tag.

"What the hell is this?" John said. He shifted the metal case so that it faced him. He thumbed the locks open on the corners and slowly raised the lid. A puff of cold vapor snuck out from the seal as the lid opened. From inside the container, a mechanical thrum sounded. John recoiled and fell back against the freezer wall.

A perfectly shaped human kidney glistened within a plastic case. Small diameter tubes ran from the organ to a battery-operated device that pushed a milky fluid through the tissue and circulated it back through the pump in a closed loop.

The message couldn't be more personal. The killer knew that John's son suffered from kidney failure.

TWELVE

"Usually, you bring me more to work with," Dr. Sandra Kelly said.

The metal case was splayed open on the autopsy table like a clamshell. The kidney, wrapped in its protective plastic cover on one side, seemed dwarfed by the size and bulk of the battery pack and pump on the other. A nest of tubes and wires ran within neat grooves and channels cut into a dense foam-insulated layer.

Dr. Kelly loosened a clamp on the part of the case that stored the kidney. "I feel like I should call in my auto mechanic for this part."

"What's the purpose of all this stuff? One of our sources said something about a trophy. Is that was this is?"

The doctor continued disassembling the protective layer of foam. "This is an organ harvested for transplant."

"Don't you have to get harvested organs for transplant to a hospital right away? Ambulances, helicopters, ice chests, and stuff?" John said.

"Sooner the better, certainly. If preserved properly, organs maintain their viability for hours. The research in this field is expanding so fast, and newer technology keeps organs viable for longer periods than anyone thought possible a few years ago." Dr. Kelly worked the clear plastic container free from the case and placed it on the stainless-steel autopsy table.

"How long would something like that last?" Paula asked.

"Hard to say. Given the right circumstances, the health of the donor, and the methods used to cool and preserve the tissue—forty-eight hours, maybe more," the doctor said.

"Two days from killing his victim to mailing out the parts and delivering them to their recipient," Paula observed.

"Two days from harvest to executed sale," John added.

The constant high-pitch thrum ceased as Dr. Kelly snapped the battery pack out of its housing. "Huh."

"What?" John asked.

"No backup. Most perfusion pumps have a redundant battery backup in case one drains. This one doesn't," Dr. Kelly said.

"Perfusion?" John said.

"Perfusion pump. This one is cutting edge. They're designed to push a specialized fluid through the organ to keep it viable for transplant. I'll test this, but I'm willing to bet it's Viaspan, Euro-Collins, or simple Ringer's lactate."

"Where can someone get a setup like that?"

"There's a dozen manufacturers. You can find the pumps on eBay," Dr. Kelly said.

"We should be able to track the purchase," Paula said. "Can't be too many people out there buying perfusion pumps."

John picked up the battery pack, and the surface was hot to the touch. "What's the significance of operating without a battery backup? I mean, other than the obvious—the pump stops working and the tissue dies."

"The choice your suspect made is . . . interesting. I guess 'interesting' is the word I'm looking for."

"Cutting up a body isn't new, but usually it's to cover up the crime," John said.

"That's not what I'm talking about. The choice to try to preserve the organ by machine perfusion over cold storage is puzzling," the doctor said.

"It was cold when we opened it," Paula said.

Dr. Kelly snapped off her latex gloves, leaned against a tall cabinet, and rubbed her temples. "I did an internship, longer ago that I'd like to admit, in cryogenic preservation."

"As in freezing people?" John said.

"It's a bit more complicated than that, but yes."

"I thought that was all science fiction," John said.

"That's why I don't bring it up very often. But the research in cryogenics has revealed useful techniques in related fields. You're looking at one of them now. Machine perfusion."

"What's puzzling about that?" John said.

"There are two primary methods of preserving an organ for transplant. Cold storage and machine perfusion. Cold storage is exactly what it sounds like. The organ is immersed in a cold solution of Euro-Collins or Viaspan and maintained at a temperature of two to six degrees Celsius."

"That cold? Won't everything turn to ice?" John asked.

"The reduction to the static temperature is gradual, one degree per minute. The preservative solutions prevent cell crystallization," Dr. Kelly said.

"The second method you mentioned—that's the machine?" Paula said.

"A perfusion pump with a plasma protein fraction perfusate solution. It's cold, but not as cold as the cold-storage solutions. If properly maintained, an organ can be kept up to five days."

"Why would our guy choose machine perfusion over the antifreeze method?" John said.

"I don't know," Dr. Kelly said. "That's more of a detective thing if you ask me. From the standpoint of a pathologist, I can say that an organ is viable for transplant for a finite amount of time."

"So he chose to keep the organ viable longer?"

"Maybe, but without the battery backup, the pump will fail. Without the circulating cooled preservative solution, the level of intracellular sodium increases. The tissue then draws water into the cell structure, resulting in lethal cell swelling. The organ ultimately develops delayed graft function and becomes useless."

"Okay then, from a pathologist's standpoint, what happens when one of these cases gets to its destination?" Paula asked.

"The activity starts long before that point," John said. "Blood typing and tissue-matching data are collected and goes into a national data registry. UNOS, the United Network for Organ Sharing, manages the allocation of transplant organs across the nation. Patients connect with a transplant center and a surgical team and wait for a match. When information comes from UNOS, the doctors and patients get notified. Transplantable organs, the recipient, and the surgical team all converge at a hospital with a transplant center."

Dr. Kelly's eyes softened. "How is Tommy doing, by the way?"

"What? What about Tommy?" Paula said.

John sighed. "Tommy has end-stage renal failure. He needs a kidney transplant."

Paula's eyes betrayed her shock. "How long . . . ?"

John leaned against a counter and faced Dr. Kelly. "He's hangin' in there. It's been three and a half years of waiting and transplant surgeries getting cancelled at the last moment. I can see why people turn to the black market to get around the UNOS wait list."

Dr. Kelly leaned on a counter. "It's not only the black market. There's an explosion in demand for human tissue. It's big business, especially in private hospitals overseas. It's spawned an entire industry—transplant tourism."

"Transplant tourism?" Paula asked.

"I've looked into it. Transplant patients travel to resort hospitals, get the surgery, and come back for postop care. China, Iran, Israel, and the Philippines have transplant destinations, and it ain't cheap," John said.

The doctor nodded. "Private hospitals, mostly. Iran's system is operated by nonprofits in the country, and they pay the expenses for both the patient and the donor. Iran actually has a waiting list of kidney donors."

"The catch is, you have to be an Iranian citizen. I checked," John said. He gestured to the swollen hunk of flesh. "How much would something like that be worth on the black market?"

"Depends. I've heard it's different from country to country, but on average, ten thousand dollars will get you one straight off the showroom floor," Dr. Kelly said.

"I bet there's no paper trail for that transaction," Paula said.

John's brow knitted. "Doc, if someone uses an off-the-books connection, how can they be sure where these organs come from? And what about the condition of the parts by the time they get there?"

"That's the risk you take when you deal with those kinds of connections. The private overseas hospitals are legitimate, so your chances of getting a matched, viable organ are decent. The black-market transactions—well, let's say, no one asks too many questions."

"I'd imagine if someone paid enough to make sure they got a transplantable organ, they'd be pissed off when it doesn't survive the trip," John said.

"That's where the black market works in your suspect's benefit. He gets paid up front. He doesn't have to worry about what happens when the organs are delivered, and there's not much the receiving end can do about it. And if your guy is trafficking in Asia, India, or Europe, there may be no way to track his transactions."

"But he only stays in business as long as the 'merchandise' meets expectations wherever he ships them to. If word got out that he sold bad product, that would be the end of his enterprise. That brings me back to the battery pack. A single battery, with no backup, means the shipment was not intended for a prolonged journey," John said.

"Long enough. Mario Guzman told us he and Cardozo delivered their crates to the air cargo terminal. There would have been plenty of battery life to ship one of these to Asia. Or this creep just didn't care," Paula added.

"Could he get the organ into the legitimate medical supply chain locally? What kind of medical facility could pull off a transplant surgery?" John said.

"You're talking about two points along a linear process, the beginning and the end. There is so much more that happens in between to ensure that the organ supply chain remains untainted. The UNOS processes exist to prevent someone from introducing contamination from a black-market connection where there is no telling what condition it's in or the condition of the donor.

"A kidney transplant isn't technically difficult. But what legitimate hospital would put their accreditation and license at risk?" Dr. Kelly asked.

"How would they know?" John countered.

"You can't simply walk in off the street with a human heart or kidney in a dirty Ziploc bag and expect the transplant team to accept it as legitimately donated tissue. It doesn't work that way. The system tracks the tissue. There are tests and protocols," Dr. Kelly said.

"Do they come with an 'Inspected by Number 43' sticker, like my boxers?" John quipped.

"In a manner of speaking, yes, smartass, they do. The data show the transplant center, when the organ was harvested, and where the organ came from. In some cases, there will be additional donor detail."

"What kind of detail?" Paula asked.

"Anything that may assist the transplanting surgeon—live donor versus deceased or any health concerns that may require additional caution to prevent infection and rejection. The point being, the system alerts the transplant team to a specific organ tagged for delivery. The allocation protocols in UNOS are rigid to protect the patient from getting the wrong organ or one without any chance of viability after transplant."

"If the transplant doctors got the alert from UNOS, they wouldn't question the origin of the donated organ," John said.

"That's right. The notification comes through the UNOS system as an online message. It's a closed system—a message goes to the transplant center, and a return message verifies the contact."

"Okay, so I can't call from the corner liquor store and claim I'm from UNOS with an organ to sell?" Paula added.

"No, and UNOS isn't involved in any financial transaction. The system is designed to collect all the information regarding the need for various transplants across the country and then allocate and notify when a match occurs in the system," the doctor said.

"If I wanted to get a harvested black-market organ to a legit hospital without the transplant center getting suspicious, how could I do that?" John asked.

"Someone on the inside would have to be deliberately manipulating the data, but no doctor would take the risk using something outside that protocol."

"What if instead of our killer selling to someone on the inside, he had access to the UNOS database? He could use the data to hunt for potential clients. It explains how this guy knew about Tommy. My son's need for a kidney is in the UNOS database."

"How many people know about what he's going through?" Paula said.

John rubbed the bridge of his nose. What he wouldn't give for a cigarette right now. "Family and a few others. Melissa and I wanted him to feel like a normal kid as much as possible. He doesn't need some Facebook stalker spreading his story all over the Internet."

"Or friends at school treating him differently," Dr. Kelly said.

"Exactly."

"Insurance representatives, pharmacists, hospital staff, his doctors," Paula continued. "Anyone involved in his care, or someone they talked to about him, knows what Tommy needs."

"That doesn't explain this," John said, tapping the organ transport case with his finger. "This is more than someone talking about my son. This was damn near gift wrapped for him. Doc, can you tell me if this is a match for my son?"

"I'll look at the tissue type against Tommy's."

Dr. Kelly placed the plastic-boxed kidney on the small pedestal and flicked a switch. A flat-panel monitor projected a display of the organ at higher magnification. "I'll run what I can on this tissue and see if I can find out more. I doubt that I'll be able to get any identification. Maybe DNA, but that could take days, if it's even in the system. Whoever harvested this wasn't too careful. There is some evidence of crushing on the main artery at the point of dissection. He used scissors rather than a scalpel."

"So?" John asked.

"The damage to the vascular tissue was avoidable, if he knew what he was doing."

"Either he didn't care or didn't know any better," Paula said.

Dr. Kelly flicked off the light over the damaged organ, and the glisten that gave the tissue purpose faded.

"Who has access to the UNOS data?" John said.

"I'm not certain, but a number of people at the transplant centers have access to patient and donor information."

"I've worked with the staff at Central Valley Hospital. It's hard to think that any of them would be involved in black-market organ harvesting," John said.

"Money is one hell of a motivator," Paula said.

"Don't forget Delta Medical Center and Southland Hospital have transplant programs too," Dr. Kelly reminded them.

"The system is interconnected, right?" John asked.

"The transplant centers are connected to the same data, but it's a closed system, so only they can access it." Dr. Kelly grabbed a blank autopsy chart that depicted the outline of the human form, where lines and dots translated into graphic illustrations of gaping lacerations and gunshot wounds. She scribbled a note on the back of the form and handed it to John. "Trisha Woods works over at Central Valley Hospital. You know her?"

"Yeah, I do. She handled all the paperwork for us when the doctors put Tommy in the transplant program."

"Tricia is the UNOS expert at the place. If there were a way to beat the system, she would know. And I trust her."

"We'll check in with her. Can you give her a call and let her know that we're pursuing something related to UNOS and not . . ."

"Using her services for personal reasons?" Dr. Kelly finished.

"I can't do anything to put Tommy's place on the list at risk. If they thought that I tried to manipulate the process . . ."

"Don't worry, I'll make the contact. Now if you don't mind, I need to get some tissue samples of this little bugger up to the lab," Dr. Kelly said.

John and Paula left Dr. Kelly in the autopsy suite and meandered back to the parking lot. At the car, Paula looked across the hood and locked eyes with her partner.

"Were you ever gonna tell me about Tommy?"

"What's to tell? It's not your problem."

"That's not what I meant. I'm your partner now."

"What would telling you do? He'd still need a kidney."

Paula's eyes narrowed. "You should have said something. Your son is on a transplant list, and our killer knows about it. If you could get Tommy on the top of the list, would you?"

"Start screwing around with that list and people die. Who could live with that?"

Paula nodded and silently got into the car.

John didn't know if his answer satisfied her. In truth, he wasn't sure how far he'd go.

THIRTEEN

Most evenings in the Penley home consisted of frantic meal preparation and homework before settling into a mellower pace. Melissa loaded the last of the dinner dishes into the dishwasher with Tommy's help before he went to finish his homework. Kari avoided eye contact with her mother and kept her head bent over her cell phone, thumbs pecking away on the keyboard at a speed that signaled the teen's world was out of balance—again.

John came in the front door, opened the closet, took off his jacket, and hung it on a hook. On the floor, he noticed a remote-control airplane kit that he had promised to put together with Tommy. One more thing put off. How many more chances would he squander?

"I have a plate warm in the oven for you. Wasn't sure when you'd be here," Melissa called out.

John strolled into the kitchen past a sulking Kari, who tapped away at another text message. "What's up with her?"

Melissa gave him an eye roll, an exact duplicate of the expression Kari worked like a world-class artist. Kari could execute a dozen variations of the eye roll. A roll one way meant exasperation, while another warned of a dark, hormonal storm on the horizon. This one was definitely of the latter variety.

John used a dish towel to pull the hot plate from the oven and pulled back the foil. He carried the dish to the counter next to Melissa and tilted his head toward Kari.

"She's been texting her friends since she got home. Something about a new school dress code. I haven't seen anything from the school about one."

Molten, cheesy strands hung from John's fork to the enchilada on his plate. He maneuvered the forkful and let it cool. "Figures that Kari and her fashion police would be the first to discover the plans to quell their freedom of expression."

"Can you imagine Kari and her friends in uniforms?" Melissa said. "I think I'll volunteer that day so I can watch the fireworks."

John polished off his enchilada and rinsed the plate in the sink. He leaned back against the counter, snaked an arm around Melissa's waist, and exhaled.

"What? I know that sigh," she said.

"I got a call from the bank today. They won't approve our loan. We don't have the equity in the house that we did a couple of years ago."

Melissa swiveled around and faced him. "They didn't even approve a loan for a smaller amount? I mean, nothing? We needed that to cover Tommy's expenses. What are we supposed to do now?" Her eyes misted over.

"We'll figure it out," John offered.

"That second mortgage on the house was our best option."

"It was the option we wanted, but it's not the only one we have."

"The social worker and financial advisor at the hospital ran the numbers for us. After the insurance pays their part, we'll have over a hundred thousand dollars in medical costs. That doesn't include the antirejection medications that Tommy will need for the rest of his life."

"I might be able to cash out my retirement accounts."

"That won't be enough," she said.

"We'll find a way to make it happen. We still have that list of foundations that the hospital gave us."

"I never thought we'd have to take donations from charity."

"Me neither. How do you think it makes me feel that I can't provide for my family? If it takes swallowing some pride and asking for help to get Tommy what he needs, I'll do it."

Melissa nodded. "If that's what it takes." Eager to change the course of the conversation, Melissa called out to Kari, "Did you finish your homework?"

"Almost," Kari said while she tapped out another text.

"Put the phone away and get to it," Melissa said.

Kari strode off to her room and announced her displeasure with a thud of her bedroom door.

"Exactly like her mother," John said.

Melissa grabbed a dish towel from the counter and snapped John's thigh. "Better watch yourself," she said before setting off across the kitchen.

John grabbed a bottle of water from the refrigerator and briefly laid it across his forehead to act as a cold compress against the tension headache that threatened to burst from behind his eyes. "When did life get so complicated?"

"It makes you appreciate all the small things," Melissa said.

"Thank you, Zen Master."

"Quit being a smartass and go see if Tommy needs help with his homework. He has a science test tomorrow."

John found his son tucked behind the family's laptop computer in the office. The boy navigated the web browser through page after page of search-engine results until he settled on a link that promised a study guide to photosynthesis. The guide, posted on his science teacher's resource web page, included last year's test answers.

"Isn't that cheating?"

"No. If Mrs. Brown didn't want the test out there, she wouldn't have posted it," Tommy said as he clicked the link.

"Shouldn't you study the material instead of the test answers?"

"It doesn't matter; I know that stuff anyway. This is like checking my work. I'm getting the right answers."

"Oh yeah? Let's see." John swiveled the laptop away from Tommy and started peppering him with questions from the test. After ten straight correct responses, John said, "Okay, you know this stuff. But tell me—how did you find this website?"

"That's easy. The answers to anything are out there, if you know where to look. Mrs. Brown always says, 'Science is fun,' even though it sucks. So I typed in *science is fun* and my teacher's name into a search box and found it."

John looked at the screen. The title of the page was "Science Is Fun" by Emily Brown. Smart kid. "That's enough studying for the night. Get ready for bed."

"Okay, Dad. Thanks for helping me."

Tommy started out the door and paused, his brow knit in a serious expression.

"Dad?"

"Yeah, Tommy?"

"What's it like when you die?"

"What do you mean?"

"When you die. What happens? Does it hurt?"

"Why are you asking?"

Tommy shifted against the doorframe and broke eye contact with his father. He stared out the window as a car passed by, and after a pause, said, "I heard Mom and Dr. Anderson talking the other day. Mom said if I don't get my kidney transplant, I could die."

John felt his stomach grow cold. "You are going to get your surgery, and you'll feel better than ever."

"What if I don't? Am I gonna die?"

"Don't worry about that. You're gonna be fine," John said with as much reassurance as he could muster. It wasn't only for Tommy.

Tommy nodded and disappeared down the hallway, his stooped shoulders and floor-bound gaze broadcasting his insecurity and fear.

John closed his eyes, tipped back his head, and let loose a breath he didn't know was trapped in his chest. A nine-year-old boy should not have to ask about what happens when you die. Kids that age are supposed to run, play sports, and not have a care in the world. It wasn't fair, and John couldn't do a damn thing about it. He felt helpless.

Tommy's words replayed in his mind: "The answers to everything are out there, if you know where to look."

John pulled the wireless keyboard over, used the mouse, and brought up a search engine. A cursor blinked in a blank white box, awaiting his command. He typed in the words *black-market organ transplant* and hit the enter key.

"Down the rabbit hole, John."

Transplants were, as Dr. Kelly had said, big business; eight billion dollars spent on organ research, preservation, and procurement, all in the name of extending life. John's Internet search confirmed what he already knew—that megahospitals, big-pharma, and insurance companies were the real gatekeepers of organ-transplant transactions. "Transaction" was the correct term because money, bundles of it, changed hands at each turn in the process. At the end of the day, everyone made a profit except for the patients. Those lucky enough to survive and receive a transplant found themselves mired in debt for the rest of their days.

John drilled deeper into the darker corners of transplants, where a husband in India sold his wife's kidney and where the harvested organs of Chinese prisoners went to the highest bidder. Humans were worth more dead than alive. Spare parts. Urban legend mixed with threads of authentic desperation. One truth among the stories captured a common theme—if you have enough money, all waiting lists disappear as long as you don't ask questions.

Black markets in human organs thrived in India, Asia, and Eastern Europe, where the accounts of the "donations" smelled of extortion and abuse. Few of the thousands of links tracked back to North American sources. An intact body was worth up to two million dollars when parsed out to those who waited in the shadows.

John plucked his cell phone from his pocket and dialed. After a single ring, Paula's voice, shrouded within a veil of sharp, off-pitch noise, responded.

"Hi, John."

"What the hell is that?"

"Oh, I was listening to Yanni, sorry. Let me turn it down." A moment later, the sound retreated. "Okay, I'm back."

"Yanni? Seriously? No wonder you have no social life."

"It's after midnight, partner. I'm entitled to some downtime," she said.

John checked his watch, surprised at how much time had gotten sucked away while he probed the dark reaches of the web.

"How did we find the warehouse?"

"What do you mean?" Paula said. "Guzman told us he and Cardozo picked up deliveries from the place. And your CI, Jimmy Franck, called in the tip about a sacrifice."

"I guess what I mean is, why were we allowed to find it? The killer made sure we'd find the place, complete with a personally autographed body part."

"You think?"

"Hey, I mean we're good, and we would have found it eventually, but he wanted it found now," John said.

"The killer wanted us to know he's killing gang members—for parts?"

"I did a quick search and found dozens of websites that claim they can get around the transplant waiting lists. I can't get over the idea that the killer could be trolling these transplant lists for desperate buyers."

"What aren't you saying, John?"

"I want to draw him out."

"If he gets wind that we're baiting him, we might lose him."

"You saw the message he left for me. He thinks he's untouchable. He might be right if we don't change tactics."

"What are you suggesting?"

"We look at who received transplants. Tomorrow we hit the UNOS network and pull the data for people who got a transplant and didn't have to wait long."

Silence was all he heard from Paula's end of the connection.

"Paula?"

"Are you certain that Tommy's long wait for a match isn't coloring your judgment?"

"I can't say it hasn't. If anything, what we've gone through with Tommy points out that transplants are a system with rules and boundaries. And with any system, some people don't think the rules apply to them."

"You're talking about thousands of records to sift through. That's if we get a judge to ignore the confidentiality of medical records and give us a warrant. We need more than a theory that someone was able to cut in line and get a transplant."

"The link is there. I know it."

"Maybe, but we have to find a way to get there without individual patient records."

"We'll figure it out tomorrow morning when we talk with Trisha Woods at Central Valley Hospital."

"The contact Dr. Kelly gave us."

"You want me to swing by your place and pick you up?" he asked.

"Sure. What time?"

They agreed on a time and hung up. John went to flick the computer monitor off, and his hand hovered over the power switch. A new e-mail message flashed on the screen and drew his attention. The subject line simply asked, *"Waiting list too long?"*

John clicked on the link, and a software file downloaded a Tor Internet browser. He'd seen this kind of anonymous Internet browser before when he worked a child pornography case. The Tor browser allowed fully anonymous, untraceable communication on the dark web, the Sodom and Gomorrah of cyberspace. A plain screen appeared without the banners, menus, and advertising that usually infected the Internet. The screen resembled an old-fashioned green-screen computer terminal with a blinking cursor parked in the upper-left corner. Pale-green letters spelled out *Log In*.

He typed in *organ* and pressed enter, but nothing happened. He tried the words *transplant, waiting list,* and *kidney*, all with the same lack of response from the web guardian. John shifted in his chair, mulling over the thousands of possibilities that would open this portal. He picked up his cell once more, this time flicking though photos he'd taken of the kidney delivery at the old ice plant. Maybe the series of random letters and numbers under his name on the tag wasn't so random.

John held his phone next to the screen, typed in the combination of letters and numbers exactly, and pressed the enter key. John ran his mouse across the screen and nothing happened. Another dead end.

As John prepared to give up and kill the power to the computer, the screen suddenly changed. The cursor blinked and moved as words flowed onto the display.

Welcome. How may I help you? The cursor blinked on a new line below the words, waiting for a reply.

"I've got you now, you son of a bitch." He tugged the keyboard toward him, poised his hands over the keys, and tapped a response. *Who is this?* He hit the return key and waited.

You may call me the Broker, came the reply after a few seconds.

John sat upright, decided to play along, and typed. *What kind of broker?*

The kind that gets things done. How may I help you?

Transplants? John typed.

Donor or recipient?

Recipient, John replied and waited.

The letters scrolled out the next question. *Are you on the waiting list?*

Yes. I don't want to wait any longer, John replied, thinking of his son.

You should allow the waiting list to take its course.

I've done that. Can you help me or not?

John waited. After a long pause, the reply spilled onto the screen. *I may be able to move things along. I will extract information from your medical records so that I can expedite the process for you.*

A cold ball of lead formed in John's stomach. The conversation teetered on the edge of all ethical boundaries, and yet nothing damned the person on the other end of the connection. Using his son's medical condition as a cover was a new low, but John needed to press the Broker for more information to get the killer to give up a vital piece of information that would bring him down.

Where do you get the organs? John pressed the return key.

Donors, of course. They don't grow on trees, which brings me to my fee for expediting this process. Ten thousand, up front.

How do I know you can do what you say? John typed.

You don't. Call it a leap of faith.

John waited, not sure of his approach.

New words scrolled out onto the screen while John watched. *Contact me when you are serious.*

The lines of the discussion disappeared from the monitor, leaving no trail that it had ever occurred. The lone, blinking cursor was all that remained on the screen. John tapped out a message on the keyboard. *I'm in. What information do you require to get started?*

His question held vigil on the screen. Not a single word response came from the other end of the computer connection.

The Broker was gone.

A twinge of panic surged, and John refreshed the screen.

I need your help, John typed.

There was a long pause with nothing but the blinking cursor, thumping in time with John's heartbeat, and then it sputtered to life.

Patient's name?

John entered Tommy's name.

Transplant center?

Central Valley Hospital, John responded.

Send full payment to this account. A long string of letters and numbers followed the demand.

John saved a screenshot of the information and closed the laptop cover as if a virus would ooze from the screen and infect his family.

But in truth, it already had.

FOURTEEN

Following a fitful night's sleep filled with images of computer screens and human organs tied up with bright ribbon, John rose hours before the rest of the family.

He made coffee for Melissa and collected the newspaper from the front drive. A quick scan of the main section revealed nothing surprising: a rehashed version of yesterday's political squabbles and budget shortfalls. His morning routine included a review of the obituaries for people that he knew. Occasionally, one of the memorials struck a chord; a young person succumbed to disease before they had a chance at life. This morning's paper listed a boy Tommy's age. The announcement didn't list the cause of death, but the family asked that donations go to Central Valley Hospital Transplant Program. John couldn't recall if he'd ever seen the boy during one of Tommy's visits at the hospital. Melissa would remember; she was good at making those sorts of connections. Networking, she called it.

At the bottom of the page was the funeral announcement for Daniel Cardozo. There was no attempt at flowery praise of Cardozo's lifetime accomplishments or mention of whom he left behind. It contained the date and time of the memorial service with a graveside service to follow, nothing more.

John refolded the paper with the child's obituary facing out and sat it next to the coffeepot for Melissa. He made a mental note to ask her about the boy.

He showered in the guest bath and dressed in the dark to avoid disturbing the family. When he returned to the kitchen, he didn't expect to find Melissa at the table huddled with a cup of coffee.

"I tried not to wake you," he said.

She lifted her head, hair still tousled from sleep. Wayward strands hung across her face, hiding her blue eyes. She tucked the stray hair behind an ear and said, "You only think you're quiet." She pointed at the newspaper. "You saw this? The Gunderson boy didn't make it."

He nodded. "I can't place him. Which one was he?"

"He had Tommy's doctor, and his mother said he had polycystic kidney disease. He went on the transplant list two months ago."

"Wow. I guess he never had a chance," John said.

"You really don't remember, do you?"

"I told you I didn't."

"He got the transplant a month ago. The same time Tommy got bumped from the top of the list."

"That was him? I wonder what happened."

"Rejection, probably. Shame. I liked his mother. She felt bad about taking 'Tommy's kidney.'"

"The kid was a better match for the donated kidney. At least that's what Dr. Anderson told us. I just don't understand why other kids get their transplants and Tommy gets put on hold."

"I know." She reached out and took hold of John's hand. "We have to be strong for Tommy."

John thought of his dark web conversation from the night before. "You think it matters where Tommy gets his donated kidney from?"

"I'm not sure I follow."

"Does it matter what kind of person the donor was? A creep, a gangbanger, or a prison inmate?"

She shook her head. "I don't think Tommy would care if it meant he was finally healthy." She kissed the back of his hand and let him go. "Where are you off to so early this morning?"

"Paula and I have some follow-up on a case."

"Anything to do with why you stayed up late last night?"

"You don't miss much, do you?"

"I'm a mom. That's what we do."

John sat across from his wife. "You know how I said I'd always separate work and home life?"

"Yeah. We both agreed the kids didn't need to see or hear about the monsters you run across."

"Paula called me on it yesterday. The case we're working looks like it involves human-organ trafficking, and Paula said Tommy's condition might cloud my judgment."

"Trafficking? Here? I've read stories about it, but always in some other corner of the world. You shouldn't have anything to do with it. It's too close to home, John. Our home."

"Someone might be manipulating the waiting list. It could affect Tommy. I can't let that happen."

"Dr. Anderson explained how the wait list works to us. There are safeguards to prevent that kind of thing from happening. Paula's right. You are letting Tommy influence your thinking. You need to get someone else to handle this one," Melissa said.

John leaned back in his chair and considered Melissa's argument. He'd never asked to have a case reassigned and took pride in that fact. Pride. Is that what this was about? He wasn't about to tell his wife about his late-night chat with a black-market organ broker.

"Maybe," he said.

"I know what maybe means. You're too stubborn and bull-headed to admit when you're wrong."

The woman was perceptive.

John stood, leaned across the table, and planted a kiss on his wife's forehead. "I'll consider it."

He left her huddled with her coffee and went out the back door so he didn't wake the kids. Light, early-morning traffic meant he got to Paula's address without much trouble. He pulled the police sedan to the curb in front of a clean, Craftsman-style home in midtown. The bronze number on the impeccable 1920s residence matched the address Paula gave him.

The neat and tidy image was so out of character for his new partner that John's first thought was that she deliberately sent him to the wrong address. John dialed Paula's number.

She picked up on the first ring. "I'm almost ready. Come on in."

John turned to the house and glimpsed Paula waving at him from the front door.

He got out of the car and followed a walkway framed with a low boxwood hedge to a wooden front porch. Paula left the massive mahogany door open for him and called out when she heard his footfalls on the porch.

"In the kitchen," Paula said.

Gleaming hardwood floors and meticulously crafted built-in cabinetry looked as if they could be featured in an issue of *Architectural Digest*. The period light fixtures, rubbed-bronze switch plates, and antique furnishings made the place seem more museum than residence. It looked so different from Paula's landfill of a work space at the station.

Paula caught him taking in the mortised woodworking detail on a glass-fronted library cabinet. "Like that one? I found it in the basement. Someone painted it blue and used it as junk storage."

"Nice. Did you restore it?"

"Don't look so surprised. Turns out it's only a copy of a Stickley piece, but it does go with the house."

"Is this really your place? I mean, don't take this all wrong, the place is beautiful, but . . ."

"It's not what you thought. I have my work life and my private life. This is my private life. Here there is order, peace, and reason. At work, it's different."

"This is like night-and-day different. At the office, your desk—"

"I know. I've heard it. Wasteland, dump, toxic-waste storage. People see that and think a certain way. They make judgments about who I am and what I can do. I like proving them wrong."

John took a few steps into the kitchen and found a renovated kitchen, modern appliances, and marble counters. "Wow. How long have you had this place?"

"About four years. I've restored the front of the house and have the bathrooms and bedrooms to go. I dump all my overtime checks into the place and work on one room at a time. I finished the kitchen last month. Took me six months, working late nights and weekends, but I like the way it turned out."

"I think Melissa and I need you to come over and work on our place. Hell, you could do remodels for half the detective bureau."

"Don't you go telling anybody at the station about this. This is what I do to unwind. Besides, half the cops don't think I should be a detective, and this will only give them more ammunition. I can hear Stark and his cronies telling me I should hang it up and be an interior decorator."

"Screw them."

Paula changed the subject. "Let me lock up and we can get over to Central Valley Hospital. You think we can get Trisha Woods to give us a list of everyone who accessed the UNOS system over the past few months? If our killer accessed the system, it would have been during that time."

"We need to find a way to connect whoever accessed the UNOS system to our victims, and I think I have an idea. But you're not gonna like it."

FIFTEEN

The administrative offices at Central Valley Hospital were mercifully separate from the building that housed the doctors, nurses, and clinical operations. Families with sick children didn't venture into this part of the building, where bean counters billed insurance carriers and shattered lives were reflected as numbers on a spreadsheet.

Steps from the elevator doors, a reception counter blocked access to the offices and the community of cubicles that lay beyond. John and Paula approached the unattended counter where a note taped to the surface directed people to use the phone on the reception desk to contact employees.

John grabbed the phone and scanned the employee directory for Trisha Woods. He tapped in her extension. "Miss Woods? John Penley and Paula Newberry here."

He listened for a moment, hung up, and heard an electric lock release the short half door set within the counter. The detectives wandered through a maze of light-blue cubicle walls to a back-corner office marked with a small plaque that identified it as the office of Trisha Woods, IT manager.

Trisha sat at a desk and faced a bank of computer monitors that threatened to encircle her work space. Lines, charts, and numbers streamed enough data to overload the senses of a NASA flight controller. She swiveled around in her chair, and her expression softened when she saw John.

"How's Tommy holding up?" she asked.

"Tommy's asking questions a kid his age shouldn't have to think about."

"It will happen for him."

"I hope so. This is my partner, Detective Paula Newberry."

Trisha stood and shook Paula's hand with an unexpectedly firm grip. She was a fraction of an inch over five feet tall but exuded a larger presence through her demeanor and confidence. "So, Dr. Kelly gave me a rundown on what you're looking for. The organ-sharing network, right?"

"We're pursuing an angle that our suspect could be using UNOS as a shopping list. He finds out who needs a transplant and goes hunting for a match," John said.

"That's a gruesome theory," Trisha said.

Paula asked, "Who has access to that kind of data?"

Trisha gestured the detectives to a small sofa. "The system operates on a private network. All patient data are encrypted, and access is restricted from the outside. No remote access. The system is password protected, and only authorized users have access to the medical information and patient data."

"How many users are there?" John asked as he moved a stack of files and parked on the sofa.

"Nationally, I'm not certain. At this transplant center, we have three categories of users, each with different levels of permissions within the system. We have users with 'read-only' permission, but most have full access to enter and edit data, and only a few superusers need access to all the code and software for reports or maintenance. Total, we have less than fifty people with access to the system."

"If I have access to UNOS, and I need to move a patient up or down on the waiting list for transplant, how do I manipulate the system?" John asked.

Trisha paused before she spoke, not certain how John would take her answer. "Strictly speaking, moving patients up and down on the wait list isn't manipulation. When the medical condition of one patient or another changes, so does the waiting list. The list doesn't look the same from one day to the next."

"I understand that, Trisha, believe me."

Trisha got the unspoken reference to the detective's son and nodded.

"What my partner and I are trying to get at is, can I move people up on the waiting list when there is no legitimate medical reason for a change?" Paula asked.

"Well, yes you could, but why would you?"

"If I have an organ to market, I'd want to get it to the person who paid me," John said.

Trisha's brow furrowed. "I see what you're saying, but it's not that simple. The transplantable organ would have to be acquired, tissue typed and cross matched, then entered into the system. Then, according to your premise, someone would change the UNOS wait list to match it to the donor."

Paula asked, "So what you're saying is that it can be done?"

"Well, yes, in theory," Trisha said.

"Who can make that kind of change in the system? I gather that it would be someone with full access to edit data?"

"Right. Each transplant center has a core set of personnel who do that kind of work. For example, at this hospital, there are two superusers, me and my deputy IT director. Then the regular permissions include the transplant team and their staff. Less than two dozen people total."

"That narrows it down a bit," Paula said.

"Can you give us a list of that UNOS user group?" John asked.

"I will check with the hospital administrator, but I don't see any problem getting that for you."

"Thanks. Is there any way to show changes in the waiting list and who made the change?" John said as he got up from the sofa.

"I can prepare a report without patient data that will show all transactions, who made changes on the waiting list, when new patients were added, and when they came off the list."

"How about just changes over the last six months?"

"No problem."

"Okay, how about patient-specific data?" John pressed.

"Release of patient data is restricted. I can't give that to you without a court order or consent, of course," Trisha said.

"What if the patient is my son?"

SIXTEEN

"That was a shitty thing to do," Paula said. "Asking for Tommy's records like that."

"I told you you weren't gonna like it," John responded.

"I only met your wife once, but I know she'll go ballistic when she finds out about this."

"Then she best not find out."

Paula looked away from her partner in frustration as they walked out of the business offices at the hospital. "She said she was willing to get us a transaction report. I don't get why you thought Tommy's info was necessary."

"The data aren't about Tommy. They give us a point in time that a change in the waiting list occurred and who made that change."

"This is not appropriate procedure . . ."

"Mr. Penley?" someone from behind them called out.

John turned and saw a familiar face, but one he couldn't quite place.

"You're Tommy's father, right?" a worn and tired woman asked.

"Yes, John Penley. I'm sorry . . ."

"Rebecca Gunderson. Steven's mom."

Steven Gunderson. The boy listed in the obituary this morning.

"Mrs. Gunderson. I'm so sorry. Melissa and I heard about Steven."

"We don't know what happened. They told us the surgery went fine. Dr. Anderson said everything would be okay. Then Steven rejected the kidney, and no one will tell us anything." She stiffened. "Why are you here? Is Tommy all right? Did something happen to him, too?"

"Tommy is still waiting. Excuse me, this is my partner, Detective Paula Newberry."

The two women exchanged glances but nothing more.

"We are tying up some loose ends on an investigation, that's all," John said.

"Mrs. Gunderson, I'm sorry about your son. When did he get his transplant?" Paula asked.

"Last month. Out of the blue. We expected a long stint on the waiting list, but my husband got a call that said they had found a match. Then . . . Steven's body rejected the transplant. All they said was that it didn't take. No one will talk to us."

"How's the rest of the family taking it?" John asked.

Rebecca Gunderson's eyes welled. "It's tearing us apart. Frank, my husband, acts like it's my fault. He won't talk to me. He stopped going to work and sits around drinking."

"Everyone handles grief differently. He can't possibly think what happened to Steven is your fault."

"I wish I could say that for certain. But that's why I'm here. I tried to get answers from these people, and they blew me off."

"Do you want us to see if we can find out anything for you?" John asked.

Paula jabbed her bony elbow into John's ribs.

"Would you do that?"

"I can't promise anything," John said before Paula cut him off.

"We can't get involved in that," Paula said.

Rebecca ignored Paula and stepped in closer to John. "Please find out what happened to Steven. We need closure."

"We will," John promised.

Paula headed toward their sedan.

As soon as Paula was out of earshot, John said, "Go meet with Trisha Woods and sign a consent form to allow me to look at your son's medical records. Without that consent, I can't help you. You know Trisha?"

Rebecca nodded.

"Good. Make sure you tell her that you want me to get those records. She's pulling together a bunch of data for me now, and I'd like to get Steven's records as well."

Rebecca grabbed John and hugged him. "We have to know what happened. You understand."

She pushed away from John, straightened her shoulders, turned, and walked back through the doors to the administrative offices.

John watched the determination in her stride and knew that no matter what he found hidden in the dead boy's medical records, the outcome would not change. Steven Gunderson wasn't coming back. It was cold, final, and unfair.

John joined Paula back at the car, and she lit into him before his butt hit the seat.

"What the hell was that about?"

"She—"

"Are you out of your mind? We can't go poking around that kid's death. It wasn't homicide. A tragic accident maybe, but there is no evidence of anything wrong here. We have rules."

"She needs answers," John said.

"We all need answers, and sometimes life hands you a steaming bag of crap instead. We have policies for this kind of thing."

"You can't hide behind policy for the rest of your career. What will some department policy do for us, other than waste my time? You heard her—all of the sudden, the boy gets bumped up on the transplant list. How did that happen? Who made that happen? The UNOS data will connect the dots."

Paula turned in the passenger seat. "You're using the kid's medical information to fill in the blanks on the transaction data that Trisha Woods wouldn't give us?"

"Yeah, and when we combine it with the information from Tommy's records, we should start to see if there are any inconsistencies in the data. Was it the same staff person making the entries? Was the data entered from the same transplant center? And when did the organ become available on the UNOS database?"

"Even if the timeline for the donated organs matches with the killings, it could be nothing but coincidence. Without knowing where all the donated organs came from, it's all speculation."

"We could ask for an autopsy on Steven Gunderson," John said.

"He died in a hospital under a doctor's care. Not likely to get an autopsy on a case like that," Paula said.

"I bet we could get the parents to push for one. Rebecca said they wanted answers."

"The hospital is gonna resist that and bring all their lawyers out of the boardroom to block the autopsy."

"What have they got to hide? They can't afford the bad press they'd get if they opposed the parents' request for an autopsy. The hospital's foundation and grant funding would dry up if they got caught on the bad side of a media storm."

"And you want to make sure the media gets wind of this?"

John shrugged.

"Won't the hospital threaten to remove Tommy from the transplant program if you do something that reckless?"

"That is why I can't be the one to leak this to the press." John looked at his partner.

"Me? They know we work together."

"They will be too busy scrambling to cover their asses to put the pieces together."

A cell-phone ring cut off Paula's response. John fished the phone from the car's center console. He'd left it behind when they went into the hospital out of habit.

He answered and then paused. His eyes narrowed, and the vein in his forehead throbbed in time with his heartbeat. "You're certain?" he said to the caller.

After another pause, he said, "Give me the address."

Paula mouthed, "Another one?"

John nodded, closed the phone, and tossed it on the console.

"Partial remains in the water in Old Sacramento. The first officer on the scene called it in."

John turned the ignition, and the sedan rumbled to life. He flipped the car into gear and sped from the hospital parking lot. "If this is our guy, we have a new worry. He's speeding up with no cooling-off period between his kills."

Paula sat without a word in response, jaw clenched so tight her lower lip turned ghostly pale.

John cut across town to I Street and pulled to a stop at the waterfront in Old Sacramento near the Delta King, a restored paddle wheel steamboat that once prowled the Sacramento River delta waters.

Paula shook her head. "The time between kills doesn't matter. If this guy is harvesting and selling organs, he's a businessman."

"How does that change anything? He's still a murderer, businessman or not," John said.

"What would you do with a white-collar criminal suspected of fraud or insider trading?" she asked.

"I don't know. Follow the money?"

"This guy is in it for the money, not the thrill of the kill, so we track him by the money trail. It's business for him," Paula said.

Two television news vans pulled to the curb at the pier and jockeyed for the best camera position to capture the exclusive breaking-news footage.

"And it looks like business is booming," John said.

SEVENTEEN

The splintered gangway angled down from the pier to the Delta King riverboat. The river level rose and fell with the seasons, and the gangway sat on hinges that adjusted with the ever-changing water level. Since the river currently ran low, only the paddle wheeler's pilothouse and twin stacks were visible from the street.

Clusters of people assembled at the edge of the pier near the gangway entrance, gazing down toward the ship's massive red-and-white paddle wheel. One man pointed at something in the water. The television news crews responded to his cue and swiveled their cameras in hopes of tagging a gruesome find in time for a broadcast at lunchtime.

John and Paula located a uniformed officer who kept onlookers and media types off the gangway and away from the ship. The officer tucked a clipboard under his arm and pulled a short section of yellow crime-scene tape back like a velvet rope at an exclusive nightclub. The detectives cleared the gangway, and the officer added their names to a list of persons who entered the scene.

The coroner's technicians had erected a tall white tarp that screened the stern of the boat and the dock from the gawking public above. In spite of the restricted view, the news cameras rolled and hoped for a tarp malfunction that would give them a front-page money shot.

As John and Paula approached the ship's deck, a pair of technicians, clad in disposable white jumpsuits, hefted a bundle wrapped in a blue plastic tarp to the surface of the dock. A river-rescue dive team untangled the package from the stern paddle wheel and lifted it to the techs on the dock.

The package settled onto the wood deck planking, and river water oozed from the folds in the plastic. The wrapping clung to the contents and molded it into a blue sculpture of semihuman form.

Behind the coroner's technicians, Lieutenant Barnes motioned for John and Paula.

"When did this get called in?" John asked when he reached the lieutenant.

Paula stopped at the plastic-wrapped remains and began jotting notes in her notebook.

"About twenty minutes ago," Barnes said.

"Damn, didn't take long for the vultures to get wind of it." John tipped his jaw toward the assembled news crews.

"The officer who responded called it in. He's a rookie and had no idea they listen to the scanners. He feels bad about it. That's one mistake he'll never make again."

"So who found the body?" John said.

Barnes pointed to a gray-haired couple leaning on the deck rail near the gangway. "They decided to walk out on the deck after they finished their brunch. The missus saw what she thought was a couple of salmon getting frisky. A large fish kept bumping up against something. Then the body rolled over, and they got a good look at the face."

"This one has a face?" John inquired.

"See for yourself," Lieutenant Barnes said.

John's footfalls sounded against the worn decking as he and the lieutenant stepped to where the bundle sat. "Was the body wrapped like this in the water?" John said.

"No, the divers wrapped the plastic around it so we could lift it. They didn't know how long it had been in the water," one of the coroner's techs said.

"Let's take a look," John said.

Paula kneeled near the head, using a pen to pull the tarp back farther. "White male in his thirties. It's not a fresh kill, from the looks of it. There's a lot of tissue damage here. His eyes are missing."

"Why did he leave the head this time?" John wondered.

"It's business, remember? The killer didn't need it. Oh, check this out. This is a new twist," Paula said as she peeled the tarp even farther back.

"He didn't remove the legs. They're bent backward, probably broken at the knee and hip. He folded them up like a suitcase and bound the legs to the torso with wire." She pointed to the narrow-gauge wire that puckered the flesh across the victim's chest.

"The wire looks like the stuff that left the marks on Cardozo's body," John said.

"Why'd he leave him like this? Looking like he went through a hay-bale machine?"

"I hope the poor bastard was dead before our guy went to work on him," John said.

John nodded to the coroner's technician, who covered the remains with the tarp and with the assistance of the second technician, lifted the water-soaked corpse onto a gurney. They covered the body with another heavy tarp and secured it to the rails that ran down the sides of the gurney. It looked less like a human body than it did a crate ready for shipping.

"Maybe the coroner's office can get some dentals for an ID," Paula said.

"And we need a time of death. This body shows signs of decomp. He might have been killed before Daniel Cardozo. If that's true, it changes our timeline."

"This might have been the source of the last delivery that Cardozo and his gangbanger friend did," Paula said.

"The case Cardozo and Guzman opened?"

"Yeah. The timing fits. This guy gets his heart ripped out, Cardozo takes a peek, and then the killer takes care of his loose end—Cardozo."

"Which brings us back to SpongeBob SquarePants. An open-water dump seems out of character for our guy."

"How do you figure? He's a frickin' butcher," she said.

"This guy wasn't butchered as precisely as Cardozo and the rest."

Paula bit her lower lip once more and watched the coroner's technicians struggle as the gurney rattled up the gangway to street level. "Is he doing all this by himself? The hunting, the computer stuff, harvesting, and distribution?"

John glanced up the gangway, where the news cameras followed the gurney in a processional toward the coroner's van. They trolled for the shot of a dangled body part or blood-soaked sheet.

"If we take your business theory, then what does our killer do himself, and what part of the work does he contract out?" John said.

Lieutenant Barnes leaned close to his detectives and said, "Get whatever you need to get this done. The chief is getting pressure to get a task force now that he's publically labeled this a serial-murder investigation, and we all know how he loves the feds in his backyard. I gotta go feed the vultures," he said, referring to the media up on the street. "The chief's office is calling this guy the Outcast Killer because he's targeting gang members on the fringes of society. Can't have the law-abiding public start to panic." He strode off in the direction of the news cameras.

John's cell phone rang, and he saw the number was Dr. Kelly's at the coroner's office.

"She must be in a hurry to get this one," he said as he pushed the button to take the call. "Hi, Doc. Your guys had to fish this one out of the water, so they are on their way now," he said.

John listened. Frown lines deepened on his forehead. "Wait, what? You're certain? No, I'm sorry, that's not what I mean." He paused and listened for a moment. "Thanks. I will pull the reports as soon as we get back." He disconnected and pocketed the phone.

"We have a cause of death on the first two victims. The lab was backed up, but Dr. Kelly got them to prioritize the Mercer and Johnson analysis when the third victim appeared. It was exsanguination. They were bled out. The toxicology report showed no drugs, but the oxygen and carbon monoxide levels in the tissue were off. Except for Cardozo. She confirmed that he was tortured and dissected while he was alive."

"A business decision. He didn't want to do anything that would compromise the sales of the product—the organs. No drugs, no gunshot wounds," Paula said.

"She also tissue typed the kidney that the killer gift wrapped for me. It matched Daniel Cardozo. The tissue was HIV positive. She's e-mailing us all the reports. She also got a call from a very perturbed Trisha Woods following our visit to Central Valley Hospital."

"Let me guess—we're not getting any of the reports because of your antics."

"Just the opposite. After Cardozo's HIV-infected kidney appeared, Dr. Kelly told her that she needed the information from UNOS to track possible transplants back to the cadavers in her morgue. Trisha refused at first, but after Dr. Kelly demands an autopsy of Steven Gunderson's body, the hospital board will likely overrule Trisha to avoid a public display that could potentially tarnish the hospital's reputation."

"She's going to do it? Agree to the autopsy and hand over the reports?"

John nodded. "She may not have a choice. I guess you don't have to join the lieutenant up there and leak anything to the press. The hospital wants it quiet."

"I'll bet they do," she said.

Paula scuffed her shoe on a ragged, splintered section of grayed deck planking. She looked down and noticed black marks on the deck where the coroner's technicians had rolled the gurney in and out of the crime scene. She knelt down, pushed a fingertip over the smudge, and wiped it from the surface.

"They tracked through something when they wheeled down here from the street," she said.

John traced the dark streaks on the wood up and down the gangway. More than one set came down the rough-hewn walkway to the main entrance of the old steamship. Thin tracks from the coroner's gurney traveled down and stopped at the wet puddle where the tarp-covered body had sat minutes earlier. A separate, thicker track went farther down the dock and disappeared off the edge at the stern paddle wheel.

"You recall anyone around the end of the ship when we got here?" John said.

Paula sat back on her haunches and looked at the now-empty dock. Her forehead drew three small creases, the kind she got when she focused on details.

"The body was here." She pointed to the wet plank boards. "Lieutenant Barnes and the dive-team supervisor were about five yards farther down." She stood and walked to the spot. "They were here." She looked down the dock. "I don't remember anyone else."

"See the wheel mark at the end of the dock?" John said.

"Yeah." Paula followed the trail to the end of the dock and looked down into the dark river water. She turned and retraced the track with her eye. "There's no second track."

"Second, as in single wheel. I saw that," he added.

"There is no return track either. See"—she pointed to the gurney tracks—"those have two separate sets of tracks, one set down to the body and one that led the way back out. This one was a one-way trip."

John walked along the trail toward Paula, stopped, and surveyed the surrounding deck surface for any other tracks, gouges, or stains. "Good catch, Detective. I missed that one." John asked a crime-scene tech to make sure they got photos of the trails.

The huge paddle wheel dominated the stern of the steamship. Two observation decks sat above the massive wooden wheel. John noticed two of the ship's crew, dressed in dark-blue work uniforms, standing at the rail. They wore harnesses with straps and buckles and leaned against the railing with their backs to the commotion on the dock below. The coveralls they wore bore dark grease stains the same color as the tracks on the dock.

Paula followed his gaze and saw the workmen. She tilted her head toward them, indicating that she would go check them out. She boarded the ship and made for an exterior stairwell that accessed the upper deck.

John heard the *clack-clack* of her boots on the stairs and saw one of the workmen toss a joint off the rail when Paula approached. The marijuana cigarette sizzled when it hit the water. The two had clearly tried to take advantage of the downtime and spark up on the deck until Paula interrupted and harshed their mellow.

Down on the dock, the older couple who had first noticed the body in the water waited on a wooden bench until they were allowed to leave. A young officer, one John didn't recognize, took their statements and dutifully scribbled into his notebook. The officer called out, "Detective, you need to speak with these folks?"

John walked to the bench and sat next to the couple. He introduced himself and learned from Joanne Watson that she and her husband, Robert, had finished their weekly brunch and had gone out for a stroll around the deck before heading home. They had paused out on the fantail of the ship to take in the view out onto the water.

"I thought it was a couple of salmon, you know, how they spawn rolling on their sides," Joanne said. A crimson blush blossomed on her cheeks at the mention of fish sex.

"Did you happen to see anything unusual? Anything out of place today?" John asked.

Robert seemed confused and on edge. He clasped his hands together so tight that his arthritic knuckles whitened. The old man's eyes darted and didn't seem to settle on anything or anyone for more than a moment. "Can we go home now, Jo?" he asked his wife as he rocked in a slight back-and-forth motion. The man looked over at John. "Who are you?"

"He told you, dear. He's a police officer," Joanne said.

"Police? What happened?" The old man's eyes widened.

Joanne patted her husband on the thigh. "It's all right, dear." Then to John, "Now that you mention it, I thought it was odd that a fisherman was bringing fish down to the river."

"What do you mean?" John asked.

"When we first arrived, a man nearly ran us off the ramp with his cart of fish. He pushed the thing and nearly hit Robert. The smell was horrible."

"He was coming down the gangway? What did the cart look like? Can you remember any markings or writing on it?"

She paused and looked up the gangway. "No, I don't think so. He went by so fast. It was a regular cart, you know the kind with one wheel in the front," Joanne said.

"Like a wheelbarrow?" John said.

"Yes—that's it, a wheelbarrow. I thought it was strange to deliver fish to the chef in something like that, but nowadays, they do all sorts of strange things."

"Mrs. Watson, did you get a look at the man with the cart? Can you tell me anything about him? Age? Height? What he wore?"

"Who are you?" Robert asked John.

"He's the police, dear," his wife said patiently. "Robert has dementia, Detective," she said matter-of-factly. "To answer your question about the fishmonger, he had long rubber boots that came to his knees. The kind you see the people on the TV wear when their houses flood. An average-looking man, I suppose."

"Anything else?"

"I'm not sure if it means anything . . ." she said.

"Tell me."

"He had a mark, here on his neck." She pointed to the front of her neck. "The kind the kids get."

"A mark? Was it a tattoo?"

"Yes. That's it. I never understood why anyone would do that to themselves."

John felt his stomach tighten with an icy knot of anticipation.

"Close your eyes and see if you can tell me what that tattoo looked like," he said.

She stiffened, straightened her back, and closed her eyes. "It had a number and it looked like a bird."

"Are you certain?"

"Yes." Her eyes popped open. "What do you think it means?"

"I don't know yet. The number—was it the number fourteen?"

"I'm sorry, I don't remember," Joanne said. "I wish I could tell you more."

"You did fine, Mrs. Watson. Thanks. You and your husband are free to go. The officer got your contact information, so if we need you to take a look at some photos or anything, we can get in touch with you."

She stood, shook John's hand, and reached for Robert. "Let's take you home now."

The couple walked up the gangway in a slow, choppy gait.

Paula finished with the potheads and joined John on the bench.

"Well, that was a waste of time. Those two guys were too busy getting a buzz on to notice what was going on down here," she said. "Get anything from the old couple?"

"Other than I don't want to get old?" He turned to her. "The body was dumped by someone with a West Block Norteños tattoo on his neck."

Less than thirty minutes later, two search-and-rescue divers went back into the dark water. Bubbles hit the river's surface in a slow, methodical fashion, moving out from the dock and back again. The trail of air bubbles released from the divers' regulators showed the grid search under way in the depths below.

A rosette of bubbles grew larger, and the orange cap of a diver burst through the surface. The relief diver tossed one end of a heavy nylon strap to his supervisor. "What do you have?" the supervisor asked.

The diver shrugged, grabbed the other end of the strap, and submerged, bubbles trailing off as he went.

In a slur of radio chatter, John picked out the word "heavy" amid the breathing and other sounds. Then the command to take up the slack must have been given, because the supervisor and relief diver began hooking the strap to an extendable boom.

A dark-brown cloud of silt rose to the surface accompanied by sets of bubbles on either side. The divers' heads popped above the water while they steadied the object they secured. The dive supervisor retracted the nylon strap in short, smooth bursts until a mud-and-slime-covered wheelbarrow cleared the river's surface.

"That what you looking for?" the dive supervisor asked.

"I think so," John said.

"Hell, I coulda picked up one for you at a yard sale and saved us some time," the relief diver said.

The boom swung over the dock and lowered the wheelbarrow upside down to the deck planks into a nest of mud and river sludge. The remaining thick layer of silt melted off the frame like hot candle wax. The dive supervisor uncoupled the strap from around the wheel frame and pulled it away.

"Huh," John said. He pointed to the back end of the wheelbarrow where black-stenciled lettering appeared beneath a thin layer of river-bottom muck. "Who do we know who works at Raley Field?" he said.

"Mario Guzman told us he worked at the ball field," Paula said. "West Block Norteños tattoo on his neck too."

"Looks like Mario knows more than he told us."

"I don't like him as our killer. Do you? He just doesn't have the brains to pull it off. He could be the killer's muscle," she said.

"At least he puts us closer to the killer." John swiveled around on his heel and surveyed the dockside, the activity, and the openness of the place. The muscles along the ridge of his jaw worked while he took stock of the place. "Why did Guzman dump the body here? The other victims were dumped while no one was watching. Now he boldly walks out into public and tosses this one in the river under our noses? Why would he do that?"

"He was in a hurry to clean up, maybe?" Paula asked.

"If he's sending us a message, let's go talk to the messenger. Let's go find Guzman," John said.

EIGHTEEN

Constructed as an upscale, minor-league ballpark, Raley Field sat a quarter mile downstream and across the river from the steamship body dump. John and Paula headed for the Tower Bridge and made for the massive light stanchions that surrounded the stadium.

The grounds crew hustled over the field, preparing the surface for an afternoon game between the hometown River Cats and their Pacific Coast League rival, the Reno Aces. A half dozen grounds keepers swept and manicured the surface to perfection. The red dirt was smooth, and two more employees guided chalk machines, laying down the foul lines. Similar tasks took place in the grassy outfield, where mowers left a tight checkerboard pattern in their wake and the warning track got a light misting.

John and Paula were walking the concourse above the first baseline toward home plate when a potbellied security guard in black pants and a yellow polo shirt noticed their approach.

"Hey," the bumblebee look-alike called out. "You can't be here. Game don't start for two hours. Dammit! Who left the gate open?"

The guard trudged up the stairs from field level to the concourse, face reddened from the unwanted effort, bearing an expression that matched. "Turn . . . around," he said between breaths.

Paula flicked her badge out. "Who's in charge around here?"

The security guard tore his walkie-talkie radio from a Velcro belt clip. "Anyone seen Lamar?" the guard said.

A voice crackled on the other end of the radio. "Lamar ain't here today. What you need?"

The guard looked at the two detectives, then said, "I got a couple of cops wanna talk to someone."

"Then talk to them. I don't have time for their crap," the voice responded.

Paula's hand snaked out and snatched the radio from the security guard. She keyed the microphone. "Make some time, or we'll shut down the field as a crime scene."

John bit back a smirk and pulled on his sunglasses, masking his amusement at his partner's diminished patience.

"Can she do that?" the security guard asked John.

"Yep, and I wouldn't want to get on her bad side."

"What crime scene is she talking about?" the man inquired in a lowered voice.

"We're investigating a murder," John said.

"Murder? Here? Man, I don't know nothing about nobody getting themselves offed around here." The guard turned to Paula and said, "Lady, I'm sorry . . ."

"That's Detective," Paula said, accompanied by a glare.

"I'm sorry, Detective lady . . ."

"Never mind," she said. She rekeyed the microphone as she turned away from the security guard. She spoke over the radio, "That's enough. Shut it down. Pull your crew off the field."

A figure popped out of the first-baseline dugout. He was a man in his fifties, dressed in pressed khaki pants and a green River Cats team polo shirt. He held a radio in his hand and looked up toward the concourse.

"There he is," Paula said.

"Who is he?" John asked the security guard.

"That's Mr. Rosedale, assistant head of operations. He don't look none too happy."

Paula handed the radio back to the security guard. "That will be all." She made a course down the bleachers in Rosedale's direction, skipping every other step along the way.

"Man, she always like that?" the security guard asked.

"No. Usually, she's pissed," John said as he followed his partner to the field.

When he reached Paula, she stood on top of the dugout, hands on hips, a vision of warrior princess.

"Mr. Rosedale, we need to talk to you," she said.

"Not a good time, sweetheart. I got a game to get ready for," Rosedale complained.

John saw his partner's fists clench with the "sweetheart" comment. For a split second, he thought Paula was going to launch her body off the dugout at the creep.

Up close, Rosedale had the ruddy complexion and red, bulbous nose of a heavy drinker. Once out of the dugout, in the sunlight, he squinted like a mole who found himself suddenly above ground.

"We need a couple minutes of your time, and then you can get on with whatever you do here," John said.

Rosedale shielded his eyes with one hand, blocking the sun. "What do you want? Make it quick."

"We need to find one of your employees, Mario Guzman," John said.

"I don't know any Guzman. What gives you the idea he works for me?"

"He said he was a grounds keeper here."

"I can't keep track of every one of the grounds crew. That's what I pay my crew boss for."

"Then we want to talk to your crew boss," Paula said with an icy tone.

Rosedale turned to home plate, where three men lined up the batter's box frames for chalking. "Johnson! Over here!"

A man looked up when Rosedale called, said something to the men working with him, and walked over to the dugout. He looked as if he was used to getting an earful from Rosedale and figured this was one more brick in that wall.

"These police officers want to talk to you about some Marco Grozman," Rosedale said.

Johnson's faced pinched up in confusion.

"Mario Guzman," John reminded.

Johnson nodded. "Oh sure, right. What about him?"

"Where is he?" Paula asked.

Johnson looked to his crew on the field and then turned back. "He came in this morning, started work, and then he got a phone call, said he had to leave. He didn't say what was up, but he was in a real hurry. Doesn't look like he made it back yet."

"You recall when he left?" John asked.

"About eight thirty," Johnson said.

John pointed to the men working in the outfield, watering the warning track. "Is that what Mario was doing before he left?" The men lugged heavy, red rubber hoses and sprayed down the dust. They all wore knee-high rubber boots, gloves, and matching ball caps.

"Yeah. Hey, is Mario all right?"

"Don't know. He may have got himself involved in something," John said.

"The gang?"

"You know that Mario is a West Block Norteños gang member?" John said.

Johnson shrugged. "This is one of the few places in the city they can work, because of the injunction. Here or the Highway Patrol Academy, and that ain't very likely. For the most part, they don't give me any trouble. They take care of any beef they have amongst each other, away from this place. Kinda like neutral territory."

Rosedale interrupted, "You have who working here? Gang members?"

"They do their job and don't cause any problem. Besides, for the pay you're willing to give, you're lucky to have them."

Rosedale's face grew ashen, and he backed toward the dugout. "We'll discuss this later," he said, then disappeared off the field.

"Sorry about that," Johnson said.

"Did you notice anything different with Mario in the past couple of months or so?"

"No, not really. He started missing work a bit. You know, a day here, an hour there. I talked to him about it, and he said it was family stuff. I didn't press him on it."

"How did he seem today, after he took that phone call?" Paula said.

"Different. Usually, the guy is laid back, kinda slow, but gets his work done. Today, he seemed on edge, even before the call. Then after he hung up, man, he was on fire. He couldn't get out of here fast enough. I never had a chance to ask him about it. He yelled, 'I gotta go,' like he was shot out of a cannon."

"Did he get the call on his cell phone?" John said.

Johnson shook his head. "No. He took it on the phone in my office."

"Your office? Did whoever talked to Mario say anything to you?" John pressed.

"Well, yeah. He asked to speak to Mario. Asked for him by name."

"What did he say, exactly?" John asked.

"The man said he needed to talk to Mario Guzman. It was very urgent."

"He didn't say who he was? You didn't ask?" John said.

"No. I figured it was his parole agent or probation officer."

"Why did you think that?"

"I don't know. The guy had that authority vibe on the phone. Like he doesn't have time to waste, you know? That and all the chatter in the background."

"Like what?" Paula said.

"It was people talking. I could hear voices over an intercom, beeping noises, and you know, office sounds. Busy sounds."

"Could you make anything out in the background?" John asked.

"No. Nothing. The sound of it all made me think of a busy place. Most of these guys are on probation or parole, so I thought it might be a parole office. You know, where a lot of people come and go at the same time."

John nodded. He changed tactics. "Could Mario have taken a wheelbarrow with him?"

"A wheelbarrow? Yeah, I suppose he could have. It's not like we have them locked down to a bike rack or anything."

"Can we have a few words with the guys he works with?" John said.

"Sure, why not. You mind doing it out here on the field? That way they won't think that you're here to arrest them."

"That happen often?" Paula asked.

"Often enough. They get called in to the office and get cuffed up. They joke that it's like they're getting called up to the majors," Johnson said.

As soon as Paula and John stepped onto the field with Johnson, the grounds crew thinned out. A few hid their faces, while others ducked out back gates. Johnson pointed to a group of three men at the center-field wall, all of whom stopped working and watched Johnson lead the strangers in their direction.

Well before John reached the group, he saw arms sleeved with tattoos, heads shaved, and a chesty, defiant posture that identified the men as Mario Guzman's brothers-in-arms, West Block Norteños gang members.

"These detectives want to talk to you," Johnson told his crew.

The gang crew held their ground, and the oldest of the three, with a wicked scar that ran across his forehead, said, "We don't have to talk to you."

"No, you don't. But we aren't here for you. Where is Mario Guzman?" John said.

"Why?" the group's spokesman replied.

"Can't really tell you that."

"Then we can't tell you nothing either."

Paula stepped forward, closed the space between the two groups, and said, "I think Mario got involved in something way over his head. He could be in trouble. We want to help him."

"Don't give me that bull, chica. No cop cares what happens to one of my brothers. If Mario got into something, then he'll find a way out," the oldest gangbanger said.

The youngest-looking member of the crew shuffled his feet, looked away from the leader, and seemed very uncomfortable. Paula picked up on the cue and pressed him.

"What was Mario into?"

"Does this have anything to do with what happened to Danny C.?" the man asked.

"Maybe," Paula said.

"Oh man, that's messed up."

The older gang member cut off his younger compatriot and said, "Mario didn't have nothing to do with that. 'Sides, if Danny hadn't turned his back on his brothers, then maybe he'd still be alive."

"You saying that Cardozo's problems with the boys led to his death?" John asked.

"I'm not saying anything like that," the gang leader said. He turned to the younger man who had spoken out of turn and said, "None of us are saying that."

The younger man bowed his head and avoided eye contact with anything except the dirt under his feet.

"Any of you know why Mario had to leave work this morning?" John asked.

That question elicited no response from the group. The crew leader expressed nothing more than a shrug of indifference, but the younger gang member fidgeted with his gloves and picked at a spot in the dirt with his toe.

"Why would Mario take a wheelbarrow from here?"

"We're done here. You got questions, you need to talk to our attorney," the older gang member said.

"Let me guess, Joseph Morrison," John said.

"That's right."

"Play it that way if you want." John looked to Mr. Johnson. "You have the employment files on these guys, right?"

"Sure," Johnson said.

"Good. I'll need copies so I can make sure West Sac. PD parks a car at each of their homes all night long. Some of the games get out late, don't they?"

"We have some late games, sure."

"That means these validated gang members violate the gang injunction curfew each and every time they leave after a night game."

"The terms of the injunction say we can go to and from employment," the gang leader said.

"Which brings me back to employment records. You paying these guys under the table?"

Johnson put up both hands. "Whoa. These guys are temporary contract workers. We pay them that way, and it's all legit."

"I bet they didn't report that income or pay taxes like good, upstanding citizens," John stated.

"You're not right. You'd really threaten us with the IRS and cops staking out our homes? That's harassment," the older gang member said.

"I call it active policing."

"Chickenshit is what it is."

"Po-tay-to, po-tah-to."

The gang member's face flushed, and his shoulders flexed for a moment. He then relaxed, considered his words carefully, and said, "Mario had a problem with his family, something he had to go rush and take care of. That's all we know about it."

"Family problems? Like what?" John said.

"Don't know, but he was in a hurry to leave. Now that's it. We cool?"

"Yeah, cool." John walked away and whispered to Paula, "What kind of family emergency would make you go dump a body?"

"Not a good one."

NINETEEN

A squalid, two-bedroom bungalow on the southern edge of West Sacramento was the place Guzman called home when he wasn't in jail. Yellowed paint chips littered the dirt at the foot of the worn wooden siding. Rusted rain gutters, dead remnants of a front lawn, and cardboard taped to a broken front window testified that the home's best days were distant memories. It was a sad backdrop for a half dozen brightly colored children's toys scattered about the yard.

John pulled the sedan behind a mideighties Chevy pickup truck parked in front of the place. Paula ran the license plate number through a tablet computer and verified that the vehicle registration came back to Guzman.

John got out of the car, walked to the front of the truck, and placed a hand on the hood. It was cool to the touch. "He's been home for a while."

"How do you want to play this?" Paula asked.

"He talked to us once. We tell him we have some routine follow-up questions."

"That was before we had witnesses who saw him dump a body in the river."

"So why not run? Why did he come back here? Let's see if we can get him to talk."

"I'd feel better with backup," she said.

John walked around the front end of the truck and stepped around a toppled tricycle on the path to the front door. The narrow wooden porch creaked under his weight and announced their arrival as sure as any doorbell.

From behind the front door came the unmistakable metallic sound of a shotgun racking a round into the chamber.

John broke left, and Paula dove on the right side of the doorway a split second before a blast sent shards of wood and shotgun pellets through the door. Slender tendrils of blue smoke hung from the ragged edges of a basketball-sized hole in the door.

"Guzman! It's Detective Penley."

Another shell chambered in response. The shotgun round readied, and a raspy warning followed. "Get away! Leave me and my family alone!" The voice quivered to the point of cracking like a teenaged boy at the prom.

"Guzman, it's us, Detectives Penley and—"

"He sent you!"

"Guzman, come out and let's talk."

"Go away! I won't let you hurt my family."

"Call it in, Paula." John pulled his weapon, and Paula followed suit.

Paula pointed to the back of the house and crept around the dry planter bed to the corner where the cardboard covered the broken front window. She pushed back a cracked section of tape and with a finger, pulled the cardboard out an inch so she could peek inside. She shook her head.

John understood that she had no visual on Guzman. "Hey, Mario, why would we hurt your family? Are they all right?" John asked.

Paula saw the barrel of the shotgun poke around an overturned kitchen table that served as a barricade. The barrel shook as it punctuated Guzman's reply.

"He sent you! You won't get them. You won't touch my family!"

Paula slipped around the side of the house, out of sight.

"Who are you talking about? No one sent us. Who is trying to hurt your family?" John said.

"You're a liar. He sent you. Stay back." Guzman let loose another shotgun blast through the front door. The blast tore the doorknob off the frame and scattered bits of wood and shrapnel on the front-porch landing. Splinters rained down on John's head. Another shotgun round chambered with a *clack-clack* of the slide.

"Dammit, Guzman! Knock it off. Tell me what's going on," John called out from his perch outside. "Guzman! Talk to me."

"I shouldn't have talked to you about Cardozo. I know that now. You told him."

The abrupt crash of shattered glass preceded a loud thump and Paula's voice. "Drop it!"

John leapt to the porch landing and quickly peeked inside the shattered front door. The front room was largely empty, except for a thrift-store coffee table and end stand tucked between a pair of threadbare chairs. Farther inside, an overturned, Formica-covered kitchen table lay on one side, blocking the path to the kitchen.

"On your knees! Now!" Paula commanded from somewhere deeper in the residence.

John covered the distance from the front door to the makeshift barricade in three steps. In the center of the kitchen, amid a sea of broken glass, Mario Guzman knelt, hands stretched overhead. Blood trailed from a deep gash on his forehead. The man blinked as the blood stung his eye. On the floor, inches from Guzman, the shotgun rested against an overturned chair. Paula stood in the open rear doorway, gun drawn.

"Hands behind your head," she said.

Guzman complied and laced his fingers together behind his thick neck.

John stepped in and grabbed Guzman's left wrist, applied a wristlock, and pulled it down behind the gunman's back. Guzman didn't resist while John snapped a handcuff on his wrist, followed by the same to the right wrist.

Once Guzman was in cuffs, Paula secured her weapon, came across the kitchen, and grabbed his shotgun. She pumped three shells from the gun in quick strokes, ejecting them onto the floor.

"What the hell were you thinking?" John said to her. "What were you trying to prove?"

"I gotta prove myself everyday around you guys," Paula said.

John pulled Guzman up from his knees and with a foot, righted a kitchen chair. He plopped the bleeding gangster into the seat. "You want to tell me what this was about?"

Guzman clinched his jaw and looked away. He nodded toward Paula and said, "You could have shot me. Why didn't you?"

Paula leaned back on a counter and kicked away broken window glass with a toe. "I should have, but then we wouldn't be having this little conversation."

"What did you hit me with?" Guzman asked.

"A brick from your broke-ass patio."

He grinned and shook his head. "You ain't right."

"I've heard that before," she said.

The grin faded, and a weighty concern replaced it. "He didn't send you, did he?"

"For crap's sake, who are you talking about?" John pressed.

"The news is calling him the Outcast Killer."

"He told you to dump the body over in Old Sacramento?"

Guzman slumped back in the chair and nodded. "He said if I didn't do exactly as he told me, he'd kill my wife and kids."

"He called you at work this morning?" John asked.

Guzman looked up. "Yeah, how did you—never mind. Yeah, dude called me and said I had thirty minutes to take care of it. He must have figured out me and Danny peeked into those shipping cases."

"Who did you dump in the river?" Paula asked.

"I don't know. I went to where he told me to go and picked him up. Man, it was unnatural. Dude's legs were folded back behind him, and he was tied up with some wire or something. It was sick."

"Why did you bring a wheelbarrow from work?" John asked.

"He told me to."

"Where did you find the body?"

"Parking garage in Old Sacramento. The package, which is what he called it, was supposed to be on the top level, behind some construction material. It was right where he said it would be, under some black plastic."

"See anyone around?" Paula asked.

"Nobody. The top level only had a couple of cars parked there. I didn't see nobody in them, and I looked to make sure no one was gonna see me load the body."

"So what next?" John said.

"I parked next to the construction pile, dropped the wheelbarrow from the truck, and loaded the body into the wheelbarrow. It was so cold, and that smell, I remember that. And it was lighter than I thought it would be. I grabbed some of the plastic and covered the dude so he wasn't lookin' at me."

"Why dump him in the river?"

"The dude told me to leave my truck parked in the garage and wheel the package to the riverboat. I was running out of time, so I did it pretty quick. Ran the wheelbarrow right off the pier near the back end of the boat. I think I might have hit the side. I saw the wheelbarrow sink, and the plastic floated away, and that dude's eye holes was starin' at me as he hit the water." Guzman shivered.

"You never saw the guy, you only talked to him on the phone, is that right?" John prodded.

Guzman nodded.

"What do you remember about his voice?" John continued.

"Cold. What I remember is that the dude was dead-calm cold about what he needed me to do. And what would happen to my family if I didn't do exactly as he said."

"Where is your family?" Paula asked.

Guzman looked up at the mention of his family, eyes glazed slightly. "They're safe. I'm not saying more than that. I can't trust no one when it comes to them."

"Fair enough," she said.

"Why did he call you?" John asked.

"Danny and me, we broke his rules. We looked at what was being shipped, and then I went and talked to you guys. He knew I talked to you."

"You ever see where the containers were getting shipped off to?"

"No. It's not like they had labels or shit. That was worked out with the cargo terminal in advance. The guy, the one who Danny met at the airport, always acted like he expected us. He'd direct us where to park, where to unload—stuff like that."

"You sure you never got a look at the guy Danny worked for? You ever get a name?"

"No, not me. Danny handled that. The only guy I ever saw was at the airport when we dropped the shit off. It was always the same dude. Long black hair, pulled back in a ponytail. Asian, maybe."

"All right. You want to call your family before we take you in?"

Guzman's face brightened. "You'd let me do that?"

John fished his cell phone out and said, "What's the number?"

Guzman gave John his wife's cell number, and he tapped the keys on the phone to connect the call. He held the phone to the gangbanger's ear.

"Hey, baby, it's me. You get to that place we talked about? You get there and stay put till I call again, okay?" He listened for a moment, looked at John, and then said, "She wants to talk to you."

John pulled the phone back from Guzman and held it to his own ear. "This is Detective Penley." After a moment, he said, "Yes, Mrs. Guzman, your husband is fine. He got himself into a bit of trouble that we are trying to sort out right now."

John listened to the excited woman on the other end of the connection and tried to calm her. "Mrs. Guzman, please do as your husband asked. He only wants you to be safe. Are you certain that no one followed you?"

The handcuffed gangster tensed in the chair as he waited for a response.

John shook his head. "You keep to yourself and call me if you get the feeling that someone is watching you, understand?" He gave her his cell number and let Guzman say a few words before he disconnected the call.

"Thank you for that," Guzman said.

"No problem."

John lifted the man out of the chair and motioned to the battered front-door frame. Guzman took a few steps, stopped, and said, "I'm sorry."

"For what?"

"I shouldn't have shot at you. I was scared for my family."

"When someone comes between you and your family, you do what you gotta do," John said.

Guzman walked to the sedan unassisted but flanked by Paula and John. A group of neighbors and curiosity seekers, drawn by the sound of gunfire, was assembled on the far sidewalk. John opened the rear door, placed his prisoner inside, and looked across the roof at the gathering crowd.

"Hey, Mario? Anybody over there you don't know?"

Guzman looked. "They're all locals. Wait, that dude on the right, the one with the black baseball cap, he's not from around here. I've seen him when I was with Danny. At the warehouse! He gave Danny a key to the warehouse on R Street!"

The man with the ball cap held his head so that the visor angled downward, obscuring his facial features. He wore a dark-blue canvas jacket, much too warm for the weather, and had his hands shoved deep in the pockets.

"I got him," Paula said as she stepped over the curb into the street.

The man in the cap backed into the crowd, and by the time Paula reached the middle of the street, he vanished, concealed by the noise and movement. She rose up on her toes but couldn't locate him. The onlookers seemed to have swallowed him. A bottle shattered in the street, and stale beer spilled on her pant leg. The gathering turned malignant.

From deep in the crowd, a gunshot sounded. Panic spread and bystanders ran in all directions, anticipating more gunfire. "The cops are shooting," one fleeing man called out. Paula crouched against a car parked on the street after the shot went off. It was close, and she could smell the burnt gunpowder. She glanced over her shoulder and saw John tucked behind their sedan, gun drawn.

The sidewalk cleared in seconds and left nothing behind except for shards of another broken bottle like the one tossed at Paula. The man in the ball cap had disappeared in the panic and confusion.

Paula peeked from her spot behind the parked car and found nothing, no bullet-riddled body, no blood trail, not even a shell casing—nothing. She stood and holstered her weapon.

John did the same and stepped into the street toward his partner. He pointed to the far street corner.

Paula sorted out the fleeing bystanders and started in their direction on foot, peering in open doorways and windows.

With Guzman secure in the rear seat, John pulled the sedan around the block and met Paula when she emerged around the corner. "You sure about that guy? He gave you a key to the warehouse?" she asked Guzman.

"Not me. He gave it to Danny. It was him. The way he moved, kind of like a boxer, you know? Always moving, staying in front of Danny. I'm sure of it."

Paula started to the passenger door and stopped midstride. "Hang on for a sec."

"What ya got?" John said.

She didn't answer. Instead, Paula went to a line of dumpsters behind a nearby restaurant. Discarded sesame-chicken scraps attracted black flies from all of Northern California. The three blue waste containers were arranged against the cinderblock wall, and the insects swarmed around the bins. All three bins were identical, and Paula swatted flies from her path to the centermost container.

"This one's been disturbed," she said.

John stood at the driver's door, pulled his weapon, and covered his partner. "What are you, the dumpster whisperer?"

She took her weapon from its holster without a sound, crept to the side of the dumpster, and with her free hand, shoved the lid up. The metal clanged off the cinderblock, and Paula peered over the rim behind the muzzle of her weapon. She paused a moment, then holstered her gun.

"That would have been too easy," John said.

Paula pulled on a pair of latex gloves, stepped up on one of the exposed ribs on the side of the dumpster, and threw her leg over. Her head bobbed below the rim of the trash container, and she surfaced with a large, paper Chinese takeout container.

"I would have stopped for lunch," John said, holstering his weapon.

"They weren't serving .38-caliber Smith & Wessons at my usual place." Paula held the container higher and displayed the wooden grip of a revolver covered in leftover rice noodles.

"Nice find," John said. "Think it belonged to our shooter?"

"Smells like it. Fresh-burnt powder."

Paula fished an evidence bag out of the car and sealed the gun and chicken chow fun inside.

"Seriously, how did you know what dumpster to look in?"

"The flies."

"Yeah, what about 'em?"

"There were more flies buzzing around that center dumpster than the other two. Something stirred them up. Had to be our guy."

She got back in the car, rested the evidence bag between her feet, and buckled up. A smirk creased her face.

John shook his head. "My partner is lord of the flies."

A midday booking at the Sacramento County Main Jail generally took an hour. Guzman was a cooperative, frequent guest at the inn, so the sheriff's personnel were able to strip him out, inventory and store his personal property—which consisted of blue jeans, a wife-beater undershirt, boxers, socks, and work boots—without delay. Guzman had nothing in his pockets; he'd kept no wallet, keys, or cash with him. It was as if he'd expected to end up in the jail's receiving and release holding cells. Or the morgue.

Some gang members routinely gave false names and phony information during booking, a game played for the sole purpose of messing with the jail staff, causing more work for them when live-scan fingerprints revealed outstanding warrants. Guzman willingly gave them all the updated information on his address and next of kin—except where his next of kin could be found.

John asked that Guzman be housed in a single cell. He told the booking officer that Guzman was on the outs with the West Block Norteños and needed segregated housing for protection. Guzman started to protest placement in a cell that might get him labeled as a protective-custody case.

"I'm no snitch," he said.

John stepped close and said, "No, but we need to keep you safe, and I don't know how this killer is targeting his gang member victims." He didn't mention that the killer seemed to know every step of their investigation and had left a gift-wrapped kidney for him.

Guzman sat on the wooden bench in his holding cell and leaned against the cold block wall. His shoulders sagged, head held down, and he let loose a long exhale, a man deflated, trapped. "If he's half as powerful as Danny thought he was, it won't matter where you put me. I'm a dead man."

Paula, as the junior detective, finished the last of the booking paperwork and joined John at the holding tank as two jail officers escorted Guzman out of the intake area to one of the housing units in the multistory downtown jail.

"You think Guzman's right, don't you? The killer can reach out and touch him, even in here?" she said.

"He was sitting right outside Guzman's place. If we hadn't gotten to him first . . ."

"We should let the techies work over the gun. Maybe they'll be able to pull a print out of that mess."

John grabbed at his belt before he had a chance to respond. The vibration surprised him. He felt the source—the pager issued by the transplant center.

He snatched the pager from his belt, nearly ripping it from his pants. The familiar black phone number stretched across the screen, a numeric cocktail of hope and frustration.

"It's the transplant center."

John's cell phone rang, and the caller ID marked the incoming call from Melissa.

John couldn't make his hand move fast enough. He fumbled with the keys on the phone and pressed the green connect button.

"Mel, I just got . . . when? You'll pick up Tommy? I'll meet you there."

"What's going on?" Paula asked.

"Melissa got a call from Tommy's doctor. They have a kidney, and the surgical team is scheduling Tommy for surgery. I gotta go. It's happening! Melissa and Tommy are on their way."

John shoved the phone and pager in his pants pocket and bolted for the door out of the booking area. The lock for the door was electronic and operated by an officer in central control. A square, perforated steel panel covered the intercom system, and a worn button stuck through a hole in the panel. John hit the button with his fist, faced left for a closed-circuit television camera, and spoke, "Detectives Newberry and Penley, sally-port door."

"Have a good day, Detectives," a voice sounded over the speaker. The door pulled back along its track, and John squeezed through sideways when the door parted enough. Paula followed into a rectangular hallway where arresting officers secured their weapons before entering the main jail. John had experienced long delays in the sally port when shift changes occurred, when disturbances in another part of the jail diverted staff, or when the officer in central control had something to prove to city cops. He let out a sigh of relief that this wasn't one of those occasions.

John quickened his step toward their car and unlocked the doors.

"Give me the keys. I'll drive you," Paula said.

The keys in his hand jangled from a slight tremor. He tossed the keys to Paula and jogged around to the passenger side.

She started the motor, navigated through the last electronic jail gate, and turned onto H Street. She activated the undercover sedan's red lights mounted in the grill and sped through the traffic down Fifth Street, toward Broadway. Paula hit the gas on Broadway and pushed toward the hospital.

"You've got to be excited, right? Tommy's getting his transplant after all this time."

John gripped his knees with his hands, knuckles white. "I'd like to get there alive to see it."

Paula shot a glance at the speedometer; the needle hovered around seventy. She let off the gas and no longer threatened the inner-city land-speed record.

"This day," John said. "We've waited for this day for a long time. I'm still worried. There is so much that can go wrong—complications, drug interaction, delayed graft function, and rejection. Now we have a whole new set of fears."

"New fears means Tommy has a fighting chance."

The tan facade of Central Valley Hospital loomed ahead, and Paula swooped across oncoming traffic and bounded into the parking lot. She turned off the red lights and circled to the patient-loading zone.

Before the sedan stopped, John had the door open and one foot on the pavement. He hopped out, ducked his head back inside, and said, "Thanks. I'll let you know what's going on as soon as we know anything. And don't do anything if you get a pop on the gun."

"I'll think about it."

John sat back in the car. "Stay cool for now." John's face was grim and ashen.

"You don't think this has anything to do with Tommy's transplant?" Paula held the evidence bag.

"I don't know what to think. But I don't like the setup, either."

"What are you gonna do?"

John got out of the car once more and said, "Whatever I have to do to keep Tommy safe." He turned and jogged inside the hospital's lobby.

TWENTY

John spotted Melissa across the lobby. She clutched Tommy close, a protective gesture and one that comforted her as much as her son. Tommy had his hospital backpack, crammed with books, video games, and personal things meant to keep him occupied and comfortable. Melissa stood when she saw her husband across the vast waiting room. She waved. Instead of the relief that the day was finally here for their son, Melissa's face betrayed something more, a mix of fear and anxiety.

John spotted Melissa with Trisha Woods, who had complained earlier about John's attempts to access transplant records. Was she here to spoil this, too?

Melissa hugged John as soon as he was within range. She felt stiff and pulled away from his embrace. Tommy glanced up from the seat and quickly refocused on the video game in his hands.

"Where's Kari?" John asked.

"She's with Andrea," Melissa said. Andrea was Melissa's younger sister, whom Kari thought was the coolest person on earth.

Trisha took out her clipboard and pen, tapping it on a form. "Now, on to Tommy's medications. When were the last doses of Tacrolimus and prednisone?"

"Noon today," Melissa said.

"I didn't take the Tacrolimus. That's the tan-and-white capsule, right?" Tommy asked.

A quicksilver ball formed in John's chest. The prescription bottles that had spilled in his car when he transported the Cardozo girl. Was Tommy's Tacrolimus among them?

"What? Why didn't you take it?" Melissa asked.

"It gives me the shakes. I can't play my video games without screwing up. The guys at school make fun of me when I take it."

Trisha got on one knee in front of the boy and asked, "When was the last time you took it?"

Tommy's eyes flicked up to his mother. "Maybe a week."

"Tommy! Why didn't you say something?"

"I knew you'd get mad."

Melissa sat on the sofa next to her son and placed an arm around him. The small tear she noticed in his eye caused one of her own. "Honey, I'm not mad. I'm surprised, I guess. Dr. Anderson told us that all your medications were important."

"I know, Mom. Dr. Anderson said all that stuff, but he's not the one who has to take it."

John moved next to Trisha. "What happens now? What does skipping his meds do to his transplant?"

"The doctor put Tommy on the immune suppressor to ready him for transplant. The chance of rejection would have been much lower if . . ."

"Will he still get the transplant? Where did the donated organ come from?" John said.

"John, don't," Melissa said.

Trisha crossed her arms and pinned the clipboard to her chest. "I don't know. That will be the doctor's call." After an awkward pause, she continued, "Let's proceed as if we are moving forward." Trisha uncrossed her arms and held out a hand to Tommy. "Time to get you checked in."

Tommy shut down his video game, stuffed it in his backpack, and hopped off the sofa. He took Trisha's hand and followed her lead through the doors that led out of the lobby.

John gripped his son's other hand as they navigated through a warren of sterile medical offices and patient rooms. Agonizing months of scans, blood tests, and biopsies ensured Tommy knew more about life and death than the average kid. The nine-year-old's pale skin, thin limbs, and dark circles under his eyes concealed a strength that outweighed most grown men. A doctor was going to slice him open, tear out a diseased clump of flesh, toss someone's leftover kidney inside, and sew him closed. To a nine-year-old, that should be the plot in a horror movie. Yet the boy moved on, only pausing to hitch up his pants, which had become too large for his withered body.

They turned down a corridor, painted a calming light blue but highlighted by anxiety-inducing signs with terse warnings about transmission of diseases to immune-compromised patients. At the far end, two scrub-clad nurses waited on either side of a doorway. Darla and Laura were Tommy's favorite nurses, and they welcomed him with practiced smiles. Their eyes betrayed something less benign.

Tommy followed Nurse Darla inside, and the second nurse stepped in behind, blocking the door. "I need a moment of your time while Darla gets Tommy comfortable," Laura said.

She guided John and Melissa to a small sofa in the corner of a bland waiting room within eyeshot of Tommy's room. Melissa sat so she could watch the room for any sign that called for a mom's immediate presence.

"I know you've completed all the preadmission paperwork, but I need to be sure that everything is up to date," Laura said. She ticked off names, addresses, phone numbers, and dates of birth to verify each of them, barely waiting for a response. Her voice held a steady tone as she asked, "Do you have an advance directive in place?"

If John wasn't sitting, the wave of fear that washed over him threatened to drop him to the floor. He heard his heart thump against his ribs, and he opened his mouth but couldn't form any words.

Laura filled in the silence. "We need to make certain that we follow your wishes, should the need arise."

She held out a small sheaf of forms. Bold letters on the visible pages outlined what happens when a patient is listed as DNR, do not resuscitate, and what procedures are considered extraordinary medical intervention to continue life.

No parent should have to make that decision. John couldn't take the documents from Laura that would end his son's life. Melissa grabbed them, tore them into small bits, and let them fall to the carpet. Not another word was exchanged, but the message was clear—we are not giving up on our son, not now, not ever.

Melissa's glare broke when a curtain shifted in Tommy's room. Tommy sat propped up in bed, his attention funneled into his video game. He'd changed into a pair of pajamas and was taking another hospital stay in stride.

Darla finished taking the boy's blood pressure and folded up the cuff, tucking it away on a bedside tray. She motioned to John and Melissa. "The doctor will be in shortly," Darla said as they passed in the hallway.

"How you doing, Tommy?" John asked.

The boy shrugged. "Fine, I guess."

"Can I get you anything?" Melissa said.

"No."

"Hi, Tommy," Dr. Anderson said as he breezed into the room, his white coat flapping behind him.

"Hi," Tommy said without looking away from his game.

"Well, you have a big day ahead of you. You all ready for it?"

"I guess so." Tommy shrugged.

"You a little scared?" the doctor said, talking to Tommy and not his parents.

"A little." Buttons clicked away on the game console.

"That's normal. What are you afraid of?"

Tommy paused the game and finally made eye contact with the doctor. "What happens if this doesn't work?"

"No reason to think that it won't work. We have a transplant-able kidney on the way. It has been matched to your tissue type, and as long as you agree to take your antirejection medications"—the doctor winked—"you should do fine."

"I will. I promise," Tommy said with a quick glance at his mother.

Dr. Anderson turned to John and Melissa. "We'll draw some blood work to make sure there are no infections or anything that would get in our way. Skipping the Tacrolimus wasn't the best thing, but we can adjust the dosage after the surgery."

Melissa stood at Tommy's bedside. John took the doctor by the elbow and led him to the far side of the room, away from his family.

"Tacrolimus is an antirejection med, right?" John asked in a low voice.

"An immunosuppression medication. We started Tommy on it to get his system ready for the transplant."

"Any other reason to give a patient that drug?"

"I'm not sure what you're getting at."

John rubbed the back of his neck. The bag of spilled medications when he brought the Cardozo girl and her mother to the hospital burned again in his memory. "Cielo Cardozo, is she a patient of yours?"

Dr. Anderson lowered his tablet computer, not expecting the question. "Mr. Penley, I cannot comment on another patient."

"You just did. She is your patient then? Her mother told us she had cancer."

"I can't get into her treatment with you, just as I wouldn't divulge Tommy's treatment to anyone else."

"Okay, hypothetically, if the girl had cancer, would a transplant treat it?"

"Many cancers include transplant as part of the treatment regimen."

"Where did the transplant come from? The UNOS wait list?"

"Well, yes, that's where a transplant comes from, after it is typed and matched."

The timing of Cielo Cardozo's rush surgery after her father's murder ate at John's mind. He should have caught that connection. Especially after the killer left a kidney gift wrapped for Tommy. Maybe he left a gift for Cielo, too. "Was the tissue HIV tested?"

The doctor's eyes narrowed. "Why would you believe it was HIV positive?"

"So she did have a transplant. Did you test it?"

The doctor let out a breath, angry with himself for divulging the little girl's transplant. "No, all the matching is done before we receive the organ."

Melissa joined the two men. "What's going on? What's wrong?"

"How long until Tommy heads into surgery?" John asked.

The doctor glanced at some notes on his tablet computer. "The organ is expected here anytime now, so we will have Tommy in the OR within an hour. I'd say we'll have the anesthesiologist put him under in about twenty minutes from now."

"That's fast," Melissa said.

"Yep. I'll bet you're all excited to finally be at this point."

"We are," she responded.

"How do you know the kidney is viable and ready for transplant when it's not here yet?" John asked.

Melissa shot a disapproving look at her husband.

The killer had connections inside the system. How much more inside could you get than a transplant surgeon, especially one who had a hand in the Gunderson boy's recent organ rejection? "How many people verify the donated tissue is viable? How many other than you?"

Melissa grabbed her husband's arm.

The doctor noticed her reaction. "No—no, that's a good question. When the organ is harvested from the donor, the surgeon who obtains it, wherever that is, examines the tissue, obtains a tissue type, and enters that information into the system."

"UNOS?" John said.

Dr. Anderson looked at John, paused, and said, "Yes. The system alerts our transplant team that a match is available, and here we are."

"How does the kidney tissue get matched?" John said.

"Actually, the kidney itself isn't matched. The tissue match is determined by blood test, the HLA mismatch pairings. The harvesting physician also removes lymphatic tissue, and those cells are used for cross-match samples."

"Where did the donated kidney come from?" John asked.

"Come from?"

"Yeah. Who was the donor?"

"I'm not sure I know, offhand. Let me check." The doctor manipulated his tablet computer and pulled up the transplant records. "Says here the donor's next of kin wished to remain anonymous."

Paranoia set its roots deep. "Do you know where the organ was harvested?"

"John, stop. You're scaring Tommy." However, Tommy wasn't paying any attention to the discussion; the boy's focus had fallen back to his video game. Melissa was pale and hugged her arms around her waist.

Dr. Anderson tapped on the tablet's display. "The transport team is picking up the organ at the cargo terminal at Executive Airport."

"Not from a local hospital?"

The doctor glanced at his tablet. "It originated from outside our region. UNOS paired the organ with Tommy because of the match and his medical necessity."

"What's wrong? Don't ruin this, John," Melissa said.

John rubbed his temples and tried to ward off the mother of all tension headaches. The harder he pressed into the thin bands of muscles around his head, the deeper the suspicion and doubt went into his brain.

"It's something I've been working on," he said.

"Can't that wait?"

"I think they are connected."

Melissa's face betrayed a combination of confusion and fear. The sparkle vanished from her blue eyes, and her lips tightened, thin and pale. "John . . ." she started.

"Doctor, is there any method to retest the donated organ before the surgery?" John asked.

"We—we examine the tissue. It will be sealed in a cold-storage bag, and while we warm up the donated tissue, we'll do a cross match for antibodies. The cross match won't prevent the transplant. It will tell us if we need to put Tommy through a course of pheresis and immunoglobulin infusion. The primary concern is the tissue type, and that matching is done before we take possession. It saves time and risk to the patients," the doctor said.

"But can you retest to verify the tissue type?"

"I don't see a reason we need to, Mr. Penley."

"John, please stop this," Melissa said.

"I need you to reexamine the organ before you put in inside my son's body. I don't think that's a lot to ask."

Dr. Anderson lowered his voice. "I understand what you're going through. You're worried and you want to make sure everything goes smoothly. The UNOS registry makes certain that the right donated tissue goes to the right patient. That's the reason for the system."

"Like the Gunderson boy? The UNOS data have been compromised," John said.

"That's simply a theory," Trisha Woods added, coming in from the hallway, drawn by the escalating conversation.

"This is the first I've heard of this. Why hasn't the transplant committee been informed?" Dr. Anderson said.

"Because it is only a theory—one Detective Penley has yet to prove," Trisha said to Dr. Anderson. She turned to John and said, "You haven't come up with any proof the data have been compromised yet, have you?"

"Not yet. But the timeline of the transplants—"

"Stop it! Stop it! This is our son we're talking about, not the ghost of some nameless victim you drag home from work every night!" Melissa turned away, went to Tommy's bedside, and sat.

"Do you have a suspect? Who tampered with the registry?" the doctor asked.

"I don't have a name," John said. The mental list of people who could manipulate the transplant data was a short one, and two of those people stood in front of him now.

"Can you tell me with absolute certainty that there is anything wrong with the kidney donated for your son?" Dr. Anderson said.

"No, I can't," John answered.

The doctor's cell phone chirped. He glanced at a text message on the screen. "The ambulance team picked up the kidney. They're on their way. ETA is fifteen minutes. We need to get Tommy prepped. Unless you're telling me that you're refusing the surgery."

John looked at his son. The boy suffered so much and missed out on what it meant to be a kid; medical appointments instead of sports and medication regimens taking instead of camping trips. Frail, pale, and weakening each day, Tommy's ability to survive without a transplant had reached its limits. Had paranoia fogged John's perception?

"Melissa?" John said in a wavering voice.

"Let's do it. Please be careful, Doctor," Melissa said.

The doctor put a hand on John's shoulder. "We will. Don't worry. We'll take good care of Tommy." Then to Trisha, the doctor said, "Let the nurses know they can get him ready. The anesthesiologist will be down in a few minutes."

Dr. Anderson nodded at Melissa and Tommy, turned, and disappeared around a hallway corner.

"We have some work to do," Trisha said, hefting her clipboard.

The next ten minutes were filled with paperwork, consent forms, inserting an IV line in Tommy's thin arm, and more blood samples. A tall, thin woman in a lab coat it looked like she borrowed from her father entered the room and introduced herself to Tommy.

"I'm Dr. Mason. I'll be giving you something to make you sleepy so we can get you off to surgery. Do you understand what you're here for today, Tommy?"

"Yeah. I'm getting a new kidney."

"That's right. So I'm going to give you something to make you sleep right through it, and when you wake up, you'll have your new kidney and you can start feeling better. Okay?"

The boy nodded.

"Any questions?" the doctor looked to the parents.

John and Melissa shook their heads.

"All right then. Tommy, let's take a nap," Dr. Mason said.

"We'll be right here when you wake up, sweetie," Melissa said as she planted a kiss on Tommy's forehead.

John held his son's hand, and in a voice that sounded calmer than he actually felt, said, "It will be over before you know it."

Dr. Mason pulled a thin syringe from her lab coat along with a vial filled with a milky-white liquid. "This is called Prophofol, and it will make you really sleepy." She plunged the needle into the vial, withdrew some into the syringe, and then stuck the needle into the valve in the IV line.

Within seconds, Tommy drifted off into sleep, and for the first time in months, the boy's face looked relaxed, completely devoid of the tension and stress that he had grown to tolerate.

Dr. Mason called in an orderly, who unlocked the gurney wheels and pulled the bed out into the hallway.

"I'm going to be with Tommy the whole time," Dr. Mason said. "I'll be giving him something a bit stronger before the surgery so he doesn't have any pain. He's in good hands now. Dr. Anderson is the best."

John and Melissa walked with the gurney as far as the doorway to the operating rooms. Melissa reluctantly let go of her son's hand as he slipped behind the doors into the surgery suite.

"I hope we did the right thing," John said.

"Can you tell me about this?" Melissa unfolded a sheet of paper and handed it to John.

"Where did you get this?" John held the printout of his laptop screen, a photo that featured the demand for a ten-thousand-dollar payment. "It's not what you think, Mel."

"You bastard! You had this at your fingertips and you didn't tell me?"

"It's not like that. The case I'm working—"

"Why couldn't you tell me that you could have had Tommy moved up on the transplant list?"

"You can't be serious. We couldn't do that. People could get hurt."

"Isn't Tommy more important than some damn case?"

"Melissa, what are you saying?"

Her eyes flashed. "I always believed, in my heart, that you'd do anything to protect your family. Now I know differently."

John reached out for her, and she jerked away. "Mel, that's not fair. You know I would give my soul for Tommy."

"Apparently not."

"You don't mean that—"

"Don't tell me what I mean, John. We could have talked about this together and come to a decision."

He crumpled the printout so hard that his knuckles went pale. "This wasn't an option. The people behind this kind of operation don't care about what happens to Tommy. I'm sorry I didn't tell you about it."

"It doesn't matter now anyway. Tommy's getting his surgery," Melissa said. The fight was out of her.

They found an empty space on a sofa in the waiting room where they could ride out the four-hour surgery. Their hearts froze in midbeat when, less than an hour into the allotted time, a grim Dr. Anderson appeared.

In his surgical garb, complete with a mask draped around his neck and head covering perched in place, Dr. Anderson surveyed the waiting room until he found John and Melissa. By the time he reached them, both were standing, waiting. The surgeon's abrupt, early appearance meant bad news. Something had happened to Tommy during the surgery.

Melissa reached out and grabbed the doctor's arm. "What is it? Is Tommy all right?"

Dr. Anderson took her hand gently. In a hushed tone, he said, "Why don't we go somewhere more private?"

"No. Tell me now! My son?" she said.

Heads from other families turned in their direction. Most had sympathetic faces, while a few wore expressions that bore relief that the bad news wasn't for them.

"Okay, please sit," Dr. Anderson said.

John and Melissa retreated to the sofa, perching on the edge, their backs rod straight with morbid resignation.

"I'm afraid I do have bad news."

Melissa tensed and grabbed her husband's hand.

The doctor moved to take her hand, but stopped when she pulled away. "First, Tommy is all right. But we had to stop the surgery."

"What happened?" John asked.

"We had Tommy ready to go for the transplant, we made the initial incisions, peeled back the muscle tissue, and exposed the iliac artery for the graft. We removed the donated kidney from the container and flushed it in sterile solution. All textbook. Since this was planned as a heterotopic transplant, where Tommy's existing kidneys were to stay in place, the next step was the graft." The doctor scanned the waiting room and leaned in closer to John. "Then I took a second look at the donated kidney, thinking about what you said."

"About where it came from?" John said.

"The UNOS system issues a unique identification number to each organ. The number issued for Tommy's new kidney came from a harvest twelve hours ago. The kidney that I examined was older than that—much older. The kidney already showed signs of delayed graft function and swelling. The perfusate solution was full of particulate matter. It was like it wasn't irrigated after harvest. That kidney wasn't viable transplant tissue."

"Did you start to graft that kidney in my son?" John asked.

"No. We caught the discrepancy in time. I closed Tommy back up, and he's in the recovery room now. He will still need a transplant, but he has to recover and get strong enough to go through this again."

John fell back against the back of the stiff sofa. "When can we see him?"

"Let's give him another ten minutes, and then it should be fine."

"How? This wasn't supposed to happen," Melissa said.

"I don't know. The system is designed to prevent this kind of problem. When the donated kidney went on the UNOS database, your son's name came up as an HLA zero mismatch, which means that it was a perfect tissue match for Tommy. It compared all the patients on the transplant list, and Tommy was the only exact match. There was no question that Tommy would end up with that donation. The thing that confounds me is how UNOS identified this as an organ harvested twelve hours ago. The condition of the tissue, swelling, and lack of elasticity is what I'd expect from a kidney well over seventy-two hours from harvest. Even with cold storage, the viability of the tissue declines rapidly."

"We need to get the kidney to the medical examiner for analysis," John said.

"Our lab has the tissue now and will share the results with them. Let's go look in on Tommy."

The doctor stood and led them to the doors of the recovery room, a few yards from the surgical suite. He paused at the door. "This shouldn't have happened. I can't tell you how sorry I am. I was minutes from putting that kidney into your son. I wouldn't have taken that extra look if it wasn't for our conversation."

"But you prevented that from happening," John said.

"It shouldn't have gone that far."

"Can we see him now?" Melissa pleaded.

Dr. Anderson nodded and stepped back from the doorway.

Melissa was first through the door. John was a step behind, and he melted when he saw Tommy with tubes, wires, monitors, and thickly packed gauze from the aborted surgery attached to him.

"What would have happened if you hadn't noticed and went on with the transplant?" John asked.

Dr. Anderson's scrubs wrinkled as he crossed his arms, revealing a small drop of blood on the surgeon's chest. John noticed the stain and couldn't look away from the spot, a small, insignificant droplet that told of Tommy's journey.

"The kidney would have failed, sooner rather than later. I would have given it a day or two, at most. Then, toxicity within Tommy's system would have spiked. Fevers, sepsis, and infection would have been bad news with his compromised immune system."

"Any way he could have fought it off and pulled through?"

"No chance. That tissue was a loaded gun. I'd be willing to bet that the lab results confirm the tissue was damaged and dying."

"How did a decaying organ get into the transplant stream?"

"I don't know. The ramifications of this—this event threatens the foundation of this hospital and the hundreds of transplants we provide each year. As soon as I report this through the transplant committee, we may be cut off from the Organ Sharing Network until we reexamine every step in our process."

John leaned on the doorframe and wished he were the one strapped down with electrodes, cords, and tubes instead of his son. The botched surgery had sapped the reserves the boy held, yet he still needed a transplant to survive. In a perverse twist, he wouldn't get the transplant until he regained some of his strength. Each succeeding day without a new kidney meant Tommy grew weaker and his blood more toxic. The boy's body lost ground in his fight to get the transplant.

Without looking away from his son, John said, "Do me a favor. Don't report what happened to the transplant committee."

"What are you saying? I have to report the condition of the organ tissue we received. The consequence of failing to alert the Organ Sharing Network presents a risk to every patient waiting for a transplant."

John locked eyes with Anderson. "Give me twenty-four hours before you report to the committee. You don't even have the lab results to confirm the report yet, do you?"

"Well, no . . ."

"You'd be like Chicken Little claiming the sky is falling without any evidence to back it up. Please, Doctor, I'm asking for twenty-four hours."

"I—I guess it can't hurt. I don't have any other transplant surgeries scheduled today. We have two possible cases tomorrow afternoon, the first at one o'clock and another at six, if the donated organs arrive. I must report before then. Why are you asking me to delay this?"

"I need to find where the kidney came from and how it got into your system. If you had any part in changing the UNOS data to make this happen, I'll find out." John grabbed the doctor by the lapels of his white lab coat. "This is your only chance to come clean."

Dr. Anderson stood motionless and stone-faced. "Mr. Penley, you're not thinking clearly. Let go of me, now."

John released his grip on the doctor's coat.

"I need to find out how this happened as much as you do," the doctor said. "I'll call the lab and have the samples brought to you."

"No, I'll get them."

"You need to trust someone, Detective."

"Not when it comes to my kid."

TWENTY-ONE

"I don't care if you're a cop. I'm not giving you anything from my lab." The starched white smock flapped behind the laboratory supervisor when he blocked John's path, an imitation of a protective goat-herder keeping a hungry coyote at bay.

John noted the blue stitching on the lab coat that bore the supervisor's name. "Listen, Martin . . ."

"That's Dr. Robinson to you. You can't barge in here and take samples from my lab."

"The tissue sample Dr. Anderson sent you is evidence in a criminal investigation. I need the medical examiner to take custody and evaluate the sample," John said.

"Then get a warrant. I have my lab protocols that must be followed. I can't release anything to you. I log in each and every tissue sample, log the testing, and log the disposition of the samples. We have a chain of custody here, and I simply can't turn over a tissue sample because you say so."

"Show me the sample. That can't violate any of your precious protocols. Can it?"

"That's highly irregular." Dr. Robinson stiffened in protest.

John probed the weakening bureaucrat. "If I get Dr. Kelly, the medical examiner herself, to tell you to release the tissue, is that within protocol?"

"I—I suppose. However, my lab will no longer be responsible for any testing associated with that tissue. Dr. Kelly will have to provide any clinical assessment and tissue typing information that's required."

"Agreed." John pulled out his cell and hit the speed-dial entry for Dr. Sandra Kelly. "Why don't you go track down the tissue sample while I speak to Dr. Kelly?"

Dr. Robinson, tight jawed from being ordered about within his own space, slunk behind the counter and retreated to the lab confines. He swiped his key card, unlocking a glass door that separated the laboratory from the outer offices.

Dr. Kelly came on the line after a few seconds. "Hi, Detective. I was just thinking about calling you. What's on your mind?"

"I need you to take a look at a tissue sample, a kidney."

"Related to our current case?"

"I think it is."

"How did you stumble upon this kidney? Find another shipping container?" she asked.

"They tried to put this one in my son."

Silence.

"The surgeon caught it before it was too late and saw that the kidney wasn't viable."

"I need that organ," she said.

"I'm trying to persuade the lab supervisor at the hospital to turn it over."

"What's his name?"

"Martin Robinson. Know him?"

"I've heard about him. Very by-the-book. More of an administrator and paper pusher than a clinical guy. Is he there? Let me talk to him. Put him on."

At that moment, Dr. Robinson returned from the lab. The lab super's face bloomed pink, and his protruding Adam's apple bobbed as he swallowed hard. "It's missing."

"I'll call you back," John said to Dr. Kelly, and he disconnected the call. "Missing? What's missing?"

"The sample. The sample Dr. Anderson sent. The whole thing. It's gone. There must be an explanation," Dr. Robinson said. He rubbed his hands together to purge the imaginary stain of a potential scandal.

"You said you kept a log. Let me see it," John said.

Robinson stepped around to his desk, opened a drawer, and pulled a thick, three-inch canvas binder from the bottom drawer. He placed it on the desk surface, opened the file to the last page of handwritten entries, and pointed. "Here is when the tissue sample came into the lab."

John read the neatly printed line. *Tissue sample (human kidney) received from Dr. Anderson for ms, vs, and bc.*

"What's that mean?" John asked.

"Mass spectrometry, vivisection, and bacterial culture. Dr. Anderson wanted those actions completed. We take small samples of the tissue, review it by mass spec, and look for abnormal tissue, cellular crystallization, edema, and foreign bodies. Fluid and tissue are tested for bacterial infection, so we grow a culture to identify the type and strain of infection."

"Where did the organ go after you logged it in?"

"Into refrigerated storage, locker number three." Robinson pointed to the entry in the log book.

"Show me," John said.

Robinson froze in place for a moment as he considered his precious protocols. The rigid rules failed him, and he needed damage control now. He gestured for John to follow him through the doors into the sterile work space.

Expansive white work surfaces, stainless-steel tables, and glass-fronted cabinets dominated the lab. The work space appeared well ordered, clean, and empty. Hulking machines with lights, vials, and dials sat along the far wall, and four refrigeration units lined the end wall to the right. The refrigerated units had tall black numbers stenciled on the glass-front panels. Bottles, racks of test tubes, and plastic-wrapped specimen dishes with red biohazard labels decorated the shelves behind the glass.

"Dr. Anderson's tissue sample went into number three."

"Are you certain?"

"Yes. I put it in there myself."

John walked to the refrigerated units and tugged on the handle of the one marked with the number three. It held tight. "Who else has access?"

"Only the lab employees have access cards. Four technicians and me," Robinson said.

Slim, metallic card readers protruded from the wall next to each glass door. Robinson unclipped his access card from his lab coat and swiped it through the card-reader slot, and a green light appeared on the door. The lock popped open.

"The sample was on the middle of the top shelf. I don't understand how it went missing."

Robinson shut the door, and an audible click indicated the door had locked, but John pulled the handle to make certain.

"The electronic lock system—can you access the history of who used an access card to open that door?" John asked.

"I suppose so. I've never had reason to do that." Robinson pivoted on his heel and took a step to a workstation. He woke up the computer with a shake of the mouse and entered his password into the secure hospital system. He scrolled down a menu of options and then clicked on the security item.

The link required a second password, and the screen refreshed with a set of menu items specifically for the hospital laboratory.

"Access log," Robinson said as he clicked on the item. The screen flickered and scrolled out line after line of dates, times, and names of the staff who had entered the secured spaces of the lab. Robinson paused the screen when the access data for refrigerated storage came on the screen.

"That can't be right."

"What is it?" John asked.

Robinson's finger shook as he pointed to the screen. "Here, precisely at 1:35, I opened the locker. That's when I secured Dr. Anderson's specimen. Twelve minutes later, the same locker opened. That's not possible."

John looked over the doctor's shoulder, and the computer indicated that at 1:47, a staff member by the name of Marsha Horn opened the locker.

"Where is Marsha Horn? I need to talk to her," John said.

"You can't."

"What do you mean, I can't?"

Dr. Robinson swallowed hard and said, "Marsha's dead. She was the lab supervisor before me. I didn't know her, but from everything I've gathered, she was a good supervisor and ran a tight lab. She died in a car accident about two years back," Robinson said.

"So how can you explain a dead woman stealing a tissue sample out of your lab?"

"I can't."

John looked around the lab quickly, assessed that there were no surveillance cameras and only two exit doors. A door in the back of the lab was marked for emergency use only and claimed that an alarm would sound if opened.

"Did Dr. Anderson call to tell you to get rid of the sample?"

"What? No."

"Who else is working here today?"

"I'm down to two assistants, and one is on vacation. So today, it's Zack Weber and me."

"Where's Zack?" John asked.

"I sent him down to admin. They're holding some of our equipment requests hostage."

John glanced at the emergency-exit door, and an uneven section on the doorframe caught his attention. He strode across the lab and grabbed the door handle.

Dr. Robinson yelled, "Wait, the alarm!" when John tugged on the handle.

The door slipped open without a crescendo of bells and buzzers.

"The door wasn't shut completely. The alarm should have gone off," John said. He slid his fingers along the metal doorframe and found thin strips of metallic tape attached to the sensors.

"Where does this exit go?"

"Stairwell, roof to basement," Robinson said.

John poked his head around the back of the door and saw no hint of a keypad or access-card reader, only a simple push bar designed for quick release in the event of an emergency evacuation. The telltale smell of cigarette smoke lingered in the stairwell.

"Are the doors alarmed all the way down?"

Before Robinson responded, the front electric door unlatched. A thin, scruffy-bearded man pushed through the door and dropped a file folder on the nearest counter. His eyes, magnified through thick lenses, blinked and shifted from Dr. Robinson to John.

"Zack, this is Detective Penley."

"Is there a problem, Dr. Robinson?" Zack asked. His voice cracked when he spoke.

Zack used a thumb to slide his glasses back up to the bridge of his nose. He crossed his arms and uncrossed them. Then he hiked up his lab-coat sleeves that were four inches too long. Zack fidgeted with the pens in his breast pocket before gathering up the files from the counter. The awkward mannerisms painted Zack as the kind of person most at home in a lab, where nothing required social interaction.

"We have experienced a breach of lab security," Robinson offered.

"Really? Who broke in?"

"How long have you worked in the lab, Zack?" John asked.

Zack kept his eyes on the paperwork. "Four years."

"So it's safe to say you know your way around this place fairly well?"

"Uh, yeah, safe to say," Zack said.

"Then you can tell me when the alarm on the fire-exit door was bypassed," John pressed.

The goggle-eyed lab assistant's face bounced up from the file in his hands. "I—I don't know anything about that," he said.

"Sure you do, Zack. You said you know your way around here. You'd notice something like that. Besides"—John pointed to a bulge in Zack's lab coat pocket—"there's a cigarette butt on the stairwell landing, and I'd bet that it's one of yours."

"There's no cigarette butt out there," Zack protested.

"How would you know that?" John countered.

His lip twitched.

"You know Marsha Horn?" John asked. "You worked here when Marsha ran the lab, right?"

"Uh-huh, so?" Zack replied.

"So how is it that Marsha accessed the refrigerated storage a couple hours ago?"

"I had—I don't know anything about that," Zack said.

John closed in on Zack. In spite of the chill in the room, small beads of moisture formed on the lab assistant's upper lip. The man smelled of nervous sweat and cigarette smoke.

"Sure you do, Zack. How often do you duck out into the stairwell for a smoke break?"

Zack looked to Dr. Robinson for a lifeline.

"Answer the man, Zack," Robinson ordered.

"Couple times a day," Zack said. His head hung low and his toe scuffed an invisible smudge on the lab floor.

"Let me see your cigarettes," John said.

"Back off! I know my rights. Get a warrant." The little man put up a rickety front of belligerence.

"I don't need one," Robinson said as he took Zack by surprise, lashed out, and snatched the cigarette package from the man's lab coat. "The coat is hospital property."

Robinson handed the cigarettes to John. The package felt stiffer than a normal, thin paper container. John opened the top, folded back the flimsy foil layer, and tucked behind a half dozen cigarettes, John spotted a thick, plastic-laminated card. John dumped the contents onto the counter, and a hospital access card slipped out. Marsha Horn's access card.

"That's no crime, using someone's card," Zack said quickly.

"Maybe, maybe not. Depends on why you used it. Why did you take Dr. Anderson's tissue sample?" John asked.

"Who says I did? You've got no proof of anything."

John spun the man around, pressed his own body weight against the smaller man, and pinned him against the counter. As John ratcheted the handcuffs tight, he whispered in Zack's ear, "You don't have the balls to pull this off by yourself. Tell me who you're working with."

"I don't have to answer to you," Zack said.

John pulled Zack around and sat him on a stool at the workbench. "Why's that?"

"Because I've done nothing wrong, even according to your laws." The little man looked smug, like he'd been waiting for this opportunity to boast. The scared lab geek transformed into someone with an edge.

"Destroying evidence, conspiracy . . ."

"Evidence of what? Conspiracy? The real conspiracy is the medical establishment and what they do to us," Zack said. His voice deepened with the bravado of a true believer.

John needed some conspiracy of his own, so he pulled out his cell and dialed.

"Detective Newberry," Paula said.

"It's me."

"How's Tommy?"

"Long story. Short version is the donated kidney was bad. It was from our 'friend,' and the hospital is compromised. We caught a break with a low-level hospital employee who destroyed evidence of the connection."

Zack's brow winced at the "low-level employee" label.

"I'll be there in ten. Did some follow-up on the gun, too. I got the name of the last registered owner," Paula said.

"You were supposed to wait for me," John said.

"Yeah. I always do what I'm told. See you in ten." She disconnected the call.

John pointed at Zack Weber. "Sit, stay."

John motioned for Dr. Robinson. "Doc, your computer records showed when Marsha Horn's access card was used in the lab. Can the system pull up any other access in the hospital systems?"

"I think so, but what do you want me to look for?"

"Did Marsha Horn access UNOS data?" John asked.

Zack postured from his chair, smug and prideful. "You have no idea what you're doing. You, of all people, Detective . . ."

John wheeled around and faced Zack. "Why screw around with a kid's life?"

"I've committed no crime."

"No, you've done something far worse," John said.

TWENTY-TWO

John arranged for a couple of uniforms to sit with Zack Weber while he checked on Tommy and Melissa. When he returned to his son's room, the boy's small chest barely rose with each breath. Melissa sat next to Tommy. She absently stroked Tommy's arm, a mother's touch, while she stared at the monitors attached to her boy, looking for any change in the blips, beeps, and lines that foretold Tommy's future.

Without glancing away from the monitor displays, Melissa said, "How could this happen?"

John perched on the side of the chair, next to his wife. He leaned in and rested his head on hers. "We'll get him through."

Melissa broke her trance away from the monitors, pulled back from her husband, and turned in the chair, facing him. "What have we done to our son?"

John recoiled as if she had slapped him. "We didn't—"

"Stop. Stop right there. We are responsible. We allowed that monster in our lives, and he nearly took Tommy from us."

John got up from the side of the chair and walked to a window that looked out on a quiet, well-maintained residential neighborhood. Monsters lurked out there, hidden behind all that Norman Rockwell veneer, monsters who preyed on the innocent and the vulnerable.

"You don't deny it, do you? That case you're working? He did this," she said.

John couldn't face Melissa. He shoved his hands in his pockets, shoulders stooped.

"What are you going to do about it?"

"I'm sorry. I'll get the case assigned to another detective," he said.

"The hell you will."

John turned.

Melissa stood and took a step toward her husband. "You'll do no such thing. Look at your son. Look what this creature made us do. You are not going to quit on Tommy. You find this son of a bitch and stop him."

Paula Newberry appeared at the doorway and cleared her throat. "How's Tommy doing?"

Melissa turned and greeted Paula with a hug. "The doctor says he's going to take a while to bounce back. He still needs a transplant."

Paula handed a small, stuffed teddy bear, dressed in a soccer uniform, to Melissa. "I know he used to like to play, so until he feels better . . ."

"Thanks. That's very thoughtful. He'll love it." Melissa clutched the stuffed animal tight.

"Let me have it," a weak voice called out. Tommy reached an arm out toward the bear.

"How are you, baby?" Melissa said, tucking the bear under his arms.

"I'm not a baby."

"You'll always be my baby. How are you feeling?" Melissa asked.

"How come I don't feel any different? I thought I was supposed to feel better. I feel the same, maybe worse. I'm sore."

John sat on the corner of the bed. "The doctor couldn't finish the surgery, Tommy," he said.

"What happened? Was I bad?"

John's throat tightened. "No, Tommy, you weren't bad. The kidney was bad, and the doctor didn't want to give you a bad one."

"Oh." Lines appeared on his small forehead. "But I still need one right?"

John nodded.

"So I have to wait some more?"

"Afraid so," John said.

"Okay. Can I have some ice cream? Last time I was here they let me have ice cream."

"I'll check," John offered.

The rattle of an equipment cart in the hallway stopped at their door. A young nurse came in with a tray laden with plastic-wrapped medical supplies and placed it on the table at Tommy's bedside.

"Hi, Tommy. I'm Katie. I need to hook you up with a new tube." The nurse checked Tommy's identification bracelet.

"Another IV?" Melissa asked. "What's wrong with the one he has?"

"This isn't for an IV. This is a shunt line for his dialysis treatment," the nurse explained.

"No one said anything about dialysis," Melissa said.

"Katie, could you excuse us for a moment? I need to speak with Mr. and Mrs. Penley," Dr. Anderson said from the doorway.

The nurse left the tray on the table and walked out into the hallway beyond Dr. Anderson. John tensed when Anderson entered the room.

"I'm sorry about that. I wanted to tell you myself," the doctor said.

"Tell us about what? Dialysis? That can't be," Melissa said.

"I'm afraid that's what we're up against. The stress from the surgery strained his kidneys. Tommy's blood work shows his GFR is below ten," Dr. Anderson said, referring to the glomerular filtration rate. He spoke softly, with a glance at Tommy to make sure he wasn't listening. "We are looking at levels that correspond with complete renal failure. We need to start him on dialysis while we search for a new kidney."

"Did the surgery cause this?" John asked.

"The anesthesia and the surgery put additional strain on his system. Tommy's renal function has been trending downward, but this event pushed him down a bit. I'm just grateful we didn't go through with the transplant with that suspect organ."

"Grateful is not what I'm feeling," John said.

Melissa returned to Tommy's bedside, her face brave, hiding a mother's darkest fears.

"The dialysis will keep his blood levels stable until the transplant." The doctor ran his hand over his short-cropped hair. "I can't understand what happened to that organ. The tissue damage I saw looked odd, like it was damaged by freezing temperature and improper perfusion."

"Perfusion? As in a perfusion pump?" John asked.

The doctor nodded. "The pump extends viability of the transplant tissue. The perfusion fluid is chilled to preserve the tissue, and in this case, the tissue samples should indicate it was too cold. The solution turned to slush and caused damage to the cellular structure of the organ. The type of fluid used will also tell us where the process went off track."

"Like Euro-Collins solution?" John said.

The doctor's eyes narrowed at the mention of the solution. "Well, yes, but Euro-Collins is very stable at low temps. I can verify once the lab does their analysis."

"The tissue samples are gone."

"No. I sent them to the lab myself."

"A lab technician, Zack Weber, took them from the lab, and he's not talking."

"Why would he do such a thing? Zack's worked in the lab since he left medical school. He's always proved reliable."

"Zack Weber went to medical school?" Paula interjected.

"My partner, Detective Newberry," John said, introducing her.

"Yes, he did. Shame he got caught up in a cheating scandal in his last year. He threw away a potential career as a fine physician."

"What happened?" John asked.

"Zack is a whiz when it comes to computer systems. I understand he hacked into the school's servers, changed a few grades for a couple of colleagues, and posted the answers for an exam online. It was a black mark for the school. Everyone involved in the scandal was kicked out."

"How did he end up here with that kind of background?" Paula asked.

"Good question," John added.

"It was a recommendation from the medical school. In spite of Zack's many failings, the dean said that Zack's superior clinical skills shouldn't go to waste. He said Zack's issues at the school were altruistic and misguided, but the young man had something to offer. The dean added that Zack didn't change his own grades or benefit from the test answers he posted. He'd taken that course a year earlier."

"They make him sound like a medical-school Robin Hood," Paula said.

"It fits with something he said about the conspiracy within the medical establishment and how 'our laws don't apply,'" John observed.

"Like he thinks he's outside the system?" the doctor asked.

"Exactly. Without the tissue sample, we have nothing to tie Weber to whoever is trafficking these organs," John said.

"What kind of tissue do you need?" Dr. Anderson asked.

"The medical examiner wanted the kidney. Now that's gone."

"What if I can give you the next best thing? I trimmed the renal artery to prep the organ for transplant. The cut from the harvest was irregular, kind of rough. I needed a uniform surface to graft the donated organ to . . ."

"My son," John said.

Dr. Anderson bit his lower lip. "Sometimes when the harvest takes place, the tissue on the edge of the incision withdraws and shrinks back. In this case, it looked more torn than it usually does, so I cut a small section off."

"Are you saying that you have that tissue?"

"I didn't send that portion to the lab. I didn't see the need."

"Where is it?"

The doctor stuffed his hands into his lab coat. "It's in a sealed biohazard container along with a vial with the perfusion fluid I drained from the kidney. The ME should be able to get somewhere with that."

"John, you stay with Tommy and Melissa while the doc takes me to get that sample," Paula said. John started to protest, but Paula cut him off. "You can't be in the chain of custody for a piece of a kidney that was supposed to go into your own kid. Besides, I think they need you." She looked toward Tommy and Melissa.

The boy clutched the stuffed animal under a frail arm. The sight made John's chest tighten.

Paula clasped John on his shoulder. "I've got this." She turned to Dr. Anderson. "Doc, take me to the tissue sample," she said before she left with him.

Fifteen minutes later, Dr. Anderson returned. His face was tight, and John couldn't recall the doctor looking as worn and worried as he did now. "I think I got your partner what she needed." The doctor glanced at his tablet. "Tommy's latest test results aren't looking good. We need to get his dialysis started."

John nodded. The test results explained the doctor's worried expression.

The doctor leaned into the hallway and whispered for the nurse. She reappeared in seconds and entered Tommy's room, her ponytail flipping side to side as she walked.

She grabbed a fresh set of latex gloves from a wall-mounted dispenser and approached the bedside.

"Okay now, Tommy, you don't like getting needles stuck in you all the time, do you?"

The boy shook his head but remained silent.

"How about if I gave you a special one that made sure that you didn't need another one while you're here? No more poking you every time we need a blood sample."

"That's good, I guess," Tommy said.

The nurse unwrapped a sterile dialysis shunt and found a vein in the boy's arm. With a gentle motion, she inserted the line. Tommy winced but didn't make a sound when the needle pierced his skin.

"Great job, Tommy. No more needles for you," she said.

"Promise?"

"Anybody tries to stick you, you tell them I said no."

The nurse finished up with Tommy and said to Melissa and John, "Let's give him some time to rest, then we'll take him down to the dialysis unit. That takes about three hours."

"Can we be with him?" Melissa asked.

"Sure, there's a place for family to sit while he gets his dialysis. Make sure you get rest too. This is a race, but it's a marathon, not a sprint."

Dr. Anderson reentered the room, leaned close to John, and said quietly, "Can I speak to you—privately?" The doctor motioned toward the hallway.

John tensed. "What's wrong?"

Dr. Anderson saw the concern etched into the father's face. "Nothing's wrong. We'll get Tommy back on track. What I wanted to talk to you about is this whole situation with the transplant tissue. We have procedures to ensure that can't happen."

"Are you saying the procedures weren't followed?" John asked as he followed the doctor into the hallway.

"On paper, everything checks out. I've pored over every document and computer entry, and everything says that the donated kidney was perfectly viable. We both know that wasn't the case."

"The documents were falsified?" John asked.

"I can't see any other possibility. You mentioned Zack Weber and the lab computers. He could have altered the documents in our system, but he wouldn't have access to the UNOS registry. That system requires a higher level of clearance than Zack had."

"Did Marsha Horn access UNOS?"

"Marsha? No, she didn't have approval for the system. When I handed what was left of the tissue sample to Detective Newberry, she asked for a list of our personnel authorized to enter and change data in the UNOS registry."

"Tricia Woods was already supposed to be gathering that report for us," John said.

"She is, but I told Detective Newberry I could do you both one better. We have a security camera in the area where the UNOS terminals are located. Once we know when our phony entry was made, we will have a record of which terminal was used."

"And the camera will show us who made that entry," John added.

"And it will prove to you that it wasn't me. I gave all the camera footage to Detective Newberry, for what it's worth."

A blue-smocked nurse came from down the hallway and interrupted the conversation. "Dr. Anderson, we have an opening in dialysis, and your orders were to get the Penley boy in as a priority. Has he recovered enough from his surgical anesthesia?"

"He should be fine to go. See if you can get him some water, nothing solid yet," the doctor directed.

She nodded and entered Tommy's room.

"Thanks for making Tommy a priority," John said.

The nurse unplugged monitors from the electric outlets, made sure the IV tubing was up away from the wheels, and rolled Tommy's gurney out the doorway as he clutched on to the stuffed animal. The boy searched over his shoulder to ensure that his mom followed close behind.

"Someone will be up in a moment to take him downstairs to dialysis," the nurse said.

John parked alongside the gurney when Melissa grabbed him gently and tugged him aside.

"I've got this, John. You go stop the son of a bitch who did this to our son."

The sight of his son, strapped down in the hospital gurney, made John's stomach fill with acid. Tommy glanced back. "It's okay, Dad," he said.

"You can't do anything sitting around here," Melissa said. "Besides, all this hovering will make Tommy worry. Go. I'll keep you updated." She stood up on her tiptoes and kissed John on the cheek.

John looked to Dr. Anderson. "If I find someone here has been playing some sick game of Russian roulette with my son . . ."

"I know these people, Detective. I've worked shoulder to shoulder with them and none of them—absolutely none of them—would get involved in something like this."

"If someone's desperate enough, there is nothing they won't do."

TWENTY-THREE

Back at the station, John found his partner tucked behind a cart-mounted video monitor rolled up alongside her desk. An extension cord ran from the back of the monitor, stretched across the aisle to the wall like a mad bomber's trip wire. Paula had her head propped back against the back of her chair; the reflection of the video played off her wire-framed glasses, the pair she was supposed to wear but usually didn't because they made her feel old. She glanced up as John plopped into his chair. She took off the glasses and rubbed her eyes.

The clear plastic evidence bag with its takeout firearm chow fun contents was balanced on a stack of file folders.

"You have a chance to lean on Zack Weber?" John asked.

She nodded. "He's not giving up anything. He's keeping up his social warrior front. He refuses to admit he knew anything about that particular sample from the lab or how it happened to go missing."

"Or how that human tissue got into the transplant pipeline?"

"Nada." Paula pointed at the gun. "But I got a hit on this. The serial number on the gun came up on NCIC as stolen. Not a big surprise there. I'll ask the techies to run a ballistics match on NIBIN to find out if this gun was used in another crime while they try to pull prints." Paula referred to the two national crime data repositories, the National Crime Information Center and the National Integrated Ballistic Information Network.

John sorted through his new phone messages and tossed his notebook on the center of his desk. "No telling how many times the gun changed hands since it was reported stolen. Local?"

Paula tabbed to another window on the computer screen, bringing up the NCIC information on the stolen firearm. "Yep, reported stolen in a residential burglary about two years ago. The reporting party was Donovan Layton, in Wilton."

"What was the address?"

She told him, and John penciled in the location of the rural neighborhood onto a blank notebook page. "I'll pull the original burglary report and look for any connection to our case."

"I already printed it out." She tossed it on his desk. "Probably some tweakers out looking for a quick score," she said. Paula let loose a sigh and pressed her palms to her temples.

"What's got you all twisted up?"

"Something's not right, and I can't figure it out," she said.

"Like?"

She sat forward and hefted a computer printout. "The UNOS access logs for the hospital terminal. We got a hit."

The hairs of the back of John's neck tingled. "Who was it?"

"The access log shows a doctor, Christiaan Barnard, entered the UNOS database the day before Tommy went into the hospital and again three hours before his surgery."

"That's just before the transplant center said they found a kidney for Tommy. That was about ten in the morning, right?"

"Yep." Paula pushed the video monitor toward John so he could see the screen. "The date and time are on the bottom-right corner. See it?"

"Yeah," John said.

The video screen showed a row of hospital office cubicles. John recognized the area from his many trips to the hospital and yesterday's interview with Trisha. The UNOS terminal sat next to her office door.

Paula tapped the rewind button on a remote, and the people who came into view ran in reverse with an awkward, disconnected motion that didn't seem human. She froze the video and pointed at the screen.

"This is the exact time the UNOS data was entered into the system, according to the log," Paula said.

The video screen glared back at them. There was no one using the hospital's UNOS terminal.

"Did you check the access logs again?" John's conversation with the online "doctor" who offered to manipulate the list scratched at the base of his brain. "There has to be an entry."

"I've looked at them upside down and sideways. The UNOS system access logs pinpoint the hospital and terminal used for that transaction. According to these logs, there was an entry made at that terminal, at that time."

"Is the video time stamp wrong?"

Paula shook her head. "No. Look at the next log entry. Trisha Woods accessed the terminal an hour later. If you fast forward to that time . . ."

Paula hit a remote button and queued up the time. Trisha strode into frame and sat at the terminal.

John's brow furrowed at the disconnect between the log entry and the videotape. "What about the second log entry? The one right before we got the call from the transplant center?"

Paula thumbed the remote and buzzed through a blur of action on the screen. People moved like busy, frantic ants in and out of the frame. They stopped when Paula tapped another button. Once more, the UNOS computer terminal sat empty.

John took the paper log and ran a finger down the listing. "How is that possible? It's the same time on both, and nobody is using the terminal. Again, Dr. Barnard supposedly used this terminal to make an entry in the UNOS database. He's not listed on the approved list of UNOS users."

"I can't explain it," Paula said.

"Wouldn't you expect to see an entry from the hospital harvesting the organ, putting the tissue in the registry, and then a second entry matching the patient, perhaps from another hospital? Dr. Anderson said it came from a hospital out of the region," John said.

Paula nodded. "Makes sense, but the logs show both entries at Central Valley Hospital at that specific terminal. Both entries made by Dr. Barnard."

John grabbed the phone from his desk and called the transplant center.

"Trisha Woods," the voice said at the other end of the connection.

"Trisha, it's Detective Penley. Thanks for the UNOS access logs, but we've hit a snag on our end. What can you tell me about a Dr. Christiaan Barnard?"

"What?" she said.

"Dr. Barnard. He accessed the UNOS database."

"There's no one by that name on staff here, Detective. Is this some kind of joke?"

"No joke. Are you certain you don't know any Dr. Barnard?"

"Dr. Christiaan Barnard was the doctor who performed the very first heart transplant in the 1960s. He's famous in medical circles."

"Is there any way for someone at the hospital to use the terminal near your office remotely?" John asked.

"No. The requirements for UNOS data access are that we have a standalone terminal, separated from our hospital network. Direct secured Internet access to the UNOS encrypted server."

John thanked Trisha and hung up the phone.

"Dr. Barnard doesn't exist, at least not here," John said.

"I figured as much, but someone made these," Paula added.

"Whoever it is knows their way around computer systems." John leaned back in his creaky wooden desk chair.

Paula shrugged. "Trisha knows how to access the system. Maybe we should take a look at her."

"First, I think we need to go spend some quality time with Zack Weber."

"The kid from the lab?" Paula asked. Her face brightened, and then she said, "Dr. Anderson said Zack was a whiz with computers."

"The Outcast Killer needed access to the system, and Zack has the skills to pull that off. You have him in holding?"

"Yep. I thought you'd want to have a shot at him before we got him booked at the jail. And I wanted to get started on reviewing these tapes," she said.

The detectives pushed back from their desks and made the short walk to the interrogation holding rooms. John opened the holding-room door and found Zack Weber slumped over the table. He could have been sleeping, except the pool of blood that collected on the floor beneath him said otherwise.

John reached for a pulse on Zack's neck and knew he wouldn't find one. The color had drained from the dead man's face.

"Son of a bitch," Paula said.

"It hasn't been long. He's still warm. Dammit, who got to him?"

Zack Weber's hands had fallen to his lap when he died, still handcuffed while awaiting interrogation. His left wrist bore a wide, jagged gash inches above the steel of the handcuff. Blood seeped from the wound, soaked the fabric of his pants, and trailed down his leg to a pool on the floor. Glistening and spreading, it had yet to congeal.

"Who even knew he was in custody?" Paula asked.

"What the hell is this?" John said as he stepped back from the table.

In front of the dead man's head, words were scrawled in blood. Zack Weber's fingers bore the red stain; his last moments in this life were spent scrawling a bloody message.

You can't stop him.

John noticed a sliver of plastic on the table near Zack's head. He didn't need to pick it up to figure out it was half of Zack Weber's hospital identification badge. "Slashing your wrist with a piece of plastic is a desperate move," John said.

"I had him cuffed behind his back. How did he get them around front?" Paula asked.

"He could have slipped his legs through. He's not a very big guy."

"I cuffed him in front," a uniformed officer said at the doorway. Ashen, the young cop looked away from Zack Weber's body. "For—for his attorney."

"What attorney?" Paula asked.

"His attorney needed him to sign some documents and asked me to cuff him in the front," the officer said. "That's the procedure for an attorney visit. That and shutting off the video feed to the room," the officer said, pointing at the camera mounted high on the wall. "Turned it back on when the attorney checked out. The prisoner was fine when he left, a little quiet and sullen maybe, but he was still alive. I swear."

"Did you have the attorney sign in?" John asked.

"That's the procedure," the officer said, holding out a clipboard with a completed form for the visit from the attorney.

John took the clipboard and found the attorney's name.

"You check his ID?"

"Yes, sir, I did."

John handed the clipboard to Paula.

She glanced at the paperwork. "Winnow? Brice Winnow, the councilwoman's chief of staff was here?" she said.

"What business did he have with Weber?" John wondered.

"The guy gave me the creeps when he met us at the warehouse. The flashy car, the clothes. Like he was trying too hard," said Paula.

"He's a politician. They're all slimy,"

"I wasn't looking for a connection between Weber and Winnow. I couldn't find much on Winnow at all," she said.

John recognized that Paula was holding something back. "And?"

"The guy is too clean. No parking tickets—nothing. It doesn't seem natural."

"He got a job with the city. They had to do a background, at the least. Let's go pick him up," John said.

"You think he went back to work after his visit with Weber?"

"City hall is a great place for a rat like Winnow to hide," John said.

Paula tossed the clipboard on the desk next to Weber. "Winnow probably won't cop to anything. Besides, we have it on video that he wasn't even here when Weber died."

"Zack Weber here is gonna tell us what Winnow had to say," John said.

"The newly dead Zack Weber?"

"The one and only."

TWENTY-FOUR

The Golden State's capital ended up in Sacramento due to the availability of hotel rooms in the 1850s. In the intervening century and a half, the city continued to be considered by many as more convenience than capital. Sacramento City Hall was a brick-and-mortar representation of local politics. The old building faced I Street and was elegant, open, and welcoming. The new addition loomed over the original building. The glass faces and cold surfaces smothered the old public hall's era of civility and birthed a time of power mongering, lobbyists, and self-promotion.

John and Paula asked for Brice Winnow's office, and a harried young woman told them he was in the city council chamber. She rushed away after jabbing a finger in the general direction. Winnow stood on the elevated dais where the city council members would reside when the council went into session later in the evening. Winnow's sleeves were rolled up, revealing muscled forearms and the hint of a tattoo that bled from beneath the starched shirt.

Winnow gave no sign of surprise at the detectives' arrival. "Here to try to condemn city hall?" he said.

"Wouldn't do any good," John said.

"Make sure the council members have copies of the district maps," Winnow directed a staffer.

"We need a couple of minutes of your time," John said.

Winnow put his hands on his hips. "I'm in the middle of something here. Can't this wait?"

Paula stepped forward to the dais where Winnow stood. "Are you an attorney?"

Winnow arranged papers at Councilwoman Margolis's seat, glanced at Paula, and said, "Do you need one, Detective?"

"Where'd you go to law school?" she asked.

"You want to be an attorney?"

"Too much deception and too many half-truths in that profession, for my taste. So where'd you say you went?"

Winnow cracked a slight grin. "I didn't say. Tell me, why the sudden interest in my educational accomplishments?"

John picked up one of the white binders, noted that the title was for a redevelopment project in the North Sacramento corridor, and tossed the thick volume back on the desk. "You came to see Zack Weber in lockup. Signed in as his attorney. I didn't know the city provided lawyers to lowlife computer hackers like him."

"I didn't hear a question there," Winnow said.

"Why'd you come see him?"

"It wasn't a city matter. A private one. I've helped Zack on legal matters from time to time."

"Like what?" John said. The detective poked around at documents on the desk, rearranging them with a fingertip.

Winnow's jaw muscles pulsed. "That's attorney-client privilege. And could you stop messing with the proposal materials?"

"That privilege only applies if you're an attorney," Paula said.

"Check with the State Bar Association," Winnow said.

"Why don't you come with us while we check?" she responded.

"I don't think that's gonna happen," Winnow said. The cords of his muscles tensed as he crossed his forearms. Defiant, untouchable.

"I think I can make it happen," Paula said.

"You do and you'll find yourself unemployed. My staff has better things to do," a voice called out from behind Winnow.

Councilwoman Susan Margolis approached. Her sharp features looked more hawkish in the harsh chamber lighting.

Paula craned her neck up at the politician. "Did you do a background check on Brice here before you took him on?"

"Excuse me?" Margolis leaned over the dais. "Who do you think you are? Does Chief Patterson know you're here, harassing my staff?"

"We're here investigating a homicide. We have a few questions for Mr. Winnow," John said.

Margolis straightened and kept her eyes on Paula. "Then ask them and get out of my chambers."

"I thought this was the public's chamber," Paula said.

"I'll be having a talk with the chief about your poor representation of the police department."

"That's Officer Newberry," Winnow said.

"Detective," Paula corrected.

"Whatever," Margolis said.

"What did you and Zack Weber talk about?" Paula pressed.

"I told you, that is privileged," Winnow said.

"Why'd he kill himself after you left?"

"Huh, sorry to hear that," Winnow said. His face remained locked in a dispassionate veneer.

"I can tell you're all broken up about it," Paula said.

"Enough!" Margolis pounded on the surface of the wooden dais. "Out."

John and Paula walked up the center aisle of the council chamber and made for the exit.

"Shame about Zack. He was always a bit too altruistic for his own good."

John turned to see Winnow grinning.

"Zack left us a message before he died," John said.

Winnow's face changed. Something darker appeared.

"Didn't know that, did you?" John added.

"I'm sure it was little more than the rantings of a haunted man."

"Maybe. Why do you think he mentioned you?" John asked.

Winnow's complexion went ashen for a heartbeat, then recovered to its usual pallor.

That was the tell John waited for. "Like I said, we'll be in touch."

TWENTY-FIVE

"Winnow's reaction, when you mentioned a message from Zack . . . you hit gold there," Paula said.

The pair dodged pedestrian traffic near Cesar Chavez Park, where they'd parked their city sedan. A crowd of a hundred gathered for an evening concert in the park, and the beer bellies masked with muscle shirts foretold the harder edge of tonight's lineup.

"It was important enough for Winnow to get to Zack before we had a chance to book him. Zack hadn't made a phone call to an attorney. Winnow magically showed up," John said.

Paula sidestepped a beer can on the sidewalk and said, "How did he know we'd picked Zack Weber up in the first place?"

"I dunno."

"Had to come from the hospital, or from the department."

"I don't like where either of those options lead," John said.

They reached the sedan, and the police radio crackled with static, followed by a call for John to meet with the lieutenant.

"Margolis already made good on her threat to call the chief," John said.

"Such a bitch."

"Such an elected bitch with control over the department's budget."

"Still, where does she get off acting like that?" she said.

John pulled out his cell phone and called Lieutenant Barnes. While he waited for a connection, he said, "You didn't have to poke her like that either. You practically begged her to call the boss."

Paula clamped her arms across her chest and stared out the window at the concert crowd.

"Lieutenant, Penley here," John said into the phone. After listening for a moment, he closed his eyes and rested his head on the seat back.

"Yes. I understand. Won't be a problem. Yes, I will pass that on to my partner."

John disconnected the call and pocketed his phone. He fished in his pocket for a piece of nicotine gum, but all he had was an empty foil pack. He balled it up and tossed it on the floor. "Dammit."

"All right, let me have it," said Paula.

"Margolis must have had the chief on speed dial. She already called him; he called the A chief, who chewed out Lieutenant Barnes . . ."

"Yeah, I know how shit flows downhill."

"Anyway, the lieutenant says we are to stay away from city hall, Margolis, and Winnow."

Paula pounded the dash with a tight fist. "They always do this! They circle up and protect the old boys' club. They can't make us stay away from Winnow. He had a hand in Zack Weber's death, and he's up to his ass in all this organ business."

"You done throwing your little tantrum?"

"It's not right."

"Is this why you got the boot from internal affairs? Your shitty attitude?"

Paula's complexion reddened. "So it's my shitty attitude when the brass turns the other way and ignores what's going on in their own evidence room?"

"Carson."

"Yeah, Carson. You were probably buddies with him too. I get it. It's my fault . . ."

"I never said—"

"I had all the logs, I turned three junkies who bought the shit. That wasn't enough for them. They just wanted to make it go away."

"Who's 'they'?"

"All you—his buddies. I had all the documentation, and the brass wouldn't approve the video surveillance. They said they didn't want to open a can of worms involving the handling of evidence."

"Yeah, it kind of hit the fan when that broke. The DA had to drop a half dozen cases because the evidence weight didn't match or the dope came up missing."

"It was a small price to pay for what Carson was doing," she said.

"Wait. Are you saying you pulled off the video surveillance without authorization?"

She turned in the seat and faced John. "What was I supposed to do, let him keep selling drugs from our evidence room? No one would listen. I had to show them proof, hard proof."

John started the engine and pulled into a gap in the traffic. "Damn, Paula, that was pretty stupid. What were you thinking?"

"We have rules—a standard of conduct, and nobody cared what Carson was doing—nobody."

"Don't we have rules about warrantless surveillance of other cops?" John said.

Paula slumped in her seat. "You sound just like them. The rules don't apply equally to everyone. You can bet your ass they can't wait until I make a mistake."

"That's what all your by-the-book rules and procedure are about? You're simply covering your ass?"

"It's called survival," Paula said.

"You can't work like that."

"Where we going?" she said. They headed south on Franklin, well past the office.

"I'm waiting until the chief cools off before I hit the bureau," he said. John handed Paula his notebook. "What was the address for the burglary? The one your gun came from?"

"Donovan Layton, off Grant Line in Wilton. You think we can get anything from him on a two-year-old burglary?"

"That pistol is the only thing we have right now, since we can't go near Winnow."

The Layton residence was hard to find. At first, John drove past the driveway because there was no address marker and the narrow drive was overgrown with vines and tree branches. The gnarled plants gave the appearance of a once-exclusive, lush enclave, now brown, entangled, and abandoned. Two jagged ruts in a broken, paved road marked the entrance to the property.

A main house sat a few hundred yards back from the access road. Tree limbs and debris littered the grounds, and deep mounds of rotting leaves hadn't been attended to in years. The rusted hulk of a farm truck deteriorated in its last resting place next to a barn. The truck bed held amorphous, moldy lumps, hay bales in a previous life.

"Big place," John said.

"Is anybody living here? The place looks abandoned," Paula responded.

"It ain't on the home-tour list." John pulled the sedan to a stop in front of the two-story ranch house. A thick film of dust clung to the windowpanes in the places where the glass remained unbroken. "Let's go see if Mr. Layton's home."

John opened his car door, and a sour smell assaulted them, a rancid mix of wet grain, manure, and uncooked meat.

"Oh man, that's awful," John said.

"City boy," she said. Paula pointed at the barn and several large pigs in a twenty-foot square pen. The pen allowed the animals to go in and out of a side barn door on their own.

"If this is country living at its best, you can have it." John went to the front door and found it ajar, open nearly six inches on a sagging frame.

"Mr. Layton? Police department," John called through the crack in the door.

Paula wiped a swath of dust off a window and pressed her face close.

"Doesn't look like anybody lives here," she said.

John needed to use his shoulder on the warped door, opening it a foot wide. "Mr. Layton? Are you in here?" He bumped the door farther open with his hip, and the dust swept back like a snowdrift against the rotting wood. "I think you're right. I don't think anybody's been in the place for a while."

A white pickup truck turned onto the driveway and carved a course down the path, missing every large pothole. The truck was at least two decades old and looked like it hadn't been scrubbed since it left the dealer's lot. A wiry, balding man with a gray complexion, sunken hollows in his cheeks, and a permanent sneer formed by sagging facial muscles stepped from the cab of the truck. The gun rack in the rear window held a cattle prod and a walking cane. The man grabbed the latter and shuffled his left leg toward the truck's front bumper.

"Who the hell are you?" the man asked. He spit a brown wad of chewing tobacco and saliva on the ground; some of the discharge dribbled down the paralyzed left side of his mouth.

John fished out his badge. "Police. You Donovan Layton?"

"What if I am? What business do you have busting inta my place?"

"We need to talk to you about a burglary a couple years back."

"Shut that door. You got no call to go in there," Layton said.

John pulled the handle, and the door rubbed against the wooden floorboards until the bottom of the door hit the frame. The warp in the old door wouldn't let it close all the way. "Sorry, sir. We were looking for you."

"Well, now you found me. Say what ya gotta say an' let me be."

Paula left the porch and stood across from Layton. "Do you live here, Mr. Layton?"

He shifted his eyes, one milky with cataracts, toward the house, then back to Paula.

"No. Not no more."

From behind the old man, one of the hogs squealed. The sound jarred Layton back to the present. "I come out here and tend to my hogs, is all."

"When did you move away from here?" Paula asked.

"A bit over two years ago, after my wife died."

"I'm sorry to hear that."

"She was always better than me. This here was her place. Too many memories here for me," Layton said.

"How long did you two live out here?"

"We married about twenty years ago. She had a kid from another marriage, and we lived here till she . . ."

"So it was just the three of you?"

"Just her and me, really. Her boy went away to school years ago. He and I didn't really see eye to eye on much. Me and her were gonna retire out here."

"You remember filing a report about a burglary and a stolen gun?"

"I may be old, but I ain't stupid. Yeah, I remember."

John came down from the front door and joined his partner.

Layton pointed the tip of his cane at John. "Someone pushed the front door in, like sonny-boy here, and walked away with my pistol."

"Any idea who would have done it?" John said.

"If I had, I'd've taken care of it."

"You don't remember seeing anybody hanging around your place?"

"It happened a few days after my wife passed. I wasn't here when it was stolen," Layton said.

The hogs grunted and squealed in the pen near the barn.

"They sound hungry," Paula said.

"Damn things are always hungry."

"How many do you have?" she asked.

Layton turned to his truck and steadied his gait with the side of the vehicle. "I got fifteen left. I don't have my stepson for help, and I can't butcher them as quickly no more." He gestured to his limp left side.

The old man reached into the back of the pickup and grabbed a grain bucket. He glanced at John. "You mind grabbing that sack of feed? I'd 'preciate it."

John hefted the fifty-pound sack out of the truck and followed Layton to the barn door. For an old, half-lame man, he cut a quick path to the barn. The smell was stronger and made the bile bubble in John's stomach.

"They always smell this bad?" John asked.

"They're a bit ripe today. You get used to it. Probably need to slop out the pens."

Layton unlocked the barn door and shoved it aside with his good arm. He shuffled into the murky barn. John followed with his grain bag while Paula held the door open.

The interior of the dark barn was difficult for John to negotiate, so he followed Layton's path. He banged into a line of chains that hung from the rafters. The links rattled and clacked together as they swayed.

"Watch out for them hooks," Layton said.

His eyes adjusting to the dim light, John saw the outline of iron meat hooks hanging from the chains at chin level. Dark spots on the wooden planks marked where an untold number of pigs had bled out. Rough-hewn fencing, constructed from wood scraps, held the hogs to half of the barn space. Their hooves trod deep ruts and tracks in the soil, where the big hogs pushed their weight around for the first feeding. They paced while Layton set up his grain bucket.

"You can drop that grain here," he said to John.

The pigs shrieked and squealed. Two of the larger hogs pushed at one another in the back of the barn. The struggle turned serious, and the larger of the two shoved his rival into the wood siding.

"What the hell got into you two?" Layton said.

"They always act like that?" John asked.

"They're usually pissy, but not this bad." Layton emptied some of the grain into his bucket and shook it, getting all of the hogs' attention. "Come on, boys."

The two distracted hogs dropped their interest in whatever kept them from the grain and trotted toward the fence in a pair of three-hundred-pound struts. The largest sniffed the grain, rejected it, and returned to rooting around in the back area of the pen.

The more the hogs moved, the stronger the rancid smell grew. It thickened within the stale barn air. A pang of recognition hit John seconds before he saw the source. The thing that preoccupied the large hog was a long, whitish bone and a mottled, yellow hunk of flesh—human flesh.

Layton dropped the grain bucket and staggered to the fence. The old man blinked, trying to register the gruesome vision.

"Oh my God!" Paula said, pointing at the exposed flesh.

"Mr. Layton," John called out.

The old man braced himself with the fence and stared at a tattoo on the exposed flesh. It writhed with each clamp of the hog's powerful jaw.

"Mr. Layton, can we get these animals out of here?" John said.

Layton nodded while the bone snapped and small shards fell from the hog's mouth. The old man moved in measured steps to the edge of the pen and whacked the flank of one of the hogs with his cane. The beast barely recognized the tap through its huge rib cage.

"Missy, could you get me the cattle prod from my truck?" Layton asked.

Paula trotted out to the vehicle and pulled the electric cattle prod from the gun rack. It had electrodes attached to a red plastic paddle and sounded like a stun gun when she fingered the trigger.

"When's the last time you came out here, Mr. Layton?" John said.

"Yesterday morning. I feed 'em every morning."

Paula returned with the prod, and Layton said, "Hit that one in the ass with it."

She laid the paddle on the designated pork rump. High-pitched squeals burst from the beast the moment she flicked the trigger.

"I didn't mean to hurt it," she said.

"They'll get over it," Layton said.

The hogs followed the shocked pig out of the side door to the pen, leaving the exposed chunk of leg behind in the sloppy barn mud.

John hopped over the fence and regretted his decision the moment his foot touched down in a pile of warm, loose pig crap. Working his way through the organic minefield, John got a closer look.

"Looks like a West Block Norteños tattoo."

"Want me to go get an evidence bag?" Paula said.

John paused, squinted in the dim light, and bent to get a better view. "Forget it. We gotta call this one in. I see a couple more bones over here."

Paula followed his gaze and noticed a gnarled hunk of bone embedded in the muck.

"Mr. Layton, why don't you come outside with me," she said.

The pig farmer was breathing hard and leaning over his cane.

John dropped a plywood barrier to keep the hogs outside, backed out of the pigsty, and shook the muck off his shoe; clumps of manure and mud clung to the soles.

"Ya just gotta let it dry," Layton said.

Paula led the old man to the front seat of his truck and got him a bottle of water from their sedan. Layton started to settle but kept shaking his head and mouthing a low moan with each breath.

John called in for a crime-scene tech unit and an ambulance to check out Layton.

"The EMTs will be here in a couple of minutes," John said.

"I don't need no EMT. I'm fine."

"Anyone else have access to your place?"

"I don't know. It ain't exactly Fort Knox."

"The name Cardozo mean anything to you? Daniel Cardozo?" John asked.

The farmer shook his head.

"Why would someone dump a body all the way out here?" Paula said.

"Them hogs would eat 'em all up, that's why," Layton said.

While they waited for the ambulance, John used the pause to call Melissa for an update on Tommy. She was tight with the response, still feeling the aftermath of the blowout in the hospital waiting room. Tommy was still getting his dialysis. When John hung up, an ambulance rolled up the drive, red lights flashing. A minute later, Layton was propped up on a gurney, an oxygen tube in his nostrils, and an EMT took his blood pressure.

John motioned Paula away from the ambulance. "That answers our question about what the Outcast Killer does with the leftover body parts."

Paula kicked a pebble and looked at the dilapidated farmhouse. "Why here? There's a hundred places more convenient to dump his extras."

"The barn was locked, so whoever accessed it had the keys."

A white panel van with the crime-scene techs pulled up the drive, and Paula waved them toward the barn. "I'll go get them started."

John walked back to the ambulance. Layton's face was a healthier shade of gray.

"Mr. Layton? Anybody have a key to the barn?"

"I don't think so. I've had that lock on there for five-plus years."

"Have a spare key?"

He thought for a moment and then bobbed his head. "Yeah, in the house."

An old Cadillac sped up the drive and skidded to a stop near the ambulance. A spry old woman in a housecoat unfolded from the front seat and propped her rail-thin torso on the driver's door. "Donovan? Is he okay?"

"Oh, crap, it's Ilene Watkins. Nosy old cow," Layton grumbled.

"He's doing just fine," John answered.

"He's getting too old to be handing those animals. Especially after his stroke last year," she scolded.

"You live nearby, ma'am?"

"Over there." She jutted a bony finger across the main road.

"You seen anything unusual going on out here? Someone who doesn't belong maybe?"

"Only Donovan and his boy," she said.

"Boy?"

"Yeah, his boy—well, stepson, truth be told."

"You sure about that?" John asked.

Layton tried to sit up, and the EMT held him back down. "Patrick ain't been around here since that drunk bastard killed Marsha."

An electric charge pricked the back of John's neck as the name fell into place. "Who?"

"My wife, Marsha."

"Marsha Layton?"

"She kept her old name, Horn. Marsha Horn."

TWENTY-SIX

After the EMTs checked Layton over, he refused any further medical treatment, and Ilene was more than willing to fawn over the old man. He blustered about her hovering but let her drive him home.

The crime-scene techs were going to take hours to sort out the human bits from the collection of waste in the barn muck. After the hogs were moved to an outside pen, little yellow flags dotted the slop where the hogs had trampled on seven pieces of human remains.

"Layton claims he doesn't know where Patrick Horn is or where he lives. I'm not buyin' it. He's not telling us everything," John said to his partner as they headed back to their sedan.

"No kidding? Like how a lab supervisor like Marsha Horn marries a hog farmer?"

"The old man has a better online dating service than you."

"He's protecting the boy."

John reached the driver's door, pulled it open as a thought crystalized. "Zack Weber was trying to protect someone too."

"Think it was Horn?"

John shrugged and climbed into the car. His shoes flaked pig waste on the floorboard. "Oh man." He swiveled in the seat and banged his heels on the doorframe. Layton was right—the dried crap-plaster cracked right off.

John closed his door, started the car, and glanced at the crop of yellow markers inside the barn door that kept sprouting. "How would someone ever think of dropping body parts in there?"

"I didn't know pigs did that—I mean, eat everything. My bacon obsession just took an ugly turn." She turned in her seat. "What Layton said, about his kid helping butcher the pigs—you'd have to know what you're doing with a knife, right?"

John pulled out onto the main road and headed back toward the city. "Weber was afraid of someone. I thought it was Winnow, but it could be this Horn kid."

"Winnow's a bureaucratic ass. Could you see him getting his manicured hands messy with pig slop?"

John chuckled at the thought. "Still, I don't know why Winnow took such an interest in Zack Weber's legal problems."

"True."

John shot a glance at his watch. "We have enough time to swing by Zack Weber's place before I need to get back to the hospital."

She nodded.

Twenty minutes later, John and Paula pulled up to the curb in front of a midtown Victorian-era home, repurposed into four small apartments. Zack Weber had left his basement apartment for the last time that morning. Using the key taken from the dead man's personal property, John unlocked the single dead bolt and pushed the heavy basement door open against its hinges.

The recently deceased Zack Weber kept a clean, orderly apartment. The morning's breakfast dishes sat in a drying rack next to the sink; laundry in a cheap, blue plastic basket awaited the trip to the Laundromat; and unread mail sat in a neat stack on the small kitchen table. Zack had left a grocery list on the refrigerator door, listing tortillas, tomatillos, and chili peppers for a Mexican dinner that would never happen.

John was not one who believed in the paranormal. He didn't have spirit guides lead him through his cases, yet the places where the dead once called home communicated. A home too tidy, all loose ends taken care of, sometimes meant the dead knew their end was approaching, or perhaps a well-planned suicide. Zack Weber's apartment gave John the vibe that Zack had intended to return. He had left his apartment without intending to take his own life today.

Both of the detectives donned latex gloves and moved deeper into the dead man's home.

"John, take a look in here," Paula called out from the narrow hallway that led to the rear of the apartment.

John passed a bathroom on the right and found Paula in a single bedroom at the end of the hall. A mattress sat on the floor, with sweat-stained bedsheets collected in a wad at the foot. Paula stood at the opposite wall where four flat-panel computer monitors were arranged in a two-by-two cluster over a cheap put-it-together-yourself desk.

"Check this out," Paula said, then wiggled a computer mouse.

All four monitors came to life. The top two scrolled line upon line of indecipherable computer code while the bottom-right monitor displayed a video feed from a hospital security camera. The bottom-left monitor held a list of names, medical data, blood types, and contact information. The header at the top of the last screen bore the logo and label of the United Network for Organ Sharing, UNOS.

"So much for their secured system. He hacked their server," John said.

"Look at the patient record," Paula said.

John stepped forward, hunched down, and stared at the monitor. He touched a gloved fingertip on the place where his son's name was displayed among matching patients.

"Zack Weber accessed the transplant list. He was the one on the inside."

Paula moved toward the desk, stood next to John, and looked at the details on the monitors. She cocked her head to one side and said, "He made the changes to the organ-donor data to make certain that Tommy got that kidney."

"He bumped two others to put Tommy on the top of the list," John said, studying the list of names.

"Weber did all this?"

"Changing the waiting list is only half of the work. This doesn't tell how the kidney got into the system in the first place. Weber was the technical mind in the deal . . ."

"And Daniel Cardozo was the muscle," she added.

"Links to the network, disappearing one by one."

John stepped back from the bank of computer monitors and pinched the bridge of his nose. He turned to a bookcase lined with medical textbooks, some of which bore a University of California–Davis medical school bookstore stamp along their spines. A dozen volumes on human anatomy, autopsy procedure, and organ transplant took up an entire shelf. A well-worn text on bioethics lay on its side, lacking the sheen of dust found on the rest of the collection. Next to it, a small photograph in a hammered copper frame occupied a central place.

John picked up the photo from the shelf, eyes drawn to two young men: Zack Weber and Brice Winnow, dressed in white smocks with the UC Davis logo emblazoned over the breast pocket.

"Dr. Anderson said Zack was booted from medical school for changing grades for his friends. I think we just found one of them." John held the photo out for Paula.

"Brice Winnow went to medical school?"

"He must have gone to law school after he got the boot from medical school."

She looked around the room and said, "That is the only photograph in the place."

"It kinda explains the attachment Winnow had with our boy Zack," John said.

John weighed the frame in his hands. It was cheap, but the placement of the photo on the shelf was special. He put the photo aside and grabbed the bioethics text, its cover worn thin from heavy use. He thumbed through the volume, and halfway through, a small, rectangular object fell out of a hole cut into the pages. The black thing rattled onto the wooden floor.

John stooped over and picked it up, holding it between his thumb and forefinger. "It's a wireless camera."

John placed the camera on the bookshelf and examined the spine of the book. A small, circular hole provided a concealed hiding place for the lens. "Why would Weber install a camera to watch what he was doing? He was too smart to do anything that would incriminate himself like that."

"Why does anyone get a nanny-cam? They want to see what others are doing when they're not home," Paula said.

Paula sat at the desk and pulled the computer keyboard toward her.

"What are you doing?" John asked.

"That kind of camera doesn't have much of a range. I'll bet he accessed the feed from here," she said while tapping the keyboard.

"Shouldn't we wait for the techies to do that?"

"Just because you don't know what side of the keyboard to use doesn't mean I don't."

The camera feed of the hospital flickered and disappeared, leaving a blank screen for a moment. Another keystroke and a menu popped up on the monitor. An obscure list of words filled the menu box on the screen.

"Riverside, Ice Man, Book, Terminal View, Farm, Wine Cave." Paula recited some of the items from the screen.

"He has an entire network of camera feeds?" John asked.

"I'm not sure." Paula scanned down the list of random words and phrases. She took the mouse and moved her right hand, causing the pointer to hover over one of the items—Terminal View. She clicked it.

The monitor snapped back to the view of the hospital above the UNOS computer.

"The computer terminal," she said.

She moved the mouse to the menu item labeled "Book" and clicked on that one. The screen flickered, and a new scene appeared.

Paula saw her face in the monitor and realized it came from the small camera John had plucked from the spine of the book. She picked up the small wireless camera from the bookshelf and rotated it, changing the view on the computer monitor as it moved.

"Who did Weber think would use his computer?" John said.

"He had to have a reason. I bet he set this up to record to a hard drive."

John edged closer to the screen. "Click on Ice Man."

She did, and the screen showed the abandoned ice plant where the refrigerators and the gift-wrapped kidney were found.

"Go to Farm." John pointed.

She clicked on the Farm menu item, and an image of the interior of the pig barn blossomed on the screen. Crime-scene technicians rolled a ground-penetrating radar unit, one that looked like a large lawn-fertilizer cart, over the barn floor.

"I'll be damned," Paula said.

"Try Riverside," John said.

Paula clicked, and the barn disappeared, replaced by a darker vision—a smaller, murky space with a stainless-steel table reflecting the light from a single fixture that hung from a wooden ceiling beam.

Paula moved the mouse and clicked on the Wine Cave menu item. The monitor displayed racks of old, cobwebbed wine bottles from floor to ceiling. In the very center, a large piece of paper was attached to the rack. It held a message.

Paula enlarged the message.

Detective Penley,
We should talk. Nine tonight, online. You know where to find me.

"You know where to find him?" Paula asked.

John steadied himself on the edge of the desk. A wave of nausea swept through him and threatened to buckle his knees. "Oh my God, what have I done?"

"What is it, John?"

John pointed at the message on the screen. "I've talked to him."

"Who? Who is he?"

"Online, I was online. I started poking around for our investigation. Then I found this website. It needed a password to get in."

"Yeah, so?"

"I had the password."

Paula squinted at him, clearly not following.

"The kidney at the ice plant, the tag had that series of numbers and letters at the bottom, remember?"

She nodded.

"That was the password. He gave it to me."

"What happened, John?"

"I tried to make contact and lure him out. I logged in and told him what I wanted. Then he demanded payment to move Tommy up the list. I stopped at that point."

"Then how come Tommy got moved up?"

"He did it so he could give Tommy a freezer-burnt piece of crap, because I didn't play along."

"There has to be more to it. Why Tommy? Why you?"

"Like I said, I didn't follow through."

"Of all the families on the transplant list, how many of them were cops investigating his kills? He knows you," she said.

"I told you, I fucked up and connected with him on the dark web."

"It's more personal than an Internet hookup. You think you've ever run across this guy before?"

"I'd remember someone targeting gang members and parting them out. If he did it to get to me, it worked."

"Since he led us to the ice plant, he's cut off anything that ties back to him. He distracted us while he reorganized his business."

"He watched us from the beginning. He wanted us at the ice plant. He left some remains there so Jimmy Franck would call it in, then got rid of them before Stark and his partner showed up. It was all designed to get me there at the ice plant to get a gift-wrapped present. He's led me on, daring me to buy a transplant for Tommy, and who knows, he may have manipulated the delays, getting the other surgeries postponed."

"Manipulated." Paula stepped back to the bookshelf and took stock of the various medical texts arranged on the shelf. "How would he get the information on where we were with the investigation?"

"Inside source. Who knew about the case, and who wanted regular updates about the status?"

"The lieutenant's handled all of that, kept us out of the line of fire. He's been briefing the media, the city council, and the mayor's office. You don't think it's the lieutenant?"

"No. Not Tim. But that briefing information had to be the way the killer knew what we were doing."

Paula paced and turned back to her partner. "Councilwoman Margolis was his pipeline, and you saw how quick she was to get us banned from city hall and her pet, Winnow."

Paula moved back to the computer and used the mouse to click on the Riverside menu item. The strangely lit room returned to the screen, but the table now held a small object, illuminated by the eerie glow. It was a small stuffed animal dressed like a soccer player.

"What?" Paula said.

"Oh God, no." John reached for his cell phone. He stabbed out Melissa's cell number. "That's Tommy's. That's the stuffed animal, the one you brought for him."

Melissa answered after the second ring. "Hi, John. Everything okay?"

"Where's Tommy?" The urgency crept into his voice.

"He's still in dialysis," she said.

"You aren't with him?"

"No, they said I should go get a cup of coffee."

"Melissa, go. Go now and find Tommy."

"What are you talking about? I'm out in the lobby near the dialysis unit. If there was a problem, they—"

"Melissa! Stop! Go get Tommy now."

"You're scaring me, John."

"You need to go find Tommy."

"All right, I'm going."

John heard background noise as Melissa entered the unit. She spoke to someone there, but John couldn't hear the conversation. The tone and volume of the speech quickly changed into a rapid, urgent chatter.

"Melissa, what's happening?"

There was no direct response from the other end, but the background noise grew in intensity.

"Melissa?"

"John, John, something's happened. They can't find Tommy," she said, nearly breathless.

"What do they mean, they can't find him?"

"He's not where he's supposed to be. The dialysis station is empty. Tommy's not there. They said he must be out for a test or something. I don't know, John, this isn't right. Something's happened."

"I'll be right there," John said, then hung up. He turned to Paula, his face ashen. "He has Tommy."

TWENTY-SEVEN

Paula guided the police cruiser back to the hospital from Weber's midtown apartment. She wasted no time with traffic lights or stop signs that blurred in the crosstown race.

John called the hospital and managed to convince a low-level security manager to lock down the hospital with the report of a missing child.

Paula fishtailed to a stop at the hospital entrance, where three Sacramento Police units blocked the access points to the hospital lobby, another blocked the parking lot exit, and a California Highway Patrol motorcycle officer roamed through the parking structure.

Frustration showed in the faces of patients who were kept from appointments inside. Nurses from the emergency room performed a triage of sorts at the entrance door, advising those who sought care to wait or directing them to another hospital emergency room.

Paula and John left the sedan in the drive and made for the entrance. A young uniformed officer was about to block their advance when Lieutenant Barnes stepped into view.

"John, Paula, this way," the lieutenant called out.

"Where's Melissa?" John said.

"I have her in the security office looking at video. I've asked for a BOLO with Tommy's description, we have the entire hospital locked down tight, and we have a five-block perimeter in place."

Lieutenant Barnes led John and Paula through a set of doors and set off down a hallway.

"What do we know?" John said.

"Tommy went into the dialysis unit and didn't come out. There are three exits out of the unit that don't dump into the lobby. The nurse with him was not a regular employee. He was a registry nurse, someone they call in when they need to cover a shift."

"Did they get an ID on the nurse?" Paula asked.

"Not yet. They only said he came from the registry. No one remembers working with him before."

"Did we get a view of him on any of the security cameras?" John said.

"Working on it," Barnes said as they reached the security offices.

A uniformed officer nodded at the lieutenant but avoided eye contact with John. John knew a missing child was painful, the kind of searing ache you want to keep from creeping into your life at any cost. Don't look directly at it and it won't burn you.

The lieutenant held the door for John and Paula. They entered a room teeming with frantic people, a stark contrast to the Zen fixtures and life-affirming artwork on the walls. The serene, calm space had transformed into a madhouse of loud-talking cops and blame-shifting hospital employees. John located Melissa in the center of the storm, hovering over a man who flicked switches at a bank of security monitors.

She leaned in and watched the screens replay security footage of the moments before Tommy disappeared. There was no glimpse of Tommy or the nurse who had wheeled him into the dialysis unit, just like the nine times she had scoured the video before this one.

Melissa sensed John before he said anything and slipped an arm around his waist. She leaned into him. John felt the quiver of her body against his. "There's no view that shows Tommy leaving the unit or who took him." She turned into her husband, buried her face in his chest, and sobbed.

Paula stopped and spoke with a cluster of hospital workers wearing light-blue scrubs. After a short conversation with the group, she broke away and came to John.

"John, check this out," Paula said.

Melissa looked up. "Did you find him?"

"Do these men look familiar?" Paula said as she passed the photo she'd taken from Weber's apartment.

Melissa took the photo in both hands and scanned the faces of the two men. She touched the image of Brice Winnow. "This is the nurse who wheeled Tommy into the dialysis unit."

"Did you get a good look at him? You're sure?" John said.

"It's him?" Paula asked.

Melissa nodded.

"The dialysis unit staff confirmed it too. I showed this photo, and all of them said this guy was supposedly a registry nurse who came in to help today because they were short on nurses."

The lieutenant joined in soon enough to hear the last part of Paula's conversation.

"Who we talking about?" Barnes said.

"He went to medical school with Zack Weber," John replied.

Barnes glanced at the photo. "Brice Winnow? As in Winnow, the aide to City Councilwoman Margolis? You were supposed to stay away from him. What happened?"

"Things kinda happened fast," John said.

"But you think he's involved?"

John stepped closer so that Melissa couldn't overhear. "Lieutenant, listen, we're close . . ."

"You aren't going to get close to anything, John. I have to pull you from the case; you know that. I can't let you investigate the disappearance of your own son."

"I have to stay on it."

"No, John, you can't, and that's final. Tommy is part of our family. Let us get him back for you. You can't be objective, and the killer is using that leverage to get to you."

"The lieutenant's right, John," Paula said. "You're too close. The rules say you shouldn't be part of this. Maybe it is time for someone to look at it with fresh eyes."

John clenched his fists, and his knuckles turned white. "Thanks for having my back, partner." He turned away from Paula and went to Melissa.

"He'll be okay," Barnes said.

"Only if we get Tommy back, Lieutenant," Paula said. She went toward John and Melissa.

John couldn't hide the disappointment etched into his face. He turned on Paula the moment she drew close. The voice that came from him sounded alien, harsh, and heavy with betrayal. "What the hell did you do? You still act like you're working IA, out to get another scalp. Partners don't do that to each other."

Paula felt the eyes of everyone in the room focus on her. She reached for John's shoulder, and he brushed her away.

"Get away from me and my family," he said from behind clenched teeth. He turned his back on Paula, took Melissa by the hand, and walked away.

Paula stood alone under the harsh lights, but it was the glare from her fellow officers that burned. A feeling that was too familiar.

TWENTY-EIGHT

Five hours. Three hundred minutes had slipped away since Tommy had vanished from the hospital. John and Melissa took up residence in a hospital waiting room where they received the search updates. Not a single report got them closer to their son. Every janitor's closet, dustbin, and open space in the hospital was searched, twice. John's friend in the county search-and-rescue team brought in his tracking dog, but the bloodhound lost the trail among all the chemical and blood odors in the dialysis unit. A team recovered all the footage from Weber's place. The killer had been careful to leave no digital trail either.

Fear and frustration form a toxic combination, a bitter cloud where self-doubt and helpless cries of panic dwell. Heaviness gathered in the room, along with darker thoughts that accompanied each negative report. The search teams came up dry. There was no sighting, trace evidence, or magic thread that promised to unravel the mystery of Tommy's abduction.

John sat on the edge of a stiff waiting-room sofa, cradling his head in his hands. Melissa perched next to her husband, her legs tucked under her. She nibbled on a thumbnail and gazed absently at a spot on the worn carpeting. They were together but so alone with their fear.

Other cops and hospital personnel checked on them frequently at first, but even that trickled off. It was another sign, and not a good one.

John lifted his red-rimmed eyes when a chair scuffed the floor near him. Lieutenant Barnes pulled a chair close to the sofa.

The lieutenant sat silently for a moment. John knew what that meant.

"Still nothing?" John said.

Barnes shook his head. "We've pulled this place apart, interviewed anyone who could have seen them, and showed them a photo of Tommy. Nothing."

"What photo of Tommy did you use? I didn't give you one."

Barnes pulled his cell from a pocket and handed it over.

The screen displayed a photo of Tommy, one that Barnes had taken at the kid's birthday party two months ago. He wore a silly-looking pirate hat.

"He wanted to be Captain Jack. I'd forgotten that," John said.

"There's nothing more to do here, John. You and Melissa need to go home, try to get some rest."

"You know how many times I've said that to people before? I know what happens next." John gave the cell phone back. "Another case comes along, and Tommy gets handed off."

"That's not how you work, John. You never give up on a case, and you should know that I don't either."

A moment of silence passed between them.

"I know," John said. He wrung his hands, sat back against the sofa, and said, "I should be out there. This guy hit my family."

"Tommy's my family too. You aren't doing any good here. Take Melissa home."

Melissa said nothing, but her eyes moistened.

"I've got a trap and trace on your home phone and your cell phone for when this guy calls," Barnes said.

"He won't call," John said.

"What makes you think that?"

"He doesn't call. He wants what he wants."

"As far as we know, this guy's never snatched a kid before. He's changed things up."

"We both know what happens when a killer dissolves. Their time between kills shrinks," John said.

"There's more to it than that. This guy went out of his way to get to Tommy. If he didn't want something specific, he would have grabbed someone else," Barnes said.

"Stop it! Stop talking like that! Like Tommy's just some piece of meat to this creep. I gave my son over to him. I handed my boy to a killer," Melissa said.

Her outburst silenced John and the lieutenant.

She stood and looked down on the two men, first locking eyes with her husband, then Lieutenant Barnes. "All this arguing isn't helping me get Tommy back home. So what are we gonna do that will actually help?"

"We wait for him to call," Barnes said.

"He's not going to do that," John insisted.

"I can't wait around and hope for the phone to ring—I have to do something," Melissa complained.

"Go home, John. I'll call you the minute I have anything," Barnes said.

"This isn't supposed to go down this way," John said.

"Promise me you will let me know if he calls."

John nodded but couldn't say the words.

Lieutenant Barnes turned away after a quick glance at Melissa. The pain and anguish had darkened her light-blue eyes into muddy, dark pools. The lieutenant couldn't look at her for more than a moment before his heart started to break.

Melissa waited until Barnes left them alone in the waiting room. She stood close to her husband. "Tell me the truth. Are they going to find Tommy? I couldn't live with myself . . ."

"This isn't your fault. I'll get him back," John said. He leaned to Melissa and whispered, "The man who took him wants me to contact him."

"Contact? How?" Melissa grabbed her husband's arm.

John hung his head and exhaled. "I didn't mean for any of this to happen."

"What do you mean?"

"This all comes back to that website you found on my laptop. I started this and almost made a deal to bump Tommy up on the wait list."

Melissa cocked her head and turned away from her husband.

"But when I didn't go through with it, I got this guy angry, and he took it out on our son," he said.

"It's not your fault, John." Melissa reached for her coat and brushed the photograph of Weber and Winnow to the floor. "I . . ." She went rigid.

"What's wrong?" he asked.

"That man, the nurse who took Tommy—I've seen him before."

"What—where?" John said, picking up the photo.

"I knew his face seemed familiar. He took my blood. The day we found out I wasn't a match for Tommy, he took my blood sample. He asked about him—about us."

"Are you sure? This guy, right here?" John said, pointing at the photo of Brice Winnow.

"I'm absolutely certain. He stuck a needle in my arm. I remember that. If he manipulated the transplant list, he could have changed the results of our tests, too." She took the coat from John and tucked it under her arm.

"He set this in motion months ago." John placed his hand around Melissa's waist and guided her out of the waiting room.

The former flurry of police activity was absent in the corridor, marking a point of surrender in the search for their son. As they walked down the hallways and through the lobby, hospital staff subtly turned away, fumbled with something on their desks, or ducked into a patient room. The maneuvers seemed all too practiced. It was the dance to avoid death and those caught in its swirling current. John had done the dance before, and he knew the hollowness of the words, "I'm sorry for your loss."

Once outside, Melissa pointed out where she had parked.

John saw a black form near the car. A person waited in the shadows.

He put his hand out, blocking Melissa's path. "Wait here."

John stepped in front of Melissa and approached the car while his hand slipped down and released the catch on his holster.

The shadow turned, faced John, but didn't move from the side of the car. The parking-lot lights angled the yellow glare away from the person's features. John's hand crept down over the pistol's grip and tightened around the polymer surface.

The shadow took a step forward into a pool of light.

John tensed before he recognized Paula's face. His hand dropped away from his weapon, and he said, "What do you want?"

"I have something for you," she said.

"Paula, we just want to get home."

"John . . ."

"Not now, Paula. I don't know why you needed to get me kicked from the case. But now that I am, leave us alone."

"Let me—" Paula held an envelope in her hand.

John ignored her and unlocked the car.

Melissa walked over and stood at John's side. She hooked an arm around her husband and felt the tension coiled inside.

"Paula, it's probably best that we leave now," Melissa said, taking the envelope from her.

Paula turned away; a slouch betrayed the hurt she felt. She faded into the shadows behind the car.

Melissa slid a finger under the envelope flap and tore it open. She extracted a copy of the photo of the two medical students, Brice Winnow and Zack Weber. Under the photo, a page torn from a medical-school yearbook held a dozen more photos, but one had a bright-red circle drawn around the image.

"John, look."

John sighed and took the paper from Melissa. It wasn't the apology he expected from his partner. The circled photo was of a younger version of Winnow, but underneath, the student's name was listed as Patrick Horn.

Horn and Winnow were the same person.

TWENTY-NINE

Melissa tossed her purse and coat on the sofa, and her shoulders fell at the sight of the big red zero that blazed on the answering machine. Hope slipped from her grasp, drifting away on the tide of passing time.

She busied herself scrubbing the already spotless kitchen and picked up the phone every minute or so, making sure the dial tone signaled the line was in working order.

John plopped down at the computer desk and went to power up the laptop. The lid was already open, and the screen sprang to life when he touched the mouse. Melissa's Pinterest page and four blank web pages were on the screen. He tapped a number into his cell phone.

"Dr. Anderson," Tommy's surgeon answered.

"Hi, Doc. It's John Penley."

"Tommy?" the doctor asked, concern fixed in his voice.

John sighed, louder than he meant to. "No. I wanted to ask you a question about Zack Weber."

"Oh, well, all right," Anderson said.

"You told me that Zack Weber got the boot from medical school for falsifying test scores and grades, right?"

"Yes."

"You said he didn't change his own grades but did hack into the school's system and changed the grades of his classmates."

"Again, yes. That's correct."

"Was one of the classmates Patrick Horn?"

The silence from the doctor's end of the phone lasted for a few seconds before he cleared his throat. "I suppose there's no harm in me talking to you about that. Zack was the one who changed the grades, and from what I understand, Patrick didn't even know about it. But he was tossed from the school along with Zack."

"Why did the hospital allow Zack Weber and Patrick Horn to work there?" John asked.

"Zack worked in the lab, as you know. Patrick didn't work for the hospital, but he worked for a local independent lab as a phlebotomist. I saw him a few times at blood drives before his mother died."

"Marsha Horn, the lab supervisor?" John asked.

"Patrick was her son. I felt like I owed it to her to put in a good word for him," Dr. Anderson said.

"How did Marsha Horn end up with Donovan Layton?"

The doctor sounded surprised at mention of Layton. "Marsha came from an old farming family. I thought she left that all behind after medical school. Until Layton came around."

"Sounds like you didn't care for him?"

"She deserved better. After her first husband died, she floundered around, and Layton was there to pick up the pieces. He didn't treat her very well."

"Any idea how Layton was with Patrick?" John asked.

"I don't know. What I picked up from Marsha was that he was fairly heavy-handed with the boy."

"So father and son didn't see eye to eye?" John said.

"Stepfather. And yes, so it seemed."

"So Patrick worked around the hospital before his mother died?"

"The independent lab runs blood drives here, not laboratory services."

"Melissa told me Patrick drew her blood once at the hospital. How did that happen?"

An uncomfortable silence from the doctor and another creak from his chair signified that he was measuring his response. "I may have opened that door. For a few months last year, I approved a contract lab to fill in for emergency-room phlebotomists. It was the company that Patrick worked with, and he could have used that access to gain entry to the transplant center."

It was John's turn for silence.

"Mr. Penley? Are you still there?"

"Thanks, Doc," John said, then disconnected the call without waiting for a response. His focus narrowed to his computer screen. He closed a handful of browser windows that Melissa must have left open—Pinterest, Facebook, and a medical financial-assistance page. The Tor dark web connection was open. He swore he had closed that application. He closed it again, clicked on a search engine icon, and typed in "Marsha Horn" and the word "obituary."

The *Sacramento Bee* obituary archives pulled up the published obituary for Marsha Jean Horn. The remembrance consisted of a few terse lines, including "Taken early from this world after a life of service to others." There was no mention of her accomplishments or how she died.

John read the last line of the obituary aloud: "Survived by her husband, Donovan Layton." The obituary omitted any reference to other living relatives, specifically Patrick Horn.

He reached for a binder on the bookshelf behind the computer and knocked over a stale cup of coffee. "Dammit, Paula," John said through clenched teeth. Her lack of organization was apparently contagious. Coffee drizzled across the tabletop and made brown spatter patterns on a pile of past-due medical insurance forms.

John hopped up, went to the kitchen, and grabbed a handful of paper towels from the counter. Melissa was bent over a section of grout on the counter and threatened to scrub it out of existence. She never looked up or acknowledged John's presence. John stood for a moment; the silent sorrow formed a cold ball in his stomach.

"I'm going to get him back," he said. The words rang with less hope than despair.

Melissa faced him with red-rimmed eyes. "Why haven't we heard anything?"

He stepped over to her, put his arms around her, and leaned in. "I—I don't know. Maybe he wants us to fear the unknown."

"Well, it's working."

He hugged her tight, then released his grasp and took a step back. "I'm on to something that might help."

"Is it the man, the one Paula named in the photo? That nurse?"

He nodded.

Melissa looked at the wad of paper towels in John's hand.

"I made a mess, tipped over a coffee cup," he said.

She wrinkled her brow. "When did you start drinking coffee at the desk? I thought that was one of your pet peeves."

John's arms went limp. He stared back at Melissa. His mouth tried and failed to form words.

"John, what is it?"

He bolted to the kitchen cabinet next to the refrigerator and flung open the door. The wooden door slammed against the refrigerator.

"What is it?" Melissa repeated.

"Gone. All of Tommy's medications are gone."

John ran down to the boy's bedroom and pushed open the door. Two dresser drawers were pulled open and empty.

"Oh my God," she said.

John turned and followed Melissa's gaze to Tommy's bed. There, on top of the quilt, lay the stuffed animal from the hospital. The bear was a flattened hulk. All of the stuffing had been ripped through a ragged incision in the animal's fabric skin. The exact method the Outcast Killer used on his victims.

With leaden legs, John approached his son's bed. The stuffed animal's corpse bore an obscene resemblance to Daniel Cardozo's body—chest flayed wide and the cavity empty. Inside, John caught a glimpse of something that didn't belong, a folded piece of paper. It looked like a small origami figure, a human form.

John picked up the paper doll and saw subtle blue lines. His fingers trembled as he unfolded the note. A message from the Outcast Killer.

You have a decision to make. Either your son gets a donor, or he becomes one. You know how to contact me. You have until 9:00.

THIRTY

Police technicians swarmed through the Penley home, swabbing, dusting, and collecting. John witnessed this process hundreds of times as a cop, but this time it felt invasive. The techs carried out their crime-scene sweep, leaving dark smudges of fingerprint powder on doorjambs and counter tops, on any surface their suspect could have touched. John had never noticed before how the blotches looked like bruises.

Two of the techs carried on a conversation about the local NBA franchise and the odds of the team leaving town after the city dumped millions of taxpayer dollars into a downtown arena deal. The shorter of the two snapped a photo of the spilled coffee mug. "I don't get why people are all worked up about losing the Kings to another city. They don't buy tickets and go to games, so what's the big surprise?"

"The city needs to step up and invest in the team," the taller one said as he brushed dark powder on the desktop surface. "Otherwise, the Kings could make more money somewhere else."

"Where are we gonna get city money, Chuck? Lay off some crime-scene techs? Why do taxpayers have to help a millionaire make more money? That ain't right, is it, Lieutenant?"

Barnes appeared in the room without John noticing.

"Why don't you guys pipe down and get to work," Barnes said.

The techs looked at one another, shrugged, and returned to their evidence-collection routine.

Barnes went to John, in a corner of the room, out of the way of the activity.

"Sorry about that," Barnes said.

"That's what we do, isn't it? We come into people's lives at the worst moment and then we act like it's no big thing. We just go on with our lives, while theirs are shattered."

"How's Melissa holding up?"

"By a thread, like me. She kept insisting it was her fault." John turned to the lieutenant. "He was here. In my house." John punctuated his words with a fist into his open palm.

"He took clothes and medications for Tommy. You know that's a positive thing," Barnes said.

"It means he plans to keep him."

"Keep him alive," Barnes corrected.

John turned away and peered out a window that overlooked the street. "I sent Melissa to her sister's place across town with Kari. I didn't want her to have to deal with this." He tilted his head to the window.

Yellow crime-scene tape draped across the driveway, secured to a tree on one end and a patrol car's door handle on the other. Official police vehicles, marked and unmarked, lined both sides of the street. Neighbors and the morbidly curious nosed up to the yellow-taped line for a peek at a real crime scene. Some left when they discovered it wasn't like one of those television cop shows, with well-dressed sexy investigators trading quips over a dead body.

Two television news crews held big, boxy cameras and filmed the spectacle for the eleven o'clock news. The police public information officer spoke with one reporter under the glare of camera light.

"What's the PIO saying?" John asked.

"The press release says Tommy was abducted. Photos and descriptions of Tommy and the nurse last seen with him are out."

John looked past Barnes to the desk where the crumpled envelope and photograph of Patrick Horn sat near the keyboard.

"You releasing the ID on the guy?" John asked.

"Patrick Horn and Brice Winnow. We're showing that surveillance photo around to anyone who might have seen him," Barnes said.

"Who's handling that?"

"Paula."

From the direction of the living room, a crime tech called out, "Lieutenant, I got something you need to see."

John followed the lieutenant out of the office to the living room, where a crime-scene tech had emptied the contents of a floor-to-ceiling bookshelf. An assortment of novels, old college textbooks, and children's storybooks lay askew, heaped on the hardwood. A single book remained on the top shelf.

"I was dusting for prints along the edge of the door, and I saw this," the tech said, pointing to gouges in the hardwood flooring near the corner of the bookshelf.

"Looks like it was moved," Barnes said.

"Exactly, but this is a built-in unit, so why would it get moved?" the tech added.

John knelt near the shelf and ran his finger along the gouge marks. "I've never noticed these."

"It's hard to see. The scratches blend in with the wood grain. But check this out," the tech said. He bent over, took hold of the lower section of millwork on the cabinet, and pulled it free. The entire five-foot-long trim piece below the bottommost shelf came loose in his hand. A single red eye reflected back from the dark, hollow space under the bookshelf.

"What the hell is that?" Barnes asked.

"A battery power supply," the tech said. He rose up and took the sole remaining book from the top shelf in his hand. "For this." A thin white wire fed from the back of the book to a small hole in the plaster wall.

The tech unplugged the wire from an input jack glued into the pages of the book and stepped away with the volume in his hands. He cracked the cover and revealed a hollowed-out core in the center of the book's pages.

"Paula and I saw something like this at the Weber kid's apartment," John said. "Cameras."

"This one is wired to the battery pack and to a recording device." The tech pushed the edge of the black plastic rectangle hidden in the book, and a memory card popped into view. "If it weren't for the scratches on the floor from the guy swapping out batteries or memory cards, I might not have found it at all."

"This asshole has been watching my family?" John asked. "How long has he been doing this?"

"No way to tell for sure. The scratches show the trim board was moved five, maybe six times. Each battery pack would last a month, maybe more, if the camera was motion activated."

"Any way we can see what's on that card?" Barnes asked.

"It's an XD card. I don't have anything with me to read it. I can get it back to the nerds at the lab."

John snatched the card. "My computer has a card reader." He quickstepped back to the computer in his office and shoved the small memory card in a slot on the computer console.

Lieutenant Barnes and the tech stood, looking over John's shoulder as the PC read the memory card. A window popped up with a single file listed in the menu. John took a breath and tapped the mouse button, pulling up the video file.

The monitor bloomed with a sharp image of the Penley living room. The lighting in the room said that it was nighttime. Streetlights, visible through a window in the background of the frame, confirmed it was well after dark.

A sudden blur filled the screen, and the camera autofocused on the source of the movement.

A male figure wearing a dark-blue hooded sweat shirt crossed the living room and disappeared toward the kitchen. Faint shuffling sounds came through the computer speakers. John hit the control to increase the volume. Faint rustling noises, cabinet doors slamming, and the crinkle of a paper bag rang through the small computer speaker. The distinct sound of pill bottles being tossed into a bag came next. The male figure crossed the screen again and made a trail to the bedrooms. The sound of his footfalls grew faint as he went down the hallway. A creaking floorboard and the sound of louder footsteps preceded the image of the hooded man in front of the camera. This time he stopped directly in front of the lens, pulled the hood down, and stared into the camera.

There was a slight pause before a smirk formed on his face. The half grin looked out of place. Patrick Horn faced the camera and made certain there was no doubt as to his identity. The man moved differently than he had when he had presented himself as Brice Winnow. The fluid stride and arrogant, self-important posture were replaced with choppy movement and a slouch. He shifted his weight from foot to foot, like a junkie impatient for the next fix.

When Horn spoke, it came out in raspy chunks of words. "Detective Penley . . . you . . . can't . . . stop me. What I do is for the greater good, for all mankind." Horn stopped to catch his breath.

"All mankind? Horn's a frickin' psycho," Barnes said.

Horn continued, "I don't expect you . . . to have the capacity . . . to understand." He lifted his arm, pointed at his watch, and said, "Tommy understands." He took a ragged breath. "I left something for you. Your son doesn't need it anymore." He sidestepped out of view and disappeared.

"Understands? Understands what?" Barnes asked.

John stood transfixed, hoping that his son would magically appear on the screen and this nightmare would end.

"What does he mean?" Barnes said. "Has he contacted you?"

John shook his head and looked to the kitchen where Horn had rummaged about. He recalled the sounds from the video. He willed his legs to propel him to the kitchen. He opened the cabinets and drawers but found nothing out of place except for the missing medications. John leaned back against the counter and rubbed a thumb into his temple to fight off the throbbing that echoed in his head.

He had looked around the kitchen and mentally ticked off each and every storage shelf when he locked eyes on the refrigerator.

He stepped across the kitchen floor and grasped the fridge door handle with his sweat-soaked palm. The crack of light spilled from the refrigerator and illuminated John's trembling hand. He pulled the door open, and his neck stiffened.

On the center of the top shelf, Horn had left a clear plastic freezer bag. A bloody mass in the outline of a human kidney.

John dropped to his knees while the killer's words replayed in his head:

"Your son doesn't need it anymore."

THIRTY-ONE

"It is a child's kidney," Dr. Sandra Kelly said. "I can confirm that much from the size and mass of the tissue." She removed her glasses and gently placed the plastic bag into a small foam container, one that looked more accustomed to holding beer at the beach, except this bore a bright-orange biohazard label on the side.

"Thanks for coming, Doc," John said.

"Of course," she said. The doctor went to the sofa, sat next to John, and placed her hand over his.

"How long can Tommy last without one of his kidneys? I mean, he was barely hanging on with both of them. Now this . . ."

John looked fragile, a shell ready to fracture. He didn't look at her, or anything really; he simply stared at a swirl in the hard-wood floorboards.

"We don't know if this . . ." Dr. Kelly caught the clinical tone in her voice. "Let me show you something."

She reached for her shoulder bag and retrieved a tablet computer. The doctor powered up the small unit, flicked through the screens, and tapped a button. The screen came alive with photos, text, and autopsy diagrams.

John never lifted his head toward the screen.

"You've seen these before, the autopsy reports for Mercer and Johnson. I completed the report for Cardozo. I don't have an ID on the body you hauled out of the water, but take a look at something." She held the tablet out for John.

His hands trembled as John took the tablet computer. A series of gruesome images were displayed on the small screen.

"What am I looking at?" he asked.

Dr. Kelly pointed at the top photo. "The Mercer autopsy. The victim's aorta transected in a downward left-to-right direction."

John's forehead wrinkled. "Okay, so?"

"This is from the Johnson autopsy." She tapped the middle photo. "The aorta is severed at nearly the same location, downward left to right."

Dr. Kelly saw that John wasn't tracking. She rotated the photo one hundred eighty degrees, so that the space where the victim's head would have been pointed downward. "The incision was made top to bottom."

John couldn't see the difference or the significance.

"Remember how I said that it was like an autopsy was already done?"

"Yeah, sure. Because of the way the chest was opened up and the Y-shaped incision." John handed the tablet back to Dr. Kelly.

"I was looking at it the same way you did, we all did. I expected to see an autopsy, and that's what I saw. When I was a little girl, my daddy took me hunting. When he'd bag a deer, he would string it up in a tree by its hind legs and do what he called 'field dressing.' He'd bleed the deer out and cut the carcass open from the top to the bottom, exactly like this."

"What made you think of that?"

"John Doe made the connection for me. Remember the body from the river? There were wounds on the back of the legs consistent with the body being hung upside down."

She let that sink in and remained silent.

John pulled the tablet closer and took another deep look at the graphic photographs of the murder victims in a new light. The recollection of the meat hooks in the Layton barn made a horrific connection. He turned to Dr. Kelly and asked, "You're certain?"

"As the medical examiner, it's kind of what I do," she said with a wry smile.

"These people were butchered."

She nodded. "It would appear so."

"Were they alive when . . . ?"

"No. The tissue samples from Johnson, Mercer, and the water-logged John Doe confirmed they were no longer alive when the organ harvesting occurred. Cardozo, well, that's a different story."

"Tox screens?" John asked, mentally checking another box.

"We did a limited tox panel, in that we didn't have blood or organ tissue, but nothing turned up."

John stood and flexed the kinks from his knees, paced to the far end of the room, and lifted a photo of his family from a mahogany side table. The picture portrayed happier times, before Tommy's diagnosis. The boy's face was fresh, happy, and innocent back then.

"Is there a way to check the DNA or find out who donated the kidney to Cardozo's daughter? Can we find out if it's a match for Cardozo?" John asked.

"I can check. She's not doing well, by the way. You're getting at the hacking of the UNOS database, aren't you?" she asked. "You know that would explain some things."

"What do you mean?" he asked.

"If the database and the waiting list were compromised, it would explain why the Gunderson boy's mother thought he received a mismatched kidney."

"The autopsy? You were able to do that?"

"Yes. I haven't gotten the entire tox panel back, but the organ was indeed a mismatch for young Mr. Gunderson. But it would have been a match for Tommy."

John stiffened. "With Zack Weber hacking into the system, Patrick Horn, or Winnow—whoever the hell he is—accessed the data on patients awaiting transplant and purposely gave patients mismatched tissue. He cancelled Tommy's transplant."

"Okay, I follow, but you're assuming that he gives a crap about tissue match. It could be that he is simply carving up people for profit," Dr. Kelly said.

"I think there is more to him than that. Zack Weber was an idealist, convinced that he was serving mankind."

"Maybe Horn threatened Weber," she said.

"He protected Horn after we uncovered the lab tampering. Weber actually believed that they were helping people the big medical corporate machine wouldn't touch."

"Daniel Cardozo's daughter needed a kidney, so Horn and company killed her father for the perfect match? Where are the idealistic values in that?"

"Daniel Cardozo was a thug, a gang member, and a drain on society, but he would have willingly given his daughter a kidney," John offered.

"So these guys play a sick game of Robin Hood with human organs—take from the undeserving and give to the poor? Tissue typing and matching isn't difficult, but I'm willing to bet it's beyond the capability of Weber and Horn. A simple blood-type match, maybe."

John paced back toward the sofa. "I don't buy the idea they were fueled by a misguided ideology. These victims weren't random. Each gang member was selected as much for who they were as for any tissue match. Do you know anything about the last victim?"

The doctor stuffed her tablet computer in her shoulder bag and said, "I'm going to see if I can pull some strings at the Department of Justice lab. They owe me, and we can't wait weeks to get a response. The first thing I'm going to ask them to do is rule out that this tissue came from Tommy."

"You can do that?"

"I've already pulled your son's DNA profile from the transplant center for comparison, so it's not like we need to search the entire DNA database for a cold hit," Dr. Kelly said.

John followed the doctor to the kitchen, where the Styro-
foam cooler containing someone's entrails waited. Dr. Kelly hefted
the case from the countertop and tucked it under one arm. She
patted the top of the insulated container. "The moment I have
anything . . ."

"I know," John said.

Dr. Kelly nodded. She understood that the contents of that
cheap foam cooler represented his son's life in many ways.

A small mass of tissue meant life or death—an end to suf-
fering or simply an end. Patrick Horn sent this flesh-and-blood
proclamation—he alone held the power over Tommy's life.

THIRTY-TWO

Alone in a house that swelled with pain, fear, and disappointment, John wandered from room to room, searching for something to replace the emptiness he carried. Instead of happy reminders of his family, he found dashed dreams and broken promises. Hope. He once held the elusive creature in his hand; now even hope disappeared as fine grains of sand through his grasp.

John poured a Scotch and leaned against the counter. He turned the crystal tumbler in his hand and became lost in the amber ripples. Melissa had found the etched glass during a trip to Europe in the days before the kids came along. An episode of food poisoning in London turned out to be morning sickness. Melissa was pregnant with Kari.

John smiled at the thought. Then he caught his reflection in the etched glass, an irregular web of lines and distortions projected on his face. The reflection of a broken man.

A faint knock at the front door broke his fixation with the image of the damaged man he had become. John placed the untouched Scotch on the counter and went to the door.

He drew the door back a few inches, expecting to see one of the nosy old women from across the street prying for gossip she could share with her bridge club.

Instead, Paula Newberry stood under the porch light. She held two white paper coffee cups, and the dark circles under the detective's eyes said she needed the caffeine fix as much as John.

John stepped aside; Paula took his lack of protest as an invitation and crossed the threshold, handing one of the coffees to him.

"Look, John, I'm sorry."

"Don't."

"You needed to get booted off the case," she said.

"You put me farther away from my son." The words didn't carry venom. They held disappointment at his partner. "Why would you do that?" John turned away and walked into the living room, leaving Paula near the open door.

"So the lieutenant pulled you off the case too? I guess you didn't count on that getting in the way of your climb to the top," John said.

"You think that's what this is about?" she said, slamming the front door shut and following him.

"A case like this would be a big stepping-stone for you. Get you back on the good side of the brass."

"Screw them! I didn't put my ass on the line for them."

"Seems to come easy for you. I get why you needed to take down Carson for what he did in the evidence room, but shit, Paula, what did I do to get on your list? Coming after me is one thing. I can deal with that. But to stop me from getting my son back?"

"You're an asshole, you know that? For a detective, you are completely clueless," she said.

"I told you I don't care what you did in the Carson case. He deserved to go down."

"You might not care, but there are a hell of lot of others who do. I hear the comments from jerks like Stark and the others. I took a risk when I forced the lieutenant to take you off the case because it was the right thing to do."

"The right thing to do? It's not that easy in this job, you know that. And when my kid is on the line—"

"John, I had—"

"Thanks for the coffee. You know your way to the front door."

"I said, you needed to be *officially* off the case," Paula said, stepping closer to him.

He squinted and shook his head. "What the hell are you saying?"

"Because of what *we* need to do."

John waited and took a sip from the coffee cup. Bitter and cold.

"How long were you waiting outside?"

"About an hour. I wanted to make sure everyone finished and got out."

He cocked his head. "Why?"

She looked at her watch. "We have two hours until you have to make contact."

"Yeah?"

"The mayor's office called in the FBI, and the feds are on their way. They won't give a damn about Tommy. Once they come in, we're gonna get pulled. We have two hours to go get Tommy before the feds do something stupid and get him hurt," she said.

John dumped the cold coffee in the kitchen sink and poured a half cup of hot coffee into the container from a carafe on the counter. "Want some?"

She poured the remnants of her coffee in the sink and handed the cup to John. "I went through Patrick Horn's apartment in Midtown. Nothing there. Completely clean. Too clean," she said.

"Anything else listed in his name?"

She shook her head. "No. Not in his name, but I got a list of properties from Marsha Horn's estate documents. Two of the three properties were sold off within a month or so of her death. Only one remains in the estate. It's abandoned and has a county tax lien on the property for back taxes. It doesn't look like Patrick Horn made any effort to claim the house."

"Any utilities accounts at the house?"

"Nothing. I couldn't get a warrant to search the place because I couldn't tie Patrick Horn to the place directly. I got it kicked back from the night judge, unless I come up with evidence that Horn was actually ever there. Judge Fogerty suggested I go sit outside the place and watch. Which brings me to why I'm here."

"We need to hit that place. He might have Tommy there. I can't wait around and hope Horn shows up," John said.

"Which is why we can't do it officially. No warrant and lack of probable cause."

John shut off the kitchen lights and grabbed a jacket on the way to the door.

Paula followed and waited on the front porch while he locked up. John paused after he withdrew his key and regarded the home that had once protected his family. The memories of carefree times deemed distant, unretrievable. Before paralysis set in, John stuffed the keys in his pocket and walked past Paula.

Paula's silver Mazda Miata sat in the driveway, tucked behind John's undercover police sedan.

John shot her a look of disbelief.

"It's not like we can cruise up to the place in a city car," she said.

The passenger door cried on rusted hinges when John tugged it open.

"This keeps getting better."

"Shut up and get in."

John ducked inside the compact car, sitting on piles of fast-food menus and crumpled hamburger wrappers. He lifted his butt and scraped the junk onto the floorboard. The paper crinkled when he moved his feet.

"Don't start with me now. I didn't have time to have the car steam cleaned for your OCD ass."

"A quick pass with a leaf blower would have been nice."

Paula turned the key in the ignition, and the small motor hummed to life. "The place is on the river, not far from the airport."

"How far from Cardozo's body dump?"

Paula backed out of the drive and popped the gearshift out of reverse. She feathered the clutch, ran through the gears, and shot up the street. "Less than a mile upriver."

John held on to the dash as Paula took a corner. She hit the Interstate 5 on-ramp at I Street at seventy-five miles an hour. The little car rattled off the uneven road where the ramp transitioned into the four northbound lanes.

She accelerated and swerved the car to the left, into the fast lane, cutting in front of a semitruck. A short blast of an air horn from the truck driver didn't seem to register with Paula as the speedometer needled to eighty-five.

"This—this is why I don't let you drive," John said with a hand clutched on the handle over the passenger window.

Paula grinned. "That trucker had plenty of room. If he wasn't so amped up on crank, he would have let it go."

The junction of Interstate 5 and State Highway 99 flew past, and Paula shot across all the traffic lanes to the far right for the next exit, marked Airport Boulevard. She turned left, away from the airport, onto North Bayou Road.

The narrow levee road forced Paula off the gas. "Look for Garden Highway."

They didn't need to wait long; the road ended at a stop sign at the intersection with Garden Highway along the riverbank.

"Where is the place?" John asked.

"Should be up here, 56723 Garden Highway," she said.

She started into the intersection but slammed on the brakes when a fire truck flew past, red lights flashing. The truck let loose a wail from the siren after it passed through the intersection. The growl of the emergency vehicle's heavy engine dissipated as it rounded the corner.

"Always a traffic accident on these river roads. Hope this one didn't slip into the water," Paula said as she checked traffic. She turned right and followed in the wake of the fire engine.

Along the riverbank, the homes sat on larger lots with expansive views, if your idea of a view was the grass-covered levee bank on the far side of the water. The homes sat on or inside a levee channel, which made them prone to seasonal flooding. It was easy to see why the flood risk in the Sacramento region rivaled that of New Orleans. Some of the homes sat atop tall pillars, ten feet or more above the ground, allowing floodwaters to ebb and flow under the home without seeping inside. Others bore witness to repeated flooding, marked by the water stains and rot on their siding.

"Should be up ahead," Paula said, scanning the homes for the number.

They could smell it before they drew near. Smoke, thick and acrid, poured from one of the riverside structures. Flashing red lights shone through the smoke in uneven patches, with an occasional tongue of orange flame lashing out like a wild creature, resisting efforts to tame its beastly nature.

John grabbed the dashboard, peering forward through an ink-black smoke plume that settled over the roadway.

Paula hesitated and tapped the brake.

"Go!" John said.

Paula stabbed the gas pedal and guided the car into the black mass. As quickly as it engulfed them, they broke through the smoke cloud into a clearing, where a dozen fire and emergency vehicles attended to a home engulfed in flame. Orange-and-yellow tendrils reached out through the windows and clutched the roof. Smoke belched from the broken underbelly of the building. Teams of fire personnel attended a snake's nest of hose lines from trucks and hydrants to the blaze. A pickup truck emblazoned with "Battalion Chief" blocked the road ahead.

"That's the place! That's the house we were looking for!" John jumped from the passenger door before Paula had come to a full stop. He ran in the direction of the house, and two firemen grabbed him as he approached.

"Hey, buddy, you can't go in there," one of the firemen said. He gripped John's arm.

"Let me go! My son is in there!"

The fireman looked at his partner, then called out, "Hey, Chief! This guy says he knows someone inside."

A burly man with a soot-stained turnout coat approached. As he drew closer, the battalion chief badge on his helmet became legible.

"This your place?" the battalion chief asked.

"No. You gotta let me go in," John said.

"Ain't no one inside anymore. We cleared it, so relax."

"You found him? Where is he?" The pumps whirred at a high pitch, making it hard to hear one another.

The chief gestured to the open doors of an ambulance on the far side of the house.

John took a step, and the chief stepped in his path. "I gotta warn you."

Those four words nearly crippled John. He was too late.

The chief pulled close so that he could look John in the face. "He's in bad shape, more than burns. He's got a chance to make it if we get him to the trauma center fast."

More than burns. The warning tumbled through John's brain. He ran for the ambulance, legs pumping hard, heart pounding.

Fifty feet from the blaze, he felt the searing heat against his skin. Tommy had suffered in that inferno.

The ambulance doors slammed shut, pulled closed by a paramedic inside. Through the glass window, John saw someone on a gurney and wisps of steam rising from the patient.

John reached the back door as the driver started up the engine. John slammed his fist on the back door and yelled, "Wait!"

The ambulance lurched and stopped. The paramedic opened the rear door. "We got to get moving."

"He's family," John repeated under a heavy, ragged breath. The cloth-draped figure smelled like burnt flesh and nearly gagged John.

"Get in."

John pulled himself up into the rear of the ambulance, and the paramedic pulled the door shut behind him. The driver pulled forward. John grabbed a storage cabinet to steady himself as the ambulance accelerated.

The paramedic adjusted the flow on a clear bag of IV fluid. The small form covered by sterile sheets looked lifeless. Gauze dressings lay over a fire-ravaged face. Exposed hair had turned to crispy wisps of ash.

The paramedic opened a bag of saline and rinsed a spot on the patient's chest to attach a heart rate monitor. He quickly cleaned the area, peeled the adhesive back from the electrode, and set it in place. A blip on a monitor screen came to life.

"I've got a pulse."

John didn't hear him because he was focused on the body's charred face. Something wasn't right. The size of the person under the sheet was off. A face too weathered for a nine-year-old. John couldn't put it together until a milky eye flicked in recognition. The eye of Donovan Layton.

John grabbed the oxygen mask, and it took all the restraint he possessed to not rip it from the patient's face.

"Don't touch that!" the paramedic said, then took John's hand.

If capable of communicating, Layton gave no indication, other than an occasional flickering glance in John's direction. Layton ignored John's repeated questions about Tommy. By the time the ambulance pulled into the portico at the hospital, the old man was unresponsive, his blood pressure and pulse weakened with each passing second.

The trauma center staff flung open the rear doors as the ambulance rolled to a stop. With efficient, practiced movements, the hospital staff unloaded the gurney and took over resuscitation and the IV bags from the paramedics.

John followed close behind Layton. This husk of a man knew where Tommy was, along with other dark secrets held in his lesioned brain. Triage began in the hallway as the gurney wheels clacked over the linoleum floors. A young woman in pale-green scrubs barked orders, and John pegged her as the doctor in charge.

One of the nurses gently peeled a section of scorched clothing from Layton's chest as the team started debridement of the wounds.

Layers of skin, fatty tissue, and muscle tissue came up with the cloth. Dark threads of fabric and ash remained behind, embedded in the open wound.

"Holy crap," one of the attending medical staff said. She lifted the sterile dressing the paramedics had placed on the patient's lower right arm. The dressing oozed a thick, crimson gel from a ragged stump were a hand should have been.

Another nurse unwrapped an IV tube from a sterile bag. She held the IV in one hand and pulled back the sheet on the opposite arm. "Son of a . . ." she said.

Donovan Layton's left hand was gone too. The raw tissue and exposed bone on the wrist had no sign of burn damage. A tight leather strap wrapped around his forearm several times, indenting his flesh, and was precisely finished off with a tight knot.

"Someone tied him off with a tourniquet. He sure as hell didn't do it himself," the attending doctor observed.

"Doctor, his legs . . ." the nurse with the IV said.

The doctor lifted the sheet at the foot of the gurney. Both legs ended four inches below the knee. Each leg bore the same leather-strapping tourniquet. The tight bands on the legs were charred into the thigh muscle, above each knee.

A thin, raspy wheeze issued from Layton's throat.

"He's crashing," a nurse said, watching the monitor display.

"I've got a new IV line in," another called out.

"Five hundred milligrams epinephrine, Ringer's lactate, and two hundred milligrams morphine sulfate in the line," the doctor ordered.

Bottles of sterile water were emptied over the burnt flesh, creating a pool of dead skin, charred fabric, and oozing fatty tissue on the gurney. Entire sections of tissue sloughed off Layton's torso.

"Heart rate steady at 150," the monitor nurse said.

"Let's get him stable and handed off to the burn unit," the doctor ordered.

Paula Newberry found John in the trauma unit and stood next to him. She smelled of soot and smoke from the fire. She held a scrap of fabric in one hand.

"Horn?" she said.

"No, old man Layton."

"He gonna make it?" she asked.

"I don't know," John said. His attention went to the piece of fabric in Paula's grasp.

"That's Tommy's sweat shirt." The words sounded final.

"They found it inside the house. No sign that Tommy was caught in there when the place went up. He isn't there, John."

John took the remnant of Tommy's charred sweat shirt. "What happened to him?"

"Maybe he got away in the confusion of the fire. He's a smart kid," she said.

"Then he would have found a way to contact me. He wasn't in the best of shape when Horn took him from the hospital. The man who did this to his own stepfather has my son," he said as he pointed to the dismembered Donovan Layton. "I'm supposed to contact Horn soon. What am I supposed to say?"

"Excuse me, are you this man's family?" a nurse said from Layton's bedside.

"No . . ." John started.

"Yes, he's my uncle," Paula blurted.

"We're doing what we can for him, but he's in very bad shape. The pain meds are helping a little. You can sit with him for a few minutes until we move him to the burn unit."

"Thank you," Paula said, then dragged John by the arm to Layton's bedside.

The nurse pulled a curtain to afford privacy for the "family."

Layton's chest fluttered; the air hissed through the respirator mask over his mouth. The burns to Horn's face left open cavities though his cheek, and the respirator air spat a pink stain on the pillow.

A groan issued from deep inside the burned man's throat. His stumped limbs wagged in agony seconds before his eyelids popped open and his eyes fought for focus.

John bent over the man. "Layton, where is my son?"

Layton lolled his head away from John, avoiding him.

John grabbed the raw flesh and pulled the man's face toward his.

A thin mewing came from Layton as the pain registered.

"Where is my son?"

Layton's eyes hardened and moved away but then focused on his interrogator when John tightened his grip, digging his fingers into exposed burnt flesh.

"Where?"

Layton drew in air to speak, but smoke-and-fire-damaged vocal cords stifled his voice to a low murmur.

"Tell me," John said.

"W. Win. Winnow. Brice Winnow has Tommy," Paula said, leaning in close to Layton's lips.

"You mean Patrick Horn?"

"He ain't Patrick no more," Layton said.

"Where is he?" John asked.

"He's waiting for you."

"Where, where is he waiting?" John said, digging his fingers a bit deeper.

Layton's eyes locked with John. A rough whisper came from the man's mouth. "I won't tell you. He's Marsha's boy. I owe that to her for what I did."

"What is he talking about?" Paula said.

John lowered his face within inches of Layton's ear. The pungent smell of burnt flesh caused a momentary gag reflex. "What did you do?"

The old man's chest heaved. His phantom limbs fought to escape the torment.

"I showed him. I showed him." Layton gagged, then shook his head. "He said you for the boy—one will die."

The exertion drained Layton, and his eyes fluttered, then closed. Seconds later, alarms sounded on the heart monitor, and the jagged, peaked lines on the displays narrowed to shallow waves.

Medical personnel rushed in and went to work on the patient, rustling John and Paula out of the space. The thin curtain couldn't contain, or dampen, the frantic, desperate sounds within.

"Call it. Time of death, nineteen thirty-three," a voice said.

John looked at his watch, not to confirm the time of Layton's demise, but in recognition there was little time left to make contact with Horn and negotiate a trade.

John's life for Tommy's. His vision shrank to a pinhole. According to Layton's last words, only one would survive.

THIRTY-THREE

"John—John, wake up." Paula's voice cut through a dark, gauzy film in his brain. The lights weren't where they were supposed to be; they were in front of him, not overhead, and cast a jaundiced glare in his half-closed eyes. An ammonia odor burned his nostrils and shot a bolt of electricity through his brain. The jump start made John press against the cold linoleum floor.

Paula read his confusion and said, "You passed out." A broken ammonia smelling salts capsule wafted under John's nose once more.

John shook his head and tried to sit up. Dizziness swept over him, and Paula caught him before he toppled over to his side.

"Easy now. You've given yourself a nice little gash on the head," the doctor said, who seconds ago, in John's memory, had attended to Donovan Layton.

"How long was I out?"

"Maybe a minute," Paula said. "You scared me when you dropped like that."

"We're slowly going to help you up and get you on a gurney, Mr. Penley," the doctor added.

"I don't need a gurney."

"I need you to lie down and be still until I suture up that wound on the back of your head."

John reached back and felt the slick, golf-ball-sized lump. He didn't need to see his hand to know it was bloody.

"I don't have time for that. Slap on a butterfly bandage and I'm fine."

"No, you're not fine. I need to close that wound, and after you bled all over my trauma room floor, you don't have much of a say in the matter," the doctor said.

The physician took one of John's arms and Paula grabbed the other. John let the two women guide him to a gurney. He tried to hide the fact that the room spun, but he involuntarily listed to one side.

Paula caught him and propped him back up. The doctor began cleaning the wound with a purple-red betadine solution.

"Can you sit still, or do we need to strap you down?" the doctor said, preparing a syringe.

"I'm good," John said, looking at Paula, who held him up.

The doctor dripped the Xylocaine anesthetic into the wound and waited a few seconds until it started to work. She jabbed the needle near the wound and injected the solution under the scalp.

"Your head might start to feel a little fuzzy. Can you feel anything?" The doctor pressed on the wound with a gloved hand. A nurse with electric clippers cut a swath of hair from his scalp.

"No, nothing."

The first suture went in, and the doctor started talking. "So who was that guy you came in with on the ambulance? I get that he wasn't a family member." Another suture went in.

"He knew the guy who took my son from Central Valley Hospital," John said. The thoughts unfogged as the unsteadiness diminished.

The doctor stopped and drew back a step. "From the dialysis unit?"

"Yes."

"I heard about that. We got the alert over here, in case someone came in." She went back to work on John's torn scalp. "I'm sorry."

"Why did I pass out like that?"

The doctor tugged on a suture, pulling the wound tight. "It's the acetone. One of my nurses got a little lightheaded too. The patient was saturated in acetone. That's why he was burnt so badly. We see that quite a bit from meth-lab fires."

"How much longer?" John asked.

"I'm going to put in another three, eight total."

"Paula, we need to get to a computer terminal so I can make contact with Winnow, Horn, or whatever he's calling himself."

"Whoa now, slow down. I want to admit you for observation. You had a serious bump to the noggin, and you have a concussion. With the loss of consciousness, we need to keep an eye on you," the doctor said.

"That's not going to happen, Doc. I have to find my son."

"Are you going to be with him?" the doctor said to Paula.

"Yep. I can keep watch over him."

"Any signs of dizziness or another fainting spell and you need to get him back here. We'll need to get a CT scan and check for a brain bleed. Watch for a mood change and increase in the intensity of his headache."

"Hear that? I get to watch *you* for mood swings," Paula said.

"I'm fine," John insisted.

"No, you're not fine," the doctor countered. "You shouldn't be doing anything except staying down and keeping quiet, but I understand." The doctor scribbled on a clipboard. "I'm signing you out AMA, against medical advice." She turned and left the room without another word.

John's cell rang, and the sound generated a disapproving scowl from a nurse in the passageway. He fumbled with it, and Paula snatched it out of his hand.

"Detective Newberry."

"Detective, it's Dr. Kelly. I have an ID on your floater, the man you and Detective Penley found at the Delta King."

"That was fast. How did you figure that out?"

"Our coroner's investigators got a hit on the missing persons database. Lawrence Travis was reported missing by his wife five days ago."

"How were you able to identify him? That body was in bad shape," Paula said.

"The wife said he had a left knee replacement while he was in prison. The body you found had an artificial knee implant, and we pulled the serial numbers from the device. It is Lawrence Travis."

"Was she able to tell you anything about when he went missing?"

"We didn't get that much from her. Only that Lawrence got a call from the blood bank, and he was supposed to drop in for a donation. He got called regularly, AB-positive blood type. Nothing more. I'll text you with the contact details so you can fill in the blanks on that part of the story," Dr. Kelly said. "One thing I can confirm, though, was that the victim was gutted like all the other cases. The tissue matches the remnant of the kidney from the aborted transplant at Central Valley Hospital."

"Tommy Penley's transplant?"

"Yep," Dr. Kelly said.

"John wanted to know . . ."

"The child's kidney left at his home was not from Tommy. It matched the tissue type of the Cardozo girl. I need some additional testing, but I think this was the kidney she had removed during her transplant. It showed signs of cancer."

"How did her kidney get to John's house?"

Tension released from John's shoulders when it registered that his son hadn't been gutted. Yet.

"Weber was working at the hospital when we brought the girl in," John said.

"Also, the first of the human remains from the barn are coming in. This is going to be nasty. Tell Detective Penley the butchering theory is holding up. We have hook marks through the victims' thighs."

"Butchering theory? What's that mean?" Paula asked.

"Detective Penley can catch you up." The doctor ended the call.

Paula handed the phone back to John. "Lawrence Travis. That name mean anything to you?" she said.

"Nope. That's our water baby?"

She nodded. "He went missing when he was supposed to give a donation at the blood bank."

"That's where the kidney came from—the one Tommy was supposed to get?"

Paula nodded again.

"The one Weber's computers found and Horn harvested," he said. John touched the back of his head and felt the short, prickly hairs where the doctor had shaved his scalp.

"Well, we can't ask Weber anything about this Travis guy," Paula said. "How rare is AB positive?"

John turned white. A cold sweat formed on his brow.

"Can you take me back to my place? I can get online and make contact with Winnow from there."

"The tech team snagged all your computer drives for prints and to find anything he may have done with them," Paula said.

She helped John to his feet, and he wobbled a bit before he steadied himself against the edge of the gurney. "Can we get to my computer?" he said.

"We can use another one, a terminal at the bureau or back at my house."

"I need to use mine."

"What are you talking about?"

"I think I know how he targeted his victims," John said.

"How's that?"

"My son's blood type is AB positive, and the blood types are listed in the UNOS database that Zack Weber hacked. Less than five percent of the population has that blood type."

"But you didn't make the buy, so why would he go forward and hunt a donor?"

"It's the blood bank. Weber had everything wired together—who needed transplants, what organs were in demand, and then they found them using the blood bank donation data. The blood bank was a shopping list."

"I'll bet Cardozo, Mercer, and Johnson tie back to the blood bank too."

John snatched his jacket from his chair and started to put it on when he noticed the bloodstain on the back of his collar. He folded the ruined jacket, tucked it under his arm, and made for the door. "Where did you park?" he asked.

Paula pointed down a warren of hallways. As they headed out, Paula watched John for any unsteadiness on his feet. A few steps worked out the kinks, and he regained his stride.

"Dr. Kelly said something about the butcher theory. What does that mean?" Paula asked.

A set of glass automatic doors opened as they approached, greeting them with a cool blast of evening air. Paula hit the remote unlock from her keys, which flicked the headlights of her car on and off, signaling their destination.

"Mercer and Johnson were hung and gutted like game animals. Butchered," John said as he opened the driver's door out of habit.

"Like Layton's hogs," she said.

Paula held the passenger door open and tipped her head, directing him to the passenger seat. He started to argue the point, then recognized it wasn't the city-issued sedan. The local anesthetic started fading, and a blossom of throbbing pain grew in its place.

He walked around, got in, and Paula took over behind the wheel.

"Is that what Layton meant? The whole 'it's my fault' deal?" Paula asked.

He pressed around the knot on the back side of his head. "Sounded like an old man with regrets. But there's something darker there."

Paula turned out of the hospital parking lot and shot through a break in the cross traffic.

Paula drifted across the lane until her tires ran over the raised dots and shook the small car's frame. "Patrick Horn and Brice Winnow ran in completely different worlds."

"Same person but different personalities."

Paula shot him a glance. "Multiple personalities?"

Paula jammed the shift lever, pumped the clutch, and shot the compact Miata down the city street, in the sweet spot, after the commuter traffic but before the nightlife erupted into a throbbing, pulsating mass of barhoppers.

"It's like two different people. Horn was conservative, from humble stock, and Winnow screams extrovert right down to his shiny, gold Rolex."

"That's what strikes you as odd? We have a whack job butchering people, and his choice of wristwatches is the thing you find odd?" she said.

They pulled into the Sacramento Police Department parking lot, and Paula aimed for an empty slot near the door. The spot belonged to the administrative captain, who rarely appeared after dark.

John released his seat belt, pushed the door open with his knee, and climbed up from Paula's low-slung car. A wave of nausea rolled through his gut, and he grabbed the doorframe for support. He recovered before Paula turned to close her door.

"I worked a case a few years back, a messy one with a dude hearing voices, telling him to do stuff," John said as they locked up Paula's Mazda and went to the door.

Paula slid an access card through a reader that looked like a debit card machine at a grocery store. The lock popped open, and they walked down the hallway into the atrium in the center of the building.

"The point is, it wasn't a clean split. One personality would come out, then another. These people are fragile and need mental health care; they're sick and can't function very well without lots of attention and medication," John continued.

"Winnow doesn't seem to have that kind of problem. He's found himself a little niche in city hall."

The detectives approached the atrium, a lush, green space in an administrative jungle. John stopped. "If Winnow is having a schizophrenic reaction, some event or trauma would have triggered it."

"Triggered how?" Paula stopped outside the tech unit's door and faced her partner with a quizzical expression etched in her brow.

"Something created Winnow. Remember Layton said something about how Patrick Horn was dead. We find what he meant, and we get a peek inside this fun house."

John reached for the door, but Paula grabbed his wrist.

"You can't do this. The nerd herd took your computer, so you can't traipse in there and snag it. It won't look right. It'll look like you're trying to cover up something," Paula said.

"I need that computer to contact Winnow. They won't let me do that. I'm nearly out of time," he pleaded.

"Leave this to me. I'll meet you back in our office. Now go," she told him.

THIRTY-FOUR

John backtracked to the detective bureau offices. Most of the investigators were out or off duty. A few of the vice cops were getting ready to head out for a prostitution sting. A female cop, new to the unit, scanned a city map displaying bright dots. Each colored dot represented a prostitution or sex-crime complaint. She tugged at the tight hot pants and fishnets, uncomfortable in the undercover hooker guise.

"You gotta act like you done this before, Lizzy. You keep trying to cover up and you won't be able to pick up a dime," a male detective said to the undercover lure.

John nodded hello to the vice detectives and stopped at the coffee urn for a shot of the thick, dark brew that fueled the detective bureau.

A voice startled him, so much that he nearly slopped his coffee across the counter.

"Why aren't you home, John?" Lieutenant Barnes asked. The same wrinkled shirt, now accompanied by stubble and heavy eyes, spoke to his weariness.

"I need to be doing something. I can't sit around and wait," John said.

"I have everyone out looking for Winnow. I heard about Layton."

John looked for any sign in the lieutenant's response that he knew Paula and John had been at the riverside house. The lieutenant didn't say anything more about it and poured the remnants of his coffee in the sink.

Barnes wiped out the dark-brown coffee residue with a paper towel. He balled up the paper, tossed it in the trash basket, and started back to his office. With his back to John, the lieutenant said, "I gave the tech unit the go-ahead to release your computer to Newberry. Make sure you guys color between the lines on this one."

A ball of ice formed in John's chest when Barnes mentioned the computer. He stood at the coffee counter and wondered how much more the lieutenant knew.

As if on cue, Paula appeared with a laptop computer under her arm and a worried look. She plopped the laptop on top of a pile of files in the center of her desk.

John returned from the coffeepot, and as he approached, Paula spoke in a hushed voice. "The tech unit called the lieutenant."

"I know," he said. "He came and told me."

"He let us have this? Why?"

"He said he knew about Donovan Layton too. That part doesn't surprise me. He would have had to assign a team to investigate the old man's death. Probably Wilson and Sikes."

Paula opened the laptop cover, found the end of the power cord, and plugged it into a wall outlet. John crossed behind her and stood over her shoulder while the laptop came to life.

"Did he know we were there, where Layton got burned?" Paula asked.

"He didn't say anything." John caught his reflection in the laptop screen, zombie-pale. "He didn't mention the bloodstains on my shirt or the shaved skunk stripe on the back of my head, either."

"So he knows what we're doing?" Paula said.

"He always seems to know."

John sat, pulled the computer close, and opened up a web browser. He thumbed the trackpad and scrolled to the list of his browser history. He found the website where he had connected with Winnow. He'd saved the random number and letter key in the laptop's password list.

"That wasn't very smart, leaving that trail," Paula said.

"I didn't know what I was doing." John tapped the trackpad and brought up the browser.

The screen was black and green, like before. A single, blinking cursor flashed on the page.

"Here we go," John said.

Winnow, are you there? He typed. The words scrolled out in green letters on the laptop screen.

The cursor blinked. No response followed his question.

A minute passed, then two more, and still nothing from Brice Winnow.

John hit the return key and typed out another line. *I want my son.*

The cursor blinked off and on and off, a heartbeat on the screen. The screen flashed, and the green cursor dimmed. It throbbed at a faster rate, and letters scrolled onto the screen, sent from an invisible hand.

You're not the only one interested in the young man.

"What does that mean?" Paula said, pointing at the screen.

John positioned his hands over the keyboard. He typed out a response: *Leave the boy out of this. It's between you and me.*

The cursor blinked for a few seconds, considering John's answer. Letters began scrolling out. *Nothing personal; this is only business. I'm willing to listen to your proposal.*

John began composing a message when the screen flickered. His keyboard strokes no longer registered on the screen. Instead, another message from Winnow appeared. *I'm disappointed in you, Detective Penley. Someone with an IP address in the police tech unit is online with us. I thought we had an understanding.*

John jabbed at the keyboard, but nothing happened. He couldn't respond.

"What's going on?" Paula said.

A sergeant from the tech unit entered the detective bureau, scanned the room until he found John and Paula. He trotted over to them and spoke in a rapid, clipped burst. "We didn't do it. We didn't have anything to do with it."

"What happened? Why am I locked out?" John said.

"IA came with some FBI gal and took over my network," the tech sergeant said.

"Hey, it wasn't me," Paula blurted.

"What is internal affairs doing with this?" John asked.

"I dunno," the sergeant said.

Paula pointed at the screen. "Look."

A new message hit the computer screen: *This is Special Agent K. Lincoln of the FBI. I trapped your IP address and know where you are.*

A quick reply shot back to the FBI from Winnow: *I doubt that very much, Special Agent K. Lincoln of the FBI. Please pass my condolences on to Detective Penley. His son would have liked to fly his kite again.*

John watched the lines of green text blink and disappear, leaving a slate-black screen behind, and along with it, all connection to the man who held his son was lost.

John felt the pressure of the room change and press down on his chest, but it wasn't from the threatening message on the computer screen. A buzz of self-importance filled the detective bureau in the form of a woman in a tailored, tight black pantsuit, along with two men in dark suit jackets over white shirts and thin ties. The woman's heels clacked off the thin linoleum in a cadence that announced she was someone who demanded attention.

"John Penley, I'm Special Agent K. Lincoln. You have no right to interfere with my investigation." She nodded to one of her associates. The man to her right moved with two quick strides and snatched the laptop computer from the desk, pulling the power cord out of the wall as he yanked it away.

"This guy has my son, so I'd say I have a right to get him back, and I didn't ask for the feds' help to do it," John said.

Lincoln moved a strand of jet-black hair away from her eyes. "I'm not here about the boy. I'm here to take down the Outcast Killer. Your mayor petitioned the FBI for assistance."

Paula stood tall behind John and squared her shoulders. The contrast between the two women was a study in opposites. Paula Newberry was a tough, gritty, get-your-hands-dirty kind of cop who wasn't afraid to get in the trenches with the guys. Lincoln, with her tailored, couture wardrobe, expensive haircut, and enough makeup to go on camera, looked the part of someone who swooped in and took credit for the hard work of others.

"Our first priority is to get Tommy back," Paula said.

"Your only priority, Detective, is to stay out of my way," Lincoln said. The title "detective" fell from her lips as if it were derogatory.

"Tommy is the only thing that matters," Paula replied.

"I'll do whatever it takes to get him back," John said.

"That will be hard to do with both of you in custody for obstruction. Besides, what proof do you have that the boy is alive? The Outcast Killer doesn't have any history of letting anyone live," Lincoln said.

"Don't tell me about this guy. I've been riding this case for months," John said.

"And you have nothing to show for it. I've been briefed on your amateurish investigation. That's why I'm here. I get results."

John stood. "I don't have to listen to this crap." Before he took a step, one of Lincoln's FBI minions stopped him with a palm flat against his chest.

"Actually, you do have to listen to me. You're going to tell me everything you know. As far as I'm concerned, you may be assisting the killer."

"You can't be serious," John said, pushing the FBI agent's hand away.

"How else would you explain not closing this case? You're in it with him, or you're a crappy cop. Which is it?"

"Fuck you, Lincoln. You think you could do better?" Paula asked.

Agent Lincoln responded to Paula with an icy gaze in her direction, then focused back on John.

"So tell me, what did the message mean, about flying a kite?" Lincoln asked.

"I don't know what Winnow meant," John said.

"I haven't established that Brice Winnow is a person of interest in this case. We don't know who put that message on the screen."

"What? Of course he is," Paula said. "Winnow is the center of the whole thing. We have the photo that ties him to—"

"An old class photo of Weber and Horn isn't enough to tie him to this crime. The prints lifted by your own department and the nursing registry identify the man as Patrick Horn, not Winnow."

"What fantasy world do you live in, lady? Winnow and Horn are the same guy," John said.

"You find any of Winnow's fingerprints? DNA, perhaps? Anything that could be admissible in court? In fact, anyone who could have given testimony against Brice Winnow is dead. One of them died in your interrogation room. Now that's certainly enough to raise some concern, wouldn't you say?"

"Winnow is the Outcast Killer," John said.

"I have nothing to prove that. The mayor's office certainly doesn't support that line of reckless speculation," Lincoln replied.

John stepped close to Agent Lincoln and said, "That's what this is about, covering for the mayor's office?"

"No one is covering for anybody. Baseless allegations have been made against someone with ties to the mayor, allegations by you that appear to be unsubstantiated and without merit. Brice Winnow has asked the court for a restraining order to keep you away from him. He doesn't want to end up dead, like every other person you two have put in the cross hairs."

"You have got to be kidding!" Paula rushed toward Lincoln, and John held her back. "Winnow is our guy. You can't honestly stand there and tell me that he's not!" Paula said.

"I don't have to tell you anything. I'm in charge of this case now." Lincoln stepped past John and took a seat in his desk chair. "So, once more, what did the message mean? The kite reference—was it a flight you arranged for the killer to escape?"

Lincoln leaned back in John's chair and crossed her legs.

"Why would I help him escape?" John said with fists balled tight.

"Wouldn't be the first time a parent arranged the kidnapping of their own child. I'll find out, you know?" She rose from the chair, leaned forward so that her face was inches from John's. "My big question is, did you arrange all this to take the boy away from his mother, or did you do it to get rid of him? He must have been a burden."

"You arrogant—" John started.

Paula stepped in between the FBI agent and John before turning on Lincoln. "You can't actually believe that John had anything to do with Tommy's kidnapping. We have video, for crap's sake."

"Did you know your partner made a rather large withdrawal from his bank account, ten thousand dollars, in the days before the boy's disappearance?" Lincoln let the words hang before she turned toward John once more. "Did that payment go to Patrick Horn?"

"Where do you make this shit up?" Paula asked.

"Nothing made up about it. Ask him," Lincoln said.

"Enough!" The booming voice came from Lieutenant Barnes, standing at the far end of the squad room, near the door. Barnes strode to the center of the cluster of FBI agents and his detectives. His face was blotchy red, with a vein that bulged near his temple. He didn't look like he was here to keep the peace, but John couldn't tell which side the lieutenant would come down on.

"As I was instructing your detectives—" Lincoln started.

"Shut up, Katy. You haven't changed one bit, have you? You may have the mayor's permission to butt in on this investigation, but know this—when it comes to my detectives and their families, you keep your mouth shut."

"If they are withholding information that I need—"

"You'll have everything relevant to this case in the chief's conference room in ten minutes. Detectives Penley and Newberry will provide you copies of all investigative notes on the case. Go. Now!"

Lincoln and her two agents started to the door out of the detective's bureau. Midway, she stopped, turned, and cast a glance at John, then onto Barnes. "The bureau appreciates your cooperation."

"What a . . . a . . ." Paula sputtered.

"A piece of work, I think is what you're looking for," Barnes said.

"She's a piece of something all right," she replied.

"You know her?" John asked Barnes.

"I was on an FBI joint terrorism task force, and Katy Lincoln was a new agent, fresh out of the academy. She had some old-money family connections and ended up posted to the joint terrorism task force instead of a field office in Omaha."

"I take it you two didn't exactly see eye to eye," John said.

"If it were only that simple. She leaked task force information to the media and blew a four-month surveillance operation on a suspected al-Qaeda recruiting cell in Riverside."

"And she didn't get canned for that?" Paula asked.

"You've seen a glimpse of how she works. Katy managed to spin the leak to the media as the reason the terror cell broke down and fled. She used some relationship with a local news reporter to play up her angle and got some face time in front of the camera. Again, the old money and family connection kept her out of the cesspool."

"Why did she come here?" Paula asked.

"She doesn't play well with others, so they send her from place to place, wherever the FBI needs to make an appearance. Believe me, it's not for her investigative prowess," Barnes said.

"You knew she was coming, though?" John said, sitting in his chair, reclaiming it from Lincoln.

Barnes rolled out a chair from an unoccupied desk and pulled it between John and Paula. "I knew the FBI was coming. I didn't know they'd send Lincoln. That's why I signed out the computer to you, Paula, before the FBI got here. If they point at you as a person of interest, we can't do anything. You'll belong to them. Were you able to get anything that will help us find Tommy?"

Paula shook her head. "No, that piece of sh . . . Lincoln hacked the computer as we got in contact with Winnow. Some convoluted message about kites."

"John, you know what that means, don't you?" Barnes asked.

"I think so," he said.

"You do?" Paula asked. "Why didn't you say so?"

"I couldn't risk Lincoln ruining my chance to find my son. I figured out the message from Winnow after Lincoln busted in."

"What did it mean?" Paula asked.

"Winnow—his message to me was, 'Tommy would have liked to fly his kite again.' The only place Tommy and I went to fly kites was in Discovery Park."

"How would he know that?" Barnes said.

"When was the last time you and Tommy went there?" Paula asked.

"Over a year ago."

Lieutenant Barnes leaned back in his chair, comfortable in the investigator role. "He's been watching Tommy long before his surgery got cancelled."

"Why watch Tommy?" John asked.

"Or was he following you, the investigator?" Paula added.

"Whatever he's doing, he's been planning this a long time," John said.

"What do we do?" Paula said.

"*We* don't do anything. I'm going to Discovery Park alone. He wants me there, and I know, sure as hell, he'll be watching."

THIRTY-FIVE

Discovery Park sits on a low section of bottomland, north of the Sacramento downtown corridor. The flood-control system of weirs and levees releases river overflow into the park during the wet season and turns the park into a vast, swampy wasteland. John slipped a car from the police motor pool and tracked through the thick muck left behind by the receding floodwater. As long as he stayed on the paved sections, the sedan's wheels wouldn't suck down into the waterlogged soil.

Yellow metal barriers blocked the road, restricting vehicle access deeper into the park. Well after sunset, the waterside recreation area transformed into a black hole enclosed by trees, riverbanks, and levee walls. The vast darkness gobbled the light a few yards from John's headlights. John peered ahead into shadows within shadows. Barren tree limbs quivered in the light breeze, like thousands of tiny skeleton hands reaching out from beyond.

John stopped at the barrier, turned off his lights, and scanned the nightscape for another car or anything that announced the exchange location. Tommy wouldn't be able to walk very far in his condition. Winnow would ensure an escape route for himself.

He cut the ignition, stepped onto the mud-slicked roadway, and listened. The breeze muffled the traffic noise from Interstate 5. Branches rubbed against one another and cracked in the distance, but nothing gave away the position of a waiting car with an idling motor.

As John's eyes adjusted to the pitch black around him, the faint outline of distant trees came into focus to his left. A large, grassy field spanned several acres between the muddy roadway and the trees on the far side of the open space.

John squatted and saw no other tire tracks in the mud, nor footprints other than his own. On the surface, at least, Winnow had yet to arrive. An uncertainty plucked at the flesh at the back of his neck. The gooseflesh came from the cold river wind. If Winnow were watching, John figured the chill would cut to the bone.

He took a position on a small rise near the roadway, where he could survey the entrance to the park and the grass field. He leaned against a tree, blending his moon-shadow with the one cast by an ancient, gnarled oak.

His mind drifted to the last time he and Tommy were in this park. The diagnosis of renal disease was fresh, and yet Tommy seemed so vibrant and alive. The boy ran in the grass field, trying to get his Spider-Man kite to take flight. John laughed so hard that day watching his son that his sides ached for hours afterward. There was a different ache now, and he hadn't laughed in months. John wiped at his cheek and rubbed a moist spot. He hadn't realized he was crying.

According to his watch, which he had checked five minutes ago and five minutes before that, he had waited two hours with nothing from Winnow. John's skin and clothing were damp from the dew in the moisture-laden air.

A rustle in the tree line to his left got his attention. He craned his neck and peered into the blackness. He listened through his throbbing skull. Nothing, not another snapped branch or imaginary footfall echoed back at him. The park fell silent; the only sounds John heard were his heartbeat and ragged breath.

A low rumble vibrated in the valley. He chalked it up to a semi-truck passing on the interstate. Then he realized the sound came from somewhere forward from his location, not from the overpass. He took a tentative step from the rise, down into the grass field.

The rumble was beyond the tree line on the other side of the park. After two more steps, thick, heavy mud and blades of grass clung to his shoes.

The source of the sound lay ahead, and he picked up his pace, slogging through the wet park bottomland. His weighted shoes made each step more difficult than the last, and his legs pumped hard to keep on course.

The rumble deepened and ramped up in volume. A throaty exhaust sound ripped the silence in the park. John recognized the sound as a boat engine. His mind fired visions of Tommy in the water as he ran toward the riverbank.

The levee bank was steep and slippery with dew-covered grass. John stumbled and fell facedown in the muck as the boat-engine sound pulled away. He clambered up the levee bank to the gravel maintenance road on the crest. The sound of the engine reverberated in the river channel, but John couldn't make out a boat, only a silver sheen in the water from the vessel's receding wake. John stood on the levee road and scanned both directions, hoping for, and fearing, a glimpse of Tommy.

He sidestepped down the levee bank toward the waterline, slipping on the slick grass. With his left arm against the bank for support, John edged closer to the bottom, moving crablike down the embankment. John tracked the ripples from the vanishing boat's wake to a spot fifteen feet upriver and discovered a deep gouge in the mud marked where a boat had touched ashore, similar to the track left when Cardozo's body was dumped.

He had no reason to trust that Winnow would deliver Tommy. The message the Outcast Killer had left on the computer screen had meaning beyond the crazed ravings of a madman. Any other explanation took John to a dark place, void of hope. His mind drifted to memories of his son calling out for him.

"Daddy?"

It was the plaintive cry of a lonely, lost boy. John shook his head to rid the imaginary voice from his mind.

"Daddy?"

John popped up, facing the direction of the voice. Even in the dim light, he could see that his son wasn't there. His pulse raced. He knew his son's voice; there was no mistaking it. It was the sound Tommy made when he was scared. But Tommy wasn't here. Was this what it was like to go insane?

John slogged through the river muck toward the sound. Tommy sounded close, but there was no one there. He pivoted, not trusting his senses, looking for his son.

"Tommy?" he called out to the invisible voice.

Silence.

John peered into the brush along the riverbank and into the rushing current, looking for the boy.

"Daddy?"

John knew he was close.

A light-blue flicker shone two paces ahead.

John tumbled over a slick rock and landed chest first into the mud.

He scrambled on his hands and knees, closer to the sound, and reached for the blue object. When he touched it, John knew what it was: the sleeve of Tommy's favorite jacket poked through the mud.

The cries for help from the unseen boy continued, buried in the mud underneath him. He clawed into the mud, pulling on the exposed section of the sleeve, and uncovered the rest of the jacket, less than an inch under the surface.

Tommy's voice came through much clearer now.

John followed the voice that came from the jacket. He felt a lump in the sleeve, and bile collected in his throat, knowing the rancid gifts Winnow left behind. A glow illuminated through the fabric, and John found the source of his son's voice. It wasn't imaginary; it came from a cell phone.

"Tommy? Tommy, where are you?" John said, holding the cell phone to his ear.

After there was no answer from his son, John looked at the screen. The phone showed an incoming call from a blocked number. Tommy's voice was set as the ringtone.

John stabbed at the green accept-call button, held the phone close to his ear, and said, "Tommy?"

It wasn't Tommy's voice that greeted him. "I was nearly ready to give up on you, Detective," Brice Winnow said.

"Where is he, you son of a bitch?"

"Oh, he's around somewhere, or maybe around several somewheres. You know how I tend to leave bits and pieces."

"What do you want from me? You left that message so I'd come out here. Well, here I am."

"Just want to get right to it, eh? No exchange of pleasantries or idle chitchat, as they say? Fine. Are you listening closely, Detective? I provided you a cell phone. Think of it as your son's lifeline."

"What do you want, Winnow?"

"Interrupt me again and we're done here. You understand?"

"Tell me," John said, kneeling in the mud.

"If I disconnect our call, your boy dies. If you hang up, the boy dies. This connection must remain open or the boy dies. You contact anyone, he dies. Understand? Do you understand?"

"I understand," John said. "How do I know you have him and that he's okay?"

Winnow laughed. "Not a trusting soul, are you? I get it. Pull up the camera on your phone."

The phone shook in his hand, and John hesitated to push any button for fear of disconnecting the call. He found a small icon with a picture of a camera on the screen. He pressed it, and the screen flashed, then went dark.

"Hello?" More than a small edge of panic seeped into John's voice.

Over the cell phone's small speaker, Winnow said, "A surveillance camera feed is linked to your phone. Look at it all you want.

That comes with a risk, as your phone battery will burn away each second you linger."

John picked up a slight movement in the picture on the screen. The camera provided a grainy, jumpy video feed, but it was enough to show Tommy, curled up on a filthy mattress.

"Tommy! Tommy, it's Dad!" John cried.

"Oh, Tommy! Tommy!" Winnow mimicked. "He can't hear you. Turn the camera off, or you won't have enough battery life and neither will Tommy."

John hesitated and took one more look before he made the video feed vanish.

"So we begin. If you do exactly as you're told, I will release your son."

"Why should I trust you?"

"Trust, Detective? This isn't about trust, it's about keeping the boy alive."

John's thumb hovered over the camera button, longing for another glimpse of Tommy.

"Warehouse, northeast corner of Tenth and R Street. Go there. Fifteen minutes."

"I can't get there in fifteen minutes," John said, already scrabbling up the levee embankment.

"You don't have a choice, Detective."

"Winnow!" John said, with no response. He looked at the phone to ensure the call remained connected and the screen counted up the call time.

John reached the top of the levee and ran across the open field toward his parked sedan. Mud clung to his feet and caused him to trip on an exposed tree root. He fell forward, still cradling the cell phone. He couldn't risk breaking his fall with his arms and took the full force of the fall on his chest, knocking the wind from his burning lungs. The concussion dizziness returned, fogging his mind for a moment.

He pushed up to his knees and struggled to pull air into his chest. With a half breath, he stood and slogged to the car. The cobwebs in his brain loosened. He held the phone up and reassured the fall hadn't broken his line to the killer, or rather his lifeline to Tommy.

John reached his car and didn't waste time knocking the river mud from his shoes or the slime from his shirt before he jumped behind the wheel. The detective started the engine, threw the transmission in reverse, and jammed the wheel to the left, spinning the car around on the slick surface.

He punched the accelerator and shot out of the park entrance, entrusting his son's future to vague promises from a sadistic serial killer.

THIRTY-SIX

The section of R Street near Tenth was a mix of commercial businesses, restaurants, and a couple of trendy bars. As directed, John pulled up to a warehouse on the northeast corner, and it appeared abandoned, with a faded sign that read, *For Sale or Lease.*

"I'm here," John said into the cell phone.

"Good. The door is locked with a combination lock. Spin the dial to 23-30-7 and go inside."

John held the phone against his chin as he worked the combination. The lock unsnapped on the first attempt. He pocketed the lock and hefted the rust-covered door, only to find it opened on smooth, well-oiled hinges.

"Is Tommy here?"

"Go inside. Light switch, on the wall by the door."

"You didn't answer me," John said.

"No, I didn't. Now do as I say, quickly."

John felt around the doorframe and located the light switches. He remembered his near electrocution at the last warehouse, but he pushed forward until he found the switch plate. He toggled the switch up, and heavy-duty industrial lights buzzed overhead, the bulbs growing brighter as they warmed. He closed the door behind him.

"All right, I'm inside," John said.

John peered into the cavernous warehouse. A separate structure sat squarely in the center of the floor. As the lights brightened, John recognized the building as a metal storage shed, large enough to cover two full-size cars. All along the outside walls of the shed, cotton pads, old mattresses, and insulation were draped over the panels—makeshift soundproofing to deaden audible noises from inside the box. The thought of Winnow eviscerating his victims in this place brought bile into John's throat.

"See the table, in front of my workroom?" Winnow asked.

A folding table, with a stained white plastic top, sat on one side of the shed. Cardboard boxes, glass bottles, and coils of clear rubber tubing covered the table's surface. Under the table, five-gallon containers of industrial solvents and cleaners lined the floor.

Mud fell from John's shoes in large clumps as he approached the table, but his attention honed in on the sliding shed doors. A sliver of light slipped through the crack between the doors from inside.

"Penley, pay attention here. On the corner of the table, there is a Bluetooth earpiece for the phone. Get it. You're going to need to use both hands."

John put the phone on the table while he put the earpiece in his right ear.

"There, you should be able to hear me now, Detective," Winnow said.

John wheeled around. The only way Winnow would know that he had picked up the earpiece was if he watched him do it. He only half expected the man to show himself and wasn't surprised when he spotted the camera mounted on a beam above.

"Yeah, I hear you," John said, staring back at the camera's black eye.

"Good. Pocket the phone. You have a lot of work to do in very little time."

"When do I get my boy?" John said. He noticed the battery meter on the cell phone registered 20 percent.

"Maybe the boy is behind those doors."

John shoved the phone in his pocket, sprinted for the shed's sliding door, and shoved it aside. The garage-sized space was a fully equipped surgical suite. Monitors, wires, and tubes hung limp from stainless-steel racks. Meat hooks, reminiscent of those John had stumbled into at the Layton barn, draped from an iron frame. Two huge boom lights shone down on a pair of autopsy tables. The lipped tables had a slight angle to contain and direct blood and bodily fluids out a drain at one end. One-inch rubber tubes connected the tables to a floor drain, and the brown discoloration was evidence of repeated use.

John's knees buckled when he recognized that one of the tables held a body, covered with a plastic tarp from the neck down. An instant rush of guilt and relief washed over him when he registered that the body was too large to be Tommy's.

He approached the body, and from the gray pallor of the skin, John knew this man was long dead. He pulled back the tarp and found the trademark Outcast Killer incisions and empty chest cavity.

"You haven't come very far from your stepfather's barn," John said.

"Layton was an animal!" It was a momentary loss of composure, a fissure in the cool facade Winnow projected.

"Whatever—Patrick. Enough of your sick game of show-and-tell."

"It is my game, don't forget that."

Winnow paused, and his voice came across cold and composed once more. "Meet James Lind. Mr. Lind's donations will allow more than a dozen transactions to occur. His A-positive blood type is very popular in certain Asian countries. That's what it's all about. The high-demand blood types, A positive, AB positive. We track them and go find them."

"Why are you telling me this?"

"Because you are going to help me," Winnow instructed.

"I can't do this."

"Want to see little Tommy again?"

"You can't ask me to cut somebody up," John said.

"No, no, Detective, I couldn't trust you to handle such a delicate task. I've harvested the good bits from Mr. Lind. See the three briefcases on the floor?"

John turned and spotted the cases, identical to the one left at the old ice plant. "Yes, I see them."

"Take them to the worktable out in the main room. I will guide you through the next steps."

John hefted all three cases at once and brought them to the worktable, setting them atop one another. The odor of chemicals, especially acetone, near the table and Lind's body burned his nose. "Okay, what am I supposed to do?"

"You are going to replace the perfusion pump in each case with a new pump and battery pack."

"I don't know how to do that."

"You'd better learn fast. You are on a deadline here, remember?"

"What do I do?"

"Open one of the cases. The perfusion pump is the clear, circular object with tubes attached to each end. Take a new pump from the boxes to your left, clip on a new battery pack, and swap out the old one in the case."

John recognized the pump from the discussion he'd had with Dr. Kelly. His fingers trembled as he popped open the first case. He raised the lid and revealed a thick, foam-padded interior with sections cut out for the battery, perfusion pump, and a clear plastic container. The case held a human heart submerged in icy-cold perfusion fluid. Liquid coursed through the pump to the stolen heart with a low hum. John winced at the grotesque display.

As instructed, John took a new pump from the box, clipped on a new battery pack, and removed the old mechanism from the case. The pump stopped its low purr when John disconnected it. He expected a burst of perfusion fluid, but the one-way valves in the lines prevented the frigid solution from escaping. John finished the swap, then closed and secured the locks on the case.

"Good. Quickly now, get to the next two," Winnow said.

John quickened his pace and swapped out the pumps and battery packs in the other two cases. One held a pair of kidneys, while the other container had a mass of tissue, which could have been liver, pancreas, or spleen to John's harried mind.

"I'm finished."

"Almost."

John faced the camera. "What?"

"Take your gun, badge, and wallet and place them on the table. No, I didn't forget about the gun, Detective. Then take the cases to the car."

"I'm your delivery boy now?" John questioned. Following the killer's instructions, the gun, badge, and wallet went on the table.

"Before you leave, look behind you."

John swiveled, hoping that the madman would reveal Tommy. Instead, an electronic *click-click-click* rattled inside the shed, followed by a quick, bright flash of flame. The Outcast Killer torched his acetone-saturated workroom by remote control.

The flames spread quickly, pouncing on Lind's body and the equipment inside. The insulation on the walls of the shed served as tinder to the flames, intensifying the height of the inferno. John put up a hand to shield himself from the heat, and in his earpiece, he heard, "Better hurry, Detective."

John lugged the cases and made it to the door as a chemical explosion lit up the interior of the warehouse. Within seconds, flames licked through the roof. The fire spread quickly; clearly, Winnow had wired the place to burn.

Patrons from a nearby bar started coming out onto the sidewalk and pointed at the burning warehouse. A couple of them yelled while John put the metal cases in his trunk. He couldn't hear what they said, but he knew what it looked like, fleeing the scene of a fire. A dozen witnesses watched him in front of the burning building, loading containers into a car that would trace back to the police motor pool. He wished the gawkers were more interested in calling the fire department than in taking cell-phone videos of the blaze.

John started the car, spun the rear wheels in reverse, shifted into drive, and sped off down R Street. In the rearview mirror, a blonde woman pointed her cell-phone camera and captured video of his escape.

"I'm not your errand boy! Let me have my son."

"I prefer to call it insurance. Don't make me cancel the policy."

John's knuckles seized hard on the steering wheel when he saw a swarm of red emergency lights flock toward him. They would stop him, arrest him for the arson, and find body parts in the trunk. Human remains would take time to explain. He couldn't afford the delay in finding Tommy.

"What am I supposed to do?" John demanded.

"Don't get caught," the voice said through the earpiece.

"I've done what you asked."

"Go to Mather Field."

The blaring siren from a fire engine drowned out the killer's instructions. A second truck followed close behind, bleating an air-powered horn. No black-and-white police units converged on the intersection to cut off John's escape.

The moment the sound diminished, John said, "Mather?"

"There is a chartered Learjet parked and waiting on the tarmac. Get there and deliver the containers to the air ambulance staff."

"How am I supposed to do that?" he asked, turning east on B Street.

"Figure it out. You have fifteen minutes."

"I can't get there in fifteen. I need more time."

"You have those containers on that plane in fifteen minutes, or Tommy takes their place."

John whipped the sedan around a white-and-blue Regional Transit bus, cutting off traffic in the lane to his left. He sped up, taking advantage of the light night traffic.

"I need more time!"

He heard nothing in return from the killer, only an extended silence.

"You hear me? I need more time!"

The cell phone remained silent.

John lifted his hips up off the seat and pulled the cell phone from his pocket. He glanced down at the screen. The call timer ticked off second by second, confirming he hadn't lost his connection. John tapped the camera icon. As before, the screen flickered, and an image of Tommy appeared. The boy faced the camera, curled up with his knees to his chest, rocking back and forth.

John couldn't look at the pitiful image without choking up. He clicked the camera off, and white-hot anger swirled in his gut. John hit the gas pedal and shot across vacant downtown intersections. Stoplights meant nothing now.

A dark sedan blowing through downtown draws attention. One with flashing red lights is residue of another gang shooting in midtown, dismissed as background noise. He flicked the switch on the dash, activating the bar of red strobe lights at the top of the front windshield. The wash of the red lights reflected off building facades, and pedestrians paid little notice.

John stabbed at the gas pedal, shot up the on-ramp that connected to the Capital City Freeway, and merged onto US 50, eastbound. He glanced down at the speedometer, and the needle edged at ninety miles per hour. The digital clock on the dash warned that he had burned five precious minutes getting to the freeway.

The Mather Field exit didn't slow John's progress. He drifted the car to the right as he made the turn toward the deactivated air force base. The sprawling facility, once the home of a B-52 bomber group, now served as a social services depot and a drop-off point for homeless shelters converted from the old barracks. The decommissioned terminal and runway serviced the local National Guard contingent and scores of air cargo flights.

John followed the signs to the cargo terminal through the maze of squat, concrete buildings.

"Two minutes, Detective. You're cutting it very close. Take the next left into the cargo delivery gate."

The killer knew John's exact location. The cell phone must have a GPS tracker so Winnow could follow his every move. *Smart*, John thought. He would have done the same thing.

He turned at the gate and slowed, unsure how he was going to explain his way into a secured terminal area. Instead, an armed security guard waved him through the open chain-link gate.

The guard pointed to a lone Learjet parked on the tarmac a hundred feet to his right.

John waved at the guard and steered to the jet, parking behind the sleek blue-and-white craft. Lettering on the side of the plane read, *Medi-Flight*. Marker lights on the wingtips flashed, and as soon as he opened his car door, a whine erupted from the twin engines mounted high on the tail section.

A man in a blue flight suit with EMT patches on the shoulders jogged down the stairway from the cabin door. He approached John at a rapid pace and extended his hand.

"I wasn't sure if you were going to make it on time," the EMT said.

"Who told you to wait?" John asked. He had to yell over the engine noise.

The EMT shrugged. "They don't tell me that. All I know is that we were to expect an organ transfer, in two cases."

"Two? I have three," John said.

"What? Where are they?"

John motioned and walked to the trunk. He unlocked the lid and pulled it open, revealing the three metal cases.

The EMT pulled a sheet of paper from a zippered flight-suit pocket and compared numbers on his document with small numbers near the handles of the cases, numbers that John hadn't noticed in the hurry to get them out of the burning building.

"These two are mine," the EMT said, lifting two of the cases out of the trunk.

"What about this one?" John asked.

"Not mine. I gotta get these going." The EMT turned to leave, and John grabbed him by the elbow.

"Where are you taking them?"

"Flight plan is filed for Mexico City. Where they go once we turn them over is a part of the book I never get to read."

"Who else is on board?"

"What?"

"Is there a patient on the flight? A boy?" John asked.

"No, only me and the two guys driving this thing."

John grabbed the handle of one of the cases. "Let me help you with that." He started walking to the foot of the stairs when a voice whispered into his earpiece.

"You are wasting my time, Detective."

John hustled up the stairs with the case. Inside the plane, the passenger cabin was vacant. Two pilots hovered over controls and checklists in the cockpit, but there was no sign of Tommy.

"Put the case on that rack," the EMT said, pointing at a sturdy frame with thick lashing straps.

The case fit into one of the open bays on the rack and locked into place.

"Thanks for the hand, but we gotta get this in the air."

"You haven't seen a little boy?"

"No." The EMT turned away and worked at the lashing straps that made certain the cases wouldn't budge in heavy turbulence.

John took his cell phone and hit the camera button once more. Tommy remained in place on the ratty mattress.

John got to the top of the stairway, and the EMT closed the cabin door before he hit the second step. A heavy clunk announced that it had locked into place. He trotted down the stairs as the engines changed pitch, growing louder. As soon as John touched the tarmac, an airport employee rolled the stairs away from the jet.

"Where's my son?" John said over the roar of the taxiing jet.

Winnow answered with, "Leave the car and walk away."

"What? I've done everything you wanted."

"My game, my rules."

John turned in time to watch the Medi-Flight jet lift off and bank off to the south.

"Congratulations! Thank you for playing. You've completed this round. Your wife is on her way to pick up the boy."

"How did you . . . ?"

"Doesn't matter, Detective. I will release the boy to her, as long as you cooperate," Winnow said.

From the corner of his eye, John noticed a small caravan of black SUVs appear from around a building. Blinking blue lights flashed on their grills. They raced toward his location.

"What's going on?"

"Cooperate," Winnow said.

The cell-phone connection went dead. John pulled out the phone, and the display confirmed that the call had terminated. John hit redial and received a recorded response: "The number you have reached is no longer in service. Please check the number and dial again."

The SUV caravan came to a stop, one vehicle behind him and one on either side. Men in black tactical vests and Kevlar helmets hopped out, stubby automatic rifles directed at John.

"FBI! Drop whatever you have in your hand! Get down on your knees!" one of the men said, edging closer.

"I'm a cop! My son's been taken," John said as he dropped to his knees.

"Face down, Penley. You know the drill."

"What are you doing?" John asked.

"Sir, we have one," another officer said from behind John's car. He lifted the case from the sedan's trunk. "No sign of Horn."

An FBI agent called out, "Penley, you're coming with us. Agent Lincoln isn't going to be a happy camper."

THIRTY-SEVEN

The holding cells in the FBI building were little more than windowless offices with a reinforced door. Everything about the room was temporary, including the government surplus chair, a bunk with a US Army property tag, and a stainless-steel sink-and-toilet combo unit that looked like it came from a scratch-and-dent sale at Leavenworth. The single thing that hinted at the room's purpose was the metal plate on the inside of the door where a doorknob should have been.

John sat on the edge of the bunk and rubbed the red welts from where the handcuffs had cut into his skin. The cuffs had come off when they'd tossed him in this custodial way station while Lincoln and company figured out their next move.

A shadow crossed the six-by-six-inch window in the door. The bunk springs creaked when John rose. Out in the hall, one of Lincoln's men sat in a chair facing the door. The man showed no expression when John peeked through the window glass.

John paced back to the bunk. He couldn't sit still while his son was out there, stashed away like last week's garbage. The worst scenarios tumbled through his mind. He knew what Winnow did to the people he kept. Tommy was a liability, an object Winnow no longer needed for leverage.

An expressionless FBI agent's face filled the small window, and the lock mechanism clacked as the bolt unlocked. The agent opened the door and stood back. Special Agent Lincoln strode into the room with two uniformed federal officers. Lincoln stopped a few feet from the doorway.

"You've lost your damn mind, Lincoln." The frustration made John's words venomous. "You people are dicking around while my son is still out there."

Special Agent K. Lincoln looked down her nose at John. She paced in front of the small metal table as she spoke.

"Between the two of us, Mr. Penley, I'd say that you're the one who's lost his mind. I mean, I get it. I get why you thought you needed to go out on your own. But you couldn't think you'd ever get away with this."

"Listen, I told you. Winnow told me to pick up those cases. I did what he told me to do so I could get Tommy back."

Agent Lincoln sat in a chair across from John and leaned forward. She spoke in a soft voice. "I understand, and I want to help you. You've gotten in way over your head, so make it easy on all of us and tell us where he is."

"I don't know where that asshole is," John said. The exasperation bubbled over in his voice.

"For a time, I wondered what you may have done with the boy."

"Boy? Wait, my son? You think I did something to my son? Find Melissa. Winnow said he was going to release Tommy to her."

"It has to be a huge financial drain, having a kid with all these medical bills. I think we've had this discussion before. I have to ask. Child abduction is a nasty thing. Did you have anything to do with Tommy's disappearance?"

"Brice Winnow has him," John said.

"I know. We all saw the video. He took him from the hospital."

One of the FBI agents handed Lincoln a file folder. She placed it in front of her and made a show of opening and turning a few pages. She relished having something John didn't.

"It says here you were recently denied a home-equity loan. I imagine you needed that to pay down some of those hefty medical bills." Lincoln didn't bother looking up from the file. "It sure would be nice to have that problem go away."

"That's why we needed the loan."

"So your idea was to get rid of the problem? Right?" she asked.

"What are you talking about? You saw him take my son on that hospital surveillance video."

"Did he take the boy for you?" she said, closing the file.

John looked across the table in disbelief. He couldn't imagine how she could make that connection. It was wild fantasy, unless . . .

Lincoln saw the uncertainty in John's face. "I know about the ten-thousand-dollar payment made to Patrick Horn's account."

John shook his head. "There was no payment."

"You paid Horn to abduct the boy and then set up this elaborate chase. Can you explain the ten-thousand-dollar deposit into Horn's account?"

"I don't know anything about a ten-thousand-dollar deposit." John remembered the web pages on his laptop—the ones he hadn't opened.

"What was that?"

"I've told you everything I know. I want my son."

"Give your wife some closure. Tell me what you did."

John fell silent.

"This is your last opportunity. Tell me. You paid ten thousand dollars to Patrick Horn, didn't you?"

"No."

She held the file in front of him. "I have your own bank records showing an electronic transfer of the money to Horn's account."

Lincoln stood from the table, tucked the file under her arm. "I know you didn't have anything to do with the human remains we recovered in the trunk of your car. Lieutenant Barnes and that partner of yours managed to get you crossed off the suspect list, for now. But there is still a connection between you and the killer—the money and your son's disappearance. That isn't easily explained away."

"Brice Winnow set all this up, the killings, the organ harvesting, and he took my son."

Lincoln paced, avoided eye contact with Penley, and said, "And your interference in this investigation put me further behind."

John started to respond, but Lincoln waved him off.

"Maybe there is a way for you to get us back on track," she said.

"Fine, let me go after him."

"Call Winnow and get him talking. We'll monitor the conversation. Get him to give up something incriminating."

"How does that help me get Tommy?"

"If Winnow is who you think he is, he'll lure you in with a chance to reclaim your son. When he does, we'll have the hostage rescue team ready to respond. HRT will put this son of a bitch down."

"He won't come out of hiding to take a phone call. He'll demand something more secure."

Lincoln leaned on the table, palms flat, and leaned in toward John. "What do you have in mind?"

"I need access to my laptop. I contacted him before, I can do it again," John said.

Lincoln pondered the idea for a moment. "He's too smart for that. He picked up that we hacked the connection last time."

"Then don't. Stand over my shoulder if you have to, but don't give him any reason to think you're listening."

Lincoln stood, straightened the hem of her jacket, and nodded. She looked to one of her men and said, "Bring her in."

The door opened, and a confused Paula Newberry entered.

"Your partner is ready to go. Pick up your laptop and wear this." Lincoln slid an undercover radio transmitter across the table.

"I'm wearing a wire?"

"You narrate what Winnow says, and I will be with the HRT on the takedown."

"Rescue, not takedown," John said.

"All the more reason for you to be precise and get him to give up the location."

THIRTY-EIGHT

"Do you trust that skank, Lincoln?" Paula asked as they pushed into the detective bureau with the liberated laptop.

"You know she can hear you, right?"

"I don't care. She knows what she is. How do you know that she didn't have the FBI cybercrime people mess with your laptop while they had it?"

"As long as Winnow pops up long enough for us to get a bead on him, it doesn't matter."

John put the laptop on his desk, plugged it in, and powered it up. Too anxious to sit, he tapped his fingertips on the desktop while the machine booted up.

Paula pulled her chair around to the desk. "What if this doesn't draw him out?"

"It will," he said as he brought the web browser up once more. There were multiple windows open on the screen. Lincoln had begun to reconstruct his browsing history and communication with Winnow over the dark web. One window didn't look familiar, and his breath caught when he read the thread. His hand shot to the mouse and closed the window. "Dammit, Mel, what have you done?"

"What?" Paula asked.

"Nothing—nothing. Lincoln must have erased all my saved passwords. I'm trying to remember where to log in."

She pointed at one of the open Tor dark web browsers.

He clicked on one of the windows, and it required him to log into the account. "Paula, pull the photo of the tag from Winnow's briefcase at the ice plant."

"Got it." She had the file in her lap, and he sorted through the documents until she found a closeup shot of the tag addressed to her partner.

"Read off the numbers on the bottom of the tag."

He entered the sequence as she read the numbers, and the screen unlocked as it did the first time John stumbled across the portal.

"I'm beginning communication with Winnow now, Agent Lincoln."

John spoke as he typed for the benefit of the feds on the other end of the transmitter.

The cursor on the screen blinked at the end of the last letter John typed.

"Maybe he's not online," Paula said.

"He is. Remember Layton's last words? He wants me in exchange for Tommy. He'll be waiting for this contact."

"The old man was insane. You can't believe anything he said."

The echo of her last word still hung in the air when the cursor began to move.

What if I told you it's too late? John read the question aloud.

John typed, *I'll kill you if anything happens to Tommy.* Then John said aloud, "I know you want me in exchange for my son."

Paula looked to John and nodded. She understood he was giving Lincoln a different account.

The screen blinked again. *I told you I'd release the boy, and I will.* "We can work something out," John said for Lincoln's benefit.

John tapped the keys. *When?*

The cursor scrolled out again with Winnow's response. *I have a client who is in a great hurry for my services. Remember when I told you to cooperate? The time for that has come.* John tensed and said, "He wants to meet."

Paula grabbed him by the elbow and raised an eyebrow, a look that asked if he was sure about this course of action.

He patted her hand and then tapped the keyboard.

It's time we continue this face to face. "I'm asking him to meet." No embellishment needed this time.

Agreed. Meet me at the place where we first met in one hour. Come alone or the boy dies. No FBI, no Detective Newberry—nobody, or your son will vanish. Understood?

John pushed back from the keyboard for a moment to compose himself. "He wants to meet. He says to meet him at Raley Field in an hour."

John scooted back to the keyboard and replied. *Understood.*

The cursor came alive once more. *What was your blood type, again?*

He shut the laptop down, closed the lid, picked it up with both hands, and slammed the laptop against the edge of the desk. The plastic and glass shattered, sending laptop shrapnel across the floor.

John's desk phone rang, and Paula grabbed it while he brushed broken laptop pieces into his trash can. She held the phone to him. "Lincoln."

He flicked a piece of plastic that pierced his palm and took the phone from Paula.

"Yeah."

"The computer went offline, what happened?" Lincoln asked.

"I dropped it."

"He said Raley Field in an hour. We'll have all of our HRT teams in place to take him down. You will stay away while I conduct this operation."

"Don't you think he'll expect to see me?"

"Doesn't matter. We'll tighten the noose before he realizes it. We'll get him."

"And Tommy?"

"Yes, of course." An afterthought. "Stay put," she commanded, then hung up.

Penley ripped the transmitter from his shirt and disconnected the feed. "You were right about Lincoln monitoring the laptop, but she didn't see what was on the screen, only that we connected with Winnow."

"You sure this is the right play here? Going in alone against this psycho?"

"I can't have Lincoln fumbling my only chance at getting Tommy so she can get good press. And I'm not gonna put you in a position where you could end your career because of me."

"You don't get to tell me what I can't do." She pushed away from the desk and took a stride, only looking back long enough to make eye contact with her partner. "Let's get your son."

They rode in silence to the abandoned ice plant off Fifteenth Street. John turned off the headlights as he slid the sedan onto the rough asphalt surface.

Paula spotted it first and pointed at the yellow sports car parked at the entrance.

"The guy drives his ego," John said.

"Pull up here, on the other side of that dumpster. We'll have some cover if he gets jumpy."

John rolled the sedan to a stop. "Paula, stay here. If he comes out with Tommy, take him."

John stepped from the car and pulled his weapon, stepping to the passenger side of Winnow's car. Empty. He moved up the metal steps that led to the warehouse door, and the old metal groaned under his weight. The sound was loud enough to announce his arrival. He crossed the threshold, where he had nearly electrocuted himself the last time he'd entered this place.

The spotlight in the center of the building that had once illuminated the remains of the dead hawk now shone down on a child-sized lump sitting in a chair.

John ran to the chair and pulled a pillowcase from over the figure. It was only a rolled-up mattress from one of the homeless people who combed through these buildings after dark.

A strong hand clamped over his mouth, and he felt a sharp jab to his neck. His vision soon narrowed to a pinprick, and his knees gave out. He couldn't control his movement. His weapon fell from his grip and clattered to the concrete floor. John felt his body moving before everything went black.

THIRTY-NINE

A bright lightning bolt of pain erupted inside John's brain. Electric hate shot through every single neuron and made his gray matter boil from the inside. Pain signaled that he wasn't dead yet.

A faraway moan rose and ebbed. The anguished, mournful cry sounded once more, and John realized the wail erupted from his own throat.

Another sound, off in the background, drew his attention. Sobbing, as soft as a lamb's bleat, came from his left. His eyes fluttered and opened a fraction of an inch. The dim light around him knifed through to the back of his skull when he tried to focus on his surroundings. Everything was sideways: the dirty concrete block walls, shelves of beakers, bottles, trays of scalpels, hemostats, and medical equipment. John realized he was the one who was sideways, flat on his back.

To his left, a dark doorway opened to another room or chamber. An irregular, yellow flicker reflected on a wall in that distant room. John recognized a similar light pattern behind him as well—candlelight. The rooms, lit with scores of candles, bore no visible sign of electric lighting, nor windows to the outside. As John's senses reawakened, the dank, musty odor of the place filled the air. An earthen, tomb-like dampness meant underground—a cellar, the wine cellar from the video at Zack Weber's place.

The sobbing from the next room distracted John. The familiarity of the cry finally sunk in. "Tommy, is that you?" he said in a weak voice.

A shadow loomed directly overhead and shifted to John's left, where the candlelight caught Winnow in profile.

"I'm very disappointed, Detective," Winnow said.

"Where's my son?"

"Near."

"I did everything you asked."

"I told you to cooperate."

"I won't cooperate with a sick bastard butchering innocent people."

Winnow's hand snaked out from the shadow and clamped down on John's face. He forcibly shook the detective's head. "No. No. No. That's not right. No one is innocent." Winnow released his grip after the scolding.

"They know all about you, Winnow, or Horn, whatever you call yourself now."

Winnow leaned and cocked his head to one side, as if inspecting an insect. "You know nothing. Patrick Horn was weak. Look what I've become—powerful, feared, and revered."

"Who the fuck reveres you?"

"Who indeed? You, for one. So did every last person who did as I instructed for a chance at life."

John didn't respond fast enough. Winnow tapped on John's forehead with a sharp fingertip in synch with his words. "You. Don't. Get. It. Every last one of you knew what you were dealing with. The organs you wanted have to come from somewhere. You chose me."

"I didn't choose you. Johnson, Mercer, and Cardozo didn't ask for what happened to them," John said.

The killer clucked his tongue. "Detective, really? They were of no value."

"How would you know?"

"I'm disappointed you didn't make the connection. Every last one of them was a drain, a parasite that needed to be cut off. Gang members sucking at the public teat. Hell, I had the gangs giving up each other. Welfare, disability, unemployment, prison, all draining resources without contributing. Until I found a way to thin the herd."

"What about me?"

"The single thing my stepfather taught me was when a pig costs more to support than it's worth, it's time to butcher it."

"What did your stepfather mean when he told me that it was his fault?" John asked.

Winnow paused as he considered the question. "Did he, now? He showed me everything I know about slaughtering pigs, all different kinds of pigs."

The dead echo of the wine-cellar walls, damp and loamy, meant any scream would disappear into the earthen tomb, unheard.

"Layton didn't teach you this."

"He's used that simple farmer persona more than once."

"It's time to stop. You got your revenge on your stepfather, if that's what this was about." The words fell hollow, more pleading than John intended.

Winnow's shoulders tensed. "Revenge? This isn't revenge. This is justice."

"Let Tommy go."

"It's a little late for that. The game has changed. Your FBI lady friend was more than a little pissed off when the news crews had nothing to show from her raid on Raley Field. As far as the feds are concerned, you found Tommy and fled."

"That can't be—how long have I been here?" John said.

Winnow ignored John's confusion, dragged a tall stool out of the shadows, and positioned it next to John. "You know what the surprising part of this was? Agent Lincoln was so eager to claim victory in solving the case and carve a notch in her bedpost that she had tunnel vision."

"You're a murderer," John said.

"I'm a harvester. When I started this, it was all about 'the greater good,' where the sacrifice of the one benefits the many. Then, I became."

"Became? What the hell are you saying?"

Winnow laughed. "I became enlightened to the almighty dollar. Not the psychobabble you had in mind?"

"You butchered innocent people and sold their organs on the black market."

"We've been over this. Garbage people. They weren't human. I harvested for those who couldn't afford to pay the outrageous medical bills, those who couldn't get on the lists for transplant because of bureaucratic red tape. They got what they wanted. I made a buck or two in the process. It's a win–win."

"Like the Cardozo girl?" John asked.

"Yes. Exactly. That girl deserved a chance."

"So you played God and decided who lived and died? How is that any different?"

"An innocent girl needed a transplant. Her father was a match, so I made that happen. He saved his daughter's life; it's probably the only decent thing that man ever did. You would have done the same."

"What about my son? Why did you put him through this?"

"You asked for my help."

"No, I didn't."

"I have ten thousand dollars that says you did."

"I didn't pay you."

"We knew you'd eventually come to us. Zack Weber was exceptionally bright. He set up an entire dark web and connected to the transplant database through a programming back door so we could make harvesting decisions to maximize profit. Really quite elegant."

"Like my son?"

Winnow nodded. "Yes, well, not at first. But when I found out you were *the* cop, it was too good to pass up. In a way, you made me what I am. At some point, we knew we would make you come to us. Zack trolled for people like you. Transplants got cancelled, donor organs disappeared. Matching blood test results were wiped from the system. We grabbed the organs for shipments to Mexico, Asia, and South America, where desperate people will pay any price, or had them slipped into the legitimate market. Laundered like drug money."

"Made you what you are? Tommy didn't do anything to deserve this."

Winnow stepped away, out of John's field of vision. He shuffled some glass bottles, which made tinkling sounds.

"I tend to agree with you. Tommy didn't, but you deserve to feel loss. But you see my predicament. I can't let him go now. You either."

"You have no reason to keep him. You have me. Let him go home."

Winnow returned to the table and looked down on John. He held a clear syringe in one hand and flicked the cylinder with a finger, chasing out the air bubbles.

"What about Agent Lincoln?"

"Agent Lincoln will believe you absconded with your son and hit the road. She's watched too many bad movies. She'll think you were making a run for the border to Mexico."

Winnow flashed the syringe in John's face.

"Good-bye, Detective. Any last words for little Tommy?"

FORTY

"Drop it, asshole!" Paula crept from the shadows of an earthen hallway.

Winnow whirled around with the syringe held tight against John's neck. "Stay where you are. Don't come any closer."

"John, are you okay?" She pressed forward, the barrel of her weapon trained on Winnow.

"Tommy's here," John said.

Winnow backhanded John with his free hand. "Shut up!" He jabbed the needle into John's neck. "You move and he's done." He positioned his thumb over the plunger. "Don't even think about it. There's enough phenobarbital in here to kill him twice."

Paula adjusted her grip on her weapon and centered the muzzle steady at her target. Her knuckles were white from squeezing the Glock's polymer surface.

"Well look at you. All ready to shoot." Winnow leaned down over John's head. "I bet you've never ended someone's life before. I have."

"Back away. It's over. You have nowhere to run," Paula said.

"Shoot me and your partner dies. Are you so eager to sacrifice him so you can bring down the big, bad man and take all the credit?"

A flicker of hesitation from Paula was all Winnow needed. He lifted the table and toppled it over with John still strapped on. Glass shattered, and trays of containers, beakers, and equipment spilled to the floor.

Paula lunged toward her partner and held his head off the floor, carefully pulling out the syringe still stuck in his neck and stopping the lethal drug from injecting into his bloodstream. Winnow used the time to run out a back tunnel.

Paula tore away at John's restraints until he was free.

Once untethered from the killing table, John took Paula's flashlight and went after Winnow. The beam revealed a narrow passageway that led deeper into the earthen complex. A flicker of a candle flame to his right revealed a small room lined with cinderblocks. John pressed his back to the wall outside of the doorway and shifted the flashlight to his left hand.

The room and the passageway were silent until a faint rustle from within the room gave away the killer's trail. John wheeled around and shined the flashlight into the space. In a corner of the room, he spotted Tommy curled up on a filthy mattress. A sheen of sweat glistened from the boy's skin in spite of the cool surroundings.

"Dad?" It was a weak voice.

"It's me, Tommy. Everything's gonna be okay." John knelt at his son's side and felt a high fever with a caress against the boy's forehead.

"I don't feel good."

Paula trained her weapon down the dark corridor outside the room in case Winnow doubled back. "How's he doing?"

"He's burning up."

"We gotta get him out of here."

"Where is here, anyway?"

"The Layton farm. This is an old root cellar under the house."

Paula ducked into the room with her partner and in a quick motion, gathered Tommy up and cradled him in her arms. "Let's go."

The candle flame flickered and brightened, signaling a change in the air within the tunnels. Winnow was on the move.

Paula handed John her weapon. "I'll get Tommy back up top. You take that son of a bitch down."

John took the Glock and extended his arms, pressing the back of his flashlight hand against his gun hand for stability, and then stepped out into the corridor.

"Go," he said, and Paula hurried back through the tunnel, clutching Tommy in her arms.

"Winnow! It's you and me now." John took a half step forward and swept the darkness with his light. With another step, he heard a heavy, metallic thud and a brief sliver of light appeared. Winnow had another exit from the cellar.

John ran toward the light. It had to be less than twenty feet away, but the claustrophobic emptiness stripped away any sense of distance. A flush of anger came over him. Winnow had kept Tommy in this soulless place.

He worked his way down one wall until a faint outline of daylight crept through a gap in a doorframe. A metal door marked the root cellar's access point, cut into the foundation of the old Layton home above. John pressed against the door, and it gave an inch before it held tight. Winnow had managed to wedge a piece of wood through the outside handles during his escape.

John shoved his shoulder into the door, and the dried wood splintered. One more push and the door flew open. Sunlight temporarily blinded him, and he raised his hands to shield his eyes. They were sensitive to the light, but he caught sight of Paula running toward him.

"Where is he?" John said.

"He went into the barn," Paula said. "I called for backup."

John hoisted himself out of the root cellar, got his bearings, and spotted the barn on the far side of the gravel-and-dirt farmyard. He took off for the hog barn in a dead run.

"Stay with Tommy," he called behind him.

"We can wait him out, John!" Paula said.

John kicked at the barn door and readied the Glock. The door swung open, casting a wash of light over the slick-bottomed hog pens. He crossed the threshold and caught a blur of movement to his left. The door flew back onto his arm, and the Glock clattered to the floor. The barn door slammed shut behind him, plunging the inside back into a foul-smelling darkness.

"Winnow. Give it up."

"I'm not giving up anything, Detective." Winnow's voice gave away his movement.

John stepped lightly on the barn floor. Ahead, a whoosh cut through the darkness seconds before a metal meat hook swung in his direction. John dodged, but the heavy hook still cracked him on the skull, above his right ear. He felt a warm, wet sensation drip from his scalp. He didn't need to touch it to know he'd need stitches if he got out of this.

A chain rattled. This time John ducked down onto his haunches as the meat hook passed overhead.

"Detective? You still there?" Winnow's footsteps shuffled on the barn floor as he changed position.

John listened and pressed closer to the origin of the sound.

An arm grabbed John around his chest, pinning his arms down.

John bent forward and held Winnow on his back. He took several rapid steps backward, hoping to pin Winnow against a wooden beam or the barn wall. Instead, he heard a chain rattle followed by a wet, rasping sound. Winnow loosened his grip.

John spun away from his attacker, ready to block another blow. But Winnow didn't make a move forward.

Winnow shuffled his feet, unable to get traction on the barn floor, and held a look of utter surprise. He attempted to reach something behind him and lost his balance. He spun in an awkward circle, and John saw the meat hook embedded in Winnow's back. The heavy chain supported him when Winnow's knees buckled. His weight drove the hook deeper into his flesh. Blood flowed from the wound and pooled beneath the killer. Winnow's feet twitched and painted a gruesome mural as he slipped in his own blood.

"Match . . ." Winnow mumbled.

John drew closer to the killer and took a knee in front of him. "What?"

A blood-speckled cough and a ragged breath steadied Winnow for a moment. He raised his eyes to John. "Your son has a match." Another cough spit more blood down Winnow's chin.

"Where is Tommy's match?" John grabbed Winnow's head and shook him to keep him alert.

Winnow coughed, and a deep laugh sounded from the dying man.

"Tell me!"

"It's you." Winnow collapsed forward, held up by a heavy chain, an ugly puppet in the dark.

FORTY-ONE

The ambulance doors opened the moment the vehicle pulled beneath the awning of the hospital entrance. Black gun barrels appeared from both sides of the open doors. FBI operators in full tactical gear, vests, and helmets emblazoned with the HRT logo of the fed's elite hostage rescue team trained their weapons on the occupants.

The EMT in the ambulance shrank back into a corner with his arms held high. John wasn't surprised by the show of force. As soon as the feds had found out Winnow still had a pulse, they'd sent in the tactical team. John moved slowly, not offering the HRT gunmen any excuse to shoot.

"Got him," one of the operators called out.

John noticed Special Agent K. Lincoln, decked out in a tailored, tight ballistic vest that looked more like a corset than a piece of personal protective equipment. Next to her, two camera crews from local news stations televised the takedown.

The television camera panned toward the back of the ambulance, where hospital staff swarmed to help the EMTs unload Tommy.

Someone from one of the news crews shouted, "Where is the killer?"

Once the first-question barrier shattered, reporters jostled for the best camera angles, and the air filled with a mass of adverb-laden mush. No single question was discernible in the fray, but a few words pierced through: "letdown," "snipe hunt at Raley Field," and "FBI failure."

The cameras turned on Agent Lincoln, and the rehearsed speech announcing the capture of Brice Winnow wasn't going to help her now. Color drained from her face as she struggled against the jostling media. "We recovered the boy, and the killer is in custody—that's all that matters," she said as she retreated inside the hospital doors.

HRT shielded John and Tommy's gurney from view. They pressed through a sliding-glass partition into the emergency room. Moments later, a second gurney with an unresponsive Winnow rolled into the room. A second team of medical staff attended to his injuries.

"Thanks for keeping him at a distance," John said.

An HRT operator nodded. "We're glad you got your boy back." The HRT members left the room, and John glimpsed Melissa standing near the nurses' station. Her face was red and blotched from sobbing. Their eyes met, and her shoulders fell in relief. Melissa came to John and hugged him while a medical team examined Tommy.

"I thought I lost you both," Melissa said.

"We need to talk." John took her by the elbow and led her to an isolated corner of the emergency room but still within view of the doctors tending to Tommy.

"I know what you did," John said in a tired voice.

Melissa's lips tightened. "John, you're exhausted. Let's talk about all this later." She turned to leave, but John took her arm and pulled her back to him. "You're hurting me."

John hadn't realized how hard he clamped onto her arm, and he let go. He stepped closer and said, "I know about the ten-thousand-dollar payment."

Her eyes hardened. "At least I did something. Why didn't you?"

"You can't make deals with these people."

"We're just supposed to sit and pray something good happens? That's not enough."

"Where did you even get the money?"

"I borrowed it from my sister."

"Why would you do this?"

"I couldn't see my son get passed over on the transplant list again. It's not right. He deserves a chance."

"It almost got him killed. Don't you get that? It's the black market."

"I couldn't just stand around and wait for him to die, John."

"Hey, guys," Paula said. The couple hadn't noticed Paula approach or the stares from hospital workers within earshot. "Keep it down, would ya?"

"I tried to tell you when Tommy's transplant fell through. I couldn't," Melissa said.

"How's Tommy?" Paula asked.

"They're checking him out now. He's gone through hell," John said.

"I'm glad you're both back. When you disappeared from the ice plant, I thought you—you had me worried."

"You and me both. How did you find me?"

"Like you figured. Winnow only had so many places he could hide. I went back to the live camera feeds. I caught Winnow digging something up in the barn, and then just a few minutes later, he was with you on the wine-cave camera. They had to be in the same place—at the Layton farm."

The curtain from around Tommy's bed split open, and a doctor joined them.

"Mr. and Mrs. Penley, I'm Dr. Philips, the emergency attending—"

"How is he?" John asked.

"Tommy is in serious condition. He's dehydrated, his kidney function is bad, and the surgical incision shows signs of severe infection."

"Can we see him?"

"Yeah, come with me."

A groggy Tommy lifted a hand. "Hi, Mom."

Melissa went to her son and stroked his cheek. "I'm so sorry, baby."

"I'm not a baby."

"I know, I know."

"We've started a course of antibiotics for the infection, pumped a couple liters of fluid in him, and we'll need to get him on dialysis as soon as possible. I've notified Dr. Anderson, and he's arranging for in-room dialysis in light of what happened."

"But he's gonna be okay, right?" John asked.

"Your son is in serious condition, Mr. Penley. The next few hours will be critical. If we can beat back the infection, he's got a chance of pulling through." The doctor looked at John's lacerated scalp. "We need to get this taken care of too."

"Thanks, Doc," John said.

"We'll get him moved out of the ER and into a private room as soon as one opens up. Mrs. Penley, get some rest. He's going to need you for the long haul. Meanwhile, Mr. Penley, you come with me, and I'll get a couple of sutures in that mess."

With Tommy settled into a room, the activity quieted and left John and Melissa with uncomfortable silence. The common bond between them—their children—pried them apart. They sat on opposite sides of the room, each with the burden of a broken promise. They had failed to keep their children safe. Evidence of their failure lay on the hospital bed. John stood and pulled aside the blinds. First light was a few hours away. John felt as dark as it was outside. Melissa wasn't the target of his anger, but she was in the room. That kind of anger cuts through silence, and it cuts deep.

"Say what you have to say," Melissa said.

"What's left to be said?"

"That is exactly how we got here. You won't say anything. You don't tell me what's going on, and you keep it all bottled up inside until something rotten escapes."

"I'm only trying to keep you safe." He rubbed the stubble of the stitches on his scalp.

A knock at the door announced a uniformed officer. The officer extended his hand when John approached. It was Officer Tucker, Stark's younger partner. He had Kari with him.

"I'm glad to see the boy back."

"Me too. Thanks for picking up Kari," John said.

"Detective Newberry said my life depended on it."

"She has people skills."

"I'm sorry. If I'd done a better search of that ice plant, this might not have happened. We could have gotten Winnow sooner, and he wouldn't have been able to take your son."

John shook the younger officer's hand. "Winnow was two steps ahead of us the entire time. There was nothing you could have done to change that. We got Tommy back, and that's what matters most. Winnow's out of moves now."

"Winnow got his," Tucker said.

"He's in a coma. They don't know if he'll regain consciousness."

Tucker waved at Tommy when he entered the room. "How ya feeling, buddy?"

"Tired."

"I'm not surprised after what you went through."

"Thanks again, Tucker," John said.

Tucker nodded and left the room.

Melissa gave her seat by the bed to Kari and walked over to John.

"This is all my fault. I'm so sorry. I should have trusted you."

"Trust is a bridge that goes both directions. It doesn't matter which side gets burnt—it makes the bridge impassable. I should have shared what I'd found with you. I thought I was shielding you from the pain, but all I did was cause more."

"Is that man still out there?" Tommy asked. The boy's eyes were puffy and yellowed.

"He'll never bother you again."

FORTY-TWO

"I have something you need to see," Paula said when she called.

John put the cell phone down on the pile of UNOS records and printouts from Zack Weber's computer, spread over his desk at home. Technically, he was on administrative leave and wasn't supposed to have the boxful of material. In between hospital visits with Tommy, he pored over the medical records, tissue-typing data, and donor information, and it left him with a scab on his soul. Numbers, charts, and dispassionate clinical terms. The raw answers were there; the "who" and the "when" of the slaughter bled from the pages. The financial deposits into nameless accounts made a strong economic argument for Winnow's dark enterprise, but the killer would be no help in determining what caused him to set out on this particular path of destruction.

A forensic analysis of the UNOS data revealed dozens of fraudulent transactions covering the trail of Winnow's illicit organ harvest. Potential donors were purged from the data, and families watched as loved ones withered and died. A thick report lay open on John's desk that contained a list of transplant patients with matching donors from a new round of blood testing. A thick circle was drawn on a single line of the report. John was a match for Tommy. Winnow had known all along and toyed with John, using Tommy as bait. Under his phone, the latest report from the medical staff provided an opinion about Winnow's health and his prognosis. The words "persistent vegetative state," "diminished neural activity," and "hospice care" were underlined in thick, hard strokes. John's pen had left a crease in the page three days ago.

John stood, grabbed his phone, and instinctively pulled the drawer open for his service weapon, only to find the drawer empty. He'd surrendered his firearm to the lieutenant when he went on administrative leave. He pushed the drawer closed harder than he needed. John closed his eyes and drew a deep breath, something that the department's assigned trauma counselor preached as a "cleansing breath." *Cleansing, my ass*, he thought. He made a quick phone call to Melissa at the hospital and let her know he'd join her and Tommy as soon as he met with Paula. John and Melissa didn't see much of one another; they took separate shifts at the hospital. Avoiding John was easier for Melissa. She still took the blame for making the ten-thousand-dollar payment to Winnow and all the trauma that followed.

Paula asked him to meet her at the Layton farm. He'd seen the photos of the place after his last encounter with Winnow. He hadn't paid attention to the forensic dig with the precise, squared sections, marked with a labyrinth of string. The entire interior of the barn was a checkerboard, and the pieces were bits of skull and fragments of long bone. Sifted, sorted, and bagged, all the human bits were gone, nothing left but residual negative energy that stained the worn barn wood.

John pulled his Toyota pickup off the main road and onto the driveway of the Layton farm. At the end of the drive, Paula sat on the trunk lid of a dark, unmarked police car, dangling her feet above the gravel. He parked the truck, and she hopped from the back of the sedan.

She didn't greet him and she seemed preoccupied, hands shoved in her pants pockets, eyes avoiding his.

"What's up?" John asked.

"I heard they are going to let Winnow walk on the criminal charges and send him to a hospice on a compassionate release."

"I'm not really surprised. That way, the case goes away quick and quiet. No public trial, no splash back on city hall."

"But a compassionate release? This guy needs release by lethal injection."

John was done talking about what Winnow deserved. "What did you want to show me?"

She nodded. "Yeah, that. Come with me."

The path to the barn door showed evidence of heavy foot traffic since the last time John had been under this roof. He wasn't one who saw ghosts in the shadows, but this place held the psychic residue to challenge his skeptical beliefs.

As they crossed the threshold at the barn door, the smell was worse than he remembered. He winced.

Paula noticed his reaction. "It's the digging. They turned over layer after layer of pig crap."

"Where are the pigs?" John noticed the side barn door was open for extra ventilation, and there was no sign of the squealing animals.

"The county took them off to the rendering plant. With what they've eaten, the public health people didn't want to run the risk of getting that into the food supply."

The barn floor glistened with a sheen of moisture seeping to the surface from decades of livestock doing their business inside the wooden walls. Even in the darkened interior, holes pockmarked the dirt surface, a greater number than John had imagined. One hole, against the back wall, was bigger than all of the others.

"Wasn't there a worktable along that wall?" John asked.

"Built over that hole there? Yeah, there was."

"More body parts?"

"Hold on," Paula said. She flicked the switch on a halogen lamp. "I asked the techies to leave this for us."

"Whoa, that's a deep hole. The pigs didn't do that."

"The pigs didn't leave an entire body in that pit either."

John followed a temporary walkway of plywood planks from the door to the edge of the large hole. "How'd they find anything in here? That's got to be four feet deep."

"Cadaver dogs. They passed over most of the small bits and went straight to that spot. They estimate the body's been there for two years."

John peered into the pit, and even though the remains no longer inhabited this hole, the image of a body covered in layers of grime and manure wasn't hard to imagine. "Think we'll ever find out who it was?"

"You're not the only detective in the world, you know." Paula had her hands on her hips and a smirk on her face. "Check this out. This is what I needed you to see." She swiveled the halogen light so the beam settled on the back wall, four or five feet from the ground.

The barn wood was scarred and gray from nearing the end of its useful life. John rubbed his hand across the grain. Letters were carved into the old surface, long enough ago that they had darkened and nearly disappeared into the swirls and knots in the wood planks.

Two names, rough cut with a sharp implement: *Patrick* and *Brice*. Next to each name, dates were carved into the wood, like Gold Rush–era tombstones.

Patrick would have been twenty-eight years old if the dates meant that he died two years ago. The date next to Brice indicated birth two years ago, with no ending date.

"But that wasn't Patrick Horn you found in that pit."

Paula joined him by the wall and handed him a file folder. She'd had it with her the entire time, but John was too preoccupied with the place to notice. He cracked the file open, and the first document inside was an accident report from the car crash when a drunk driver had run Marsha Horn off the road.

"Suspect in that hit-and-run was one William Brice Winnow, a Skinhead gang member out of Stockton. The DA declined prosecution. It seems his blood samples for alcohol-level testing went missing."

"That's my signature on this report. I recommended the DA drop the case because of the missing evidence. This was around the time Carson was up to his dealings in the evidence room. Did you try to track—?"

"William Brice Winnow was reported missing a week after the accident." She pointed at the pit. "Not anymore. We got a match on dentals."

"You're sure it's him?"

"We got a DNA hit on the body too."

"And it matched the dentals?"

"I'm talking about DNA *on* the body. We got a match for Patrick Horn on the guy's body. There was some evidence of bodily trauma that made it look like the vic was strung up on those steel hooks in the barn."

"The date on the report—it's the same one carved on the wall," John said.

"Sure is. Like *our* Brice was born that day."

John lowered the file. "Winnow said Patrick Horn was weak, and look at what he's become."

"He became Brice Winnow. Patrick Horn died two years ago after his mother's accident. He got revenge on her killer and assumed a new identity," she said.

"Winnow told me I could have prevented this. He blames me for letting his mother's killer go free."

"There is nothing you could have done. When did all the organ harvesting start?"

John hooked a thumb over his shoulder at the pit. "I bet it started right there. It would be impossible to prove, but Winnow had a sore spot for old man Layton. He claimed his stepfather showed him how to do it. I thought he was talking about butchering hogs, but I think he meant this."

"Neither one's gonna say anything. Layton's dead, and Winnow is in a coma. We were right about the blood bank, by the way."

"What's that?"

"The blood bank. That was the connection between all the victims. Mercer, Johnson, Travis, even Cardozo—they all went there. Johnson and Mercer donated plasma for money; Cardozo tried to donate, but his blood tested HIV positive; and Travis—"

"Got a call to donate because of his AB-positive blood type."

"Makes you wonder if Winnow made that call," she said.

Paula switched off the halogen light, plunging the barn into shadow. Something dark moved in the corner. For a moment, John had a vision of the trapped souls of those once buried in the place.

Paula was on the phone when John emerged from the barn behind her. She glanced up. "Yeah, he's here with me. Hold on." She handed the phone to John. "It's the lieutenant."

"Penley."

"I wanted to give you a heads-up, before you hear it on the news."

"Yeah?"

"Brice Winnow died at South Valley Memorial."

"How?"

"The hospital spokesman said something about brain swelling. He died fifteen minutes ago. But get this. Winnow was a registered organ donor. And he's a match for the Cardozo girl."

"That's a fitting end. Can't say that I'll miss him," John said.

"Me neither. Just wanted you to know. Give Melissa a hug from me," Lieutenant Barnes said.

"Will do." John disconnected the call and handed the phone to Paula.

The pager on John's belt vibrated. He glanced down at the display, gave a slight nod in recognition, and switched it off. "Everything okay?" Paula asked.

"Everything is fine. That was the transplant center confirming Tommy's and my surgeries tomorrow."

"I'm so happy Tommy is healthy enough for the transplant. Everything he's been through—everything you've been through to make it happen . . ."

"That's what you do for your kids—at whatever cost."

ACKNOWLEDGMENTS

At What Cost would still be an idea in my cluttered mind if not for the support, encouragement, and occasional well-timed prod from so many.

I'm eternally grateful to my agent, Elizabeth K. Kracht of Kimberley Cameron and Associates Literary Agency, for her unwavering belief in *At What Cost*. She is every author's dream agent, and I'm lucky to have her by my side.

Thanks to the early readers of the manuscript, Brenda Pandos and Karen Crain-Hedger, who offered the right mix of "Atta boy" and "Are you crazy?" to keep me motivated.

My heartfelt appreciation goes to Matt Martz and Sarah Poppe of Crooked Lane Books, who believed in the book and pressed me to make it better. *At What Cost* found the perfect home at Crooked Lane.

Technical aspects of the story were influenced by Dr. Christian Swanson, chief of surgery, Mercy Medical Group; Dr. Roopinder Poonia, nephrology; and Dr. Christopher Olson, internal medicine, who provided valuable medical insight and critical detail for the story. Any misstatement or simplification of medical procedure or terminology is mine and designed to feed the fictional story line within *At What Cost*.

My kids, Jessica Windham and Michael L'Etoile, are a constant source of wonder and pride. They indulge their father's writing-induced craziness without judgment. Keep those "geospastic" forces going. I love you guys more than you can imagine.

Thanks to my wife, Ann-Marie, for reading countless drafts of the book and giving me the freedom and encouragement to write without the slightest hint that she truly thinks I'm nuts. You continue to be my inspiration and partner in all things. I love you.

2/17